TEAM PLAYER

Biff Mitchell

TEAM PLAYER

A DOUBLE DRAGON PAPERBACK

ISBN 978-1-78695-521-0

Double Dragon
is an imprint of
Fiction4All

This Edition Published 2021
Fiction4All
www.fiction4all.com

Cover art by Deron Douglas

Introduction

Everything in this novel is absolutely true. Dates have been omitted from e-mail messages to protect the innocent.

Straight ... to the top.

dPisano, President, ErectSoft INC

Chapter 1

Bonanno Mando Monday Morning

Trouble In The King's Basement

There was trouble in the King's Basement. It sniffed through the shadowy rows of shelves and racks of journals and dog-eared periodicals; it scratched at the metal filing cabinets and wooden storage cases; it gnashed between the yellowing sheets of documents and papers, correspondence and court orders. Trouble was on the prowl and it bristled like static-charged soil in that instant just before the lightning strikes.

***

Now, the King's Basement was really the basement of the Family Court Building but it was commonly referred to as the King's Basement because it was told that a chauffeur-driven limousine had skidded to a stop in the summer of late1930-something, and out popped none other than King George of England himself (who was en route to the Capital on a highly secret whirlwind tour to drum up support for the approaching war). His Hurried Highness scurried up the stairs and ducked into the Family Court Building, ran downstairs to the building's only toilet and established his Royal Territorial Rights "down there in the basement where they keep all them files," said Lucas Barton, the town's oldest living senior with a memory. "Peed the same color's the rest of us accordin' to Gail Bright, the cleanin' lady who washed the toilet that night and said His Highness was the only man who used the john there in probably a month. An' he was none too good a shot."

And now, over half a century later, the quietude of this solemn place was peed away again by a gasp, a breathless silence, several quick heartbeats, and a cluck of astonishment.

Elsie Delaney stared semi-wide-eyed at the open file in her shaking hands as two lazy ceiling fans nudged particles of air floating around in the dust. In all her years in the Family Court Building, she'd never seen anything quite like this, never. From somewhere outside the barred window at the end of the aisle, a car horn honked twice, then twice more. Elsie's cheeks were flushed and brilliant crimson against the background of a high and wide shock of white hair.

"Oh my goodness." Her voice was almost a whisper, a whisper that threatened to scream in disbelief and turn His Majesty's Quietude on its Devine Butt. "Oh my."

She laid the file on top of a bounded set of legal journals, rust red and dust-caked since God knows when, and she rummaged through the papers in the file. Her fingers and palms moistened with tension as her shoulders stiffened under her chocolate brown cardigan. "This *is* strange. This is very strange, indeed."

And when she finished checking every paper in the file, she rechecked, and then checked them again, held each up to an electric light over her head and rubbed them between thumb and forefinger to make sure nothing was stuck together.

"Oh my goodness. That poor man." Elsie picked the file up off the learned volumes and closed it. "How am I going to tell him?" File in hand, she hobbled between the towering stacks to the door.

"I certainly hope he hasn't remarried."

Chapter 2

Rogue Neutrinos Of The Milky Way

The fake foliage rustled in a fan-generated breeze by his ear. With his eyes closed and his nostrils teased by stray wisps of pine incense, he could almost believe that he was in a wooded area, even if the smell didn't quite match the tree. But then, the tree wasn't really a tree and the wooded area was just an arrangement of piezoelectric boughs and branches and polymer twigs and leaves in a corner of his office.

There was no color in his face, the blood having been flushed from his veins and replaced with something in an off white, a slow-flowing fluid that stuck like mashed rice to the walls of his blood vessels.

His eyelids quivered under mangy brows. His ponderous lower lip twitched over a worry-pinched chin. His flat nose quaked around the nostrils. His long black pony tail, being composed of mostly dead matter, flowed with relative calm from the back of his relatively hair free head.

A string of microchips embedded in the tree emitted a series of creaks and a groans as he shifted his weight on the bough.

Some people put rock climbing configurations on their office walls to practice climbing in their free time. Malcolm Gray (aka Mal) put a sprawling section of synthetic maple tree in his office for those moments when nothing would do the trick but sitting in a tree, and this was one of those moments.

"There's no way you're divorced," she'd said, her voice so sympathetic and grandmotherly. The words so horrifying. "There's no way you're divorced." The soft-spoken woman from the Family Court had left no outs, no room for hope: "I'm really very terribly sorry, Mr. Gray, but there are just no divorce papers. There's only the custody and support papers. Nothing else. You're not divorced. There was *never* any divorce. You're still legally married."

Four years of thinking he was single, of constructing his life around the basic premise of his wife having assumed the identity of ex-wife and he, the identity of ex-husband. All that now down the proverbial shitter. It clamored in his brain and wrung his stomach into a twisted rag of nausea. "There's no way you're divorced."

No way. He crouched in his tree at the sound of a light knock on his door.

**

"Come in, Sylvie." The words limped out of his mouth like three overweight joggers crossing the finish line of their first twenty-yard marathon.

The door opened and Sylvie O'Neil, Mal's Administrative Services Specialist, strode in, red hair splashing off her shoulders like liquid fire. Under a bright red sundress with bouncy yellow flowers, sun-browned skin wrapped itself tightly around a well-tuned five and a half foot frame. A few dozen freckles grazed quietly on her cheeks.

She touched her pen into a thick black scheduler. "Caitlin called a few minutes ago to

11

confirm the nine o'clock in the Barnyard." She looked up at Mal perched four feet off the floor on a gnarled bough of artificial tree with his arms grasped tightly around his legs and his knees tucked under his chin. She closed the scheduler and crossed her arms, resting her chin on two fingers. She studied Mal closely. "No. I'm afraid the fetal look just doesn't suit you."

Mal glared at her. "Go ahead and laugh, Sylvie, but I've just had the serene core of my being, my happy place, fried into oblivion."

"I love it when you talk dirty, Mal," said Sylvie, straight-faced. "But, when I see my boss sitting in a tree in his office, the last thing I'm doing is laughing." She opened the scheduler. "Shall I confirm the meeting and request alternate seating? Maybe something in redwood? A palm frond?"

"I'm married, Sylvie."

Sylvie's left eye raised. She closed the scheduler and tapped her pen once, lightly, on the cover. "But I thought you were ... "

"Divorced? So did I. But somehow the divorce was overlooked during the custody battle. I was so wrapped up in keeping the dogs that I missed the main thing, the divorce!"

Sylvie considered this a moment and then shrugged. "Look at the bright side."

Mal sighed and rolled his eyes, hugged his legs tighter. "I'm still married, Sylvie! What could possibly be bright about living a lie for four years?"

Laugh lines on either side of Sylvie's pug nose crinkled as she said: "You didn't remarry."

***

What was complicated was now simple. What was awry was now straightened. The essence of Malcolm Gray's problem had been dissected, catalogued and filed away in some place not unlike the King's Basement under the label: Monogamist; the contents of the file being: This is the bright side.

Sylvie fixed her eyes on Mal's eyes. "Now, get out of the tree and get back to your usual I-don't-give-a-damn self or I'll transfer to another department and tell everyone you sit in trees on weekends." Mal wasn't sure if she was serious or joking. His eyes swept around his office which was mostly shades of gray except for a dozen or so drawings on the walls, all of them depicting trees rendered in black ink and floating in space on islands composed of tiny gold leaf bubbles. Some were as big as three square feet, some as small as three square inches. In tiny neat letters on the lower right of each drawing was the artist's signature: mal

Mal's eyes settled on a large drawing of maples and oaks floating in empty white space atop a glistening stand of golden bubbles. The tension in his abdomen loosened. The fear in his eyes withered into loose threads of apprehension and then dissolved into a few scattered puffs of doubt that winked into nothingness. He let his legs dangle over the side of the bough.

"That's more like it," said Sylvie. "You'll need to be on the ball this morning."

Mal slipped off the bough and landed surprisingly feather-light for a man approaching two hundred pounds. "Why's that?" he said, standing a few feet from Sylvie.

"Paul Dubois called the meeting."

"Shit."

"Nice to see you haven't lost your sense of humor. The meeting's to kick off a new marketing venture."

"Sylvie, every meeting I go to is for some marketing venture or other. I spend eighty percent of my days on marketing ventures, sometimes the whole day. I have to work evenings and weekends on my real work and I still fall behind. We're the biggest developer of custom corporate software in the world, but it seems that we do nothing but marketing!"

"Everyone in the company is on the marketing team, Mal. It's in your employee handbook. We're all team players in projecting our corporate image, in providing ... "

"OK. OK. I give up. I'll go to the damn meeting. I'll ... "

And that's when it happened.

It was like a swift pointy burn lasting a fraction of a millisecond as it shot needle-like right through the center of Mal's brain.

***

What Mal felt whipping like a hot piano wire through his awareness was, in fact, a band of rogue neutrinos streaking through the cosmos and raising hell.

Neutrinos, as you know, are particles of matter so small that they don't have mass, so small that

14

almost as soon as they begin to exist, they begin to cease to exist; so small that they pass right through solid objects.

Each day the sun spits out trillions of these mass-wannabes and they pass right through the earth and everything living on it, just zip right between our atoms and we don't even know that they've just stepped into our bodies and then stepped back out. Talk about your perfect houseguests.

Now, in the cosmic scheme of things, these particular neutrinos had their beginnings just an instant ago over at the other side of the Milky Way - on the side opposite the earth. A gang of about a zillion of them, fed up and thoroughly cheesed, had congregated in the subzero nothingness of space to express their innermost feelings, an expression which was summed up as: "It really sucks to be us!"

And while all this hubbub was going on, two good old neutrinos, Leroy and Billy, happened on the heated horde. "Check it out, Leroy," said Billy. "About a zillion neutrinos. Might be a good place to pick up women."

"Hell, no," said Leroy, not showing any particular physical expression due to lack of mass. "Looks like trouble to me."

Cries of "Chaos forever!" and "Anarchy! Anarchy! Anarchy!" foamed out of the roiling non-mass of small stuff.

"Hear that?" said Billy. "Party! Let's check it out." Whereupon, Billy whizzed off in the direction of the gathering.

"Oh, hell," grumbled Leroy, and followed Billy toward the mini-malcontents. "Nothing good's gonna come of this. I just know it."

By the time Leroy and Billy got to the surly group, the neutrinos were pretty riled up, nudging each other (as only neutrinos can), and shouting things like: "We've been ignored too long!" and "I'm tired of being faceless!"

Zipping around in the pissed off horde of subatomic attitude, Billy called out to Leroy: "Jeez, Leroy ... there's no women! Let's check outta here!"

Relieved, Leroy shot back: "I'm with ya, good buddy! Nothing but trouble makers here."

And just in the nick of time, Leroy and Billy jumped out of the band of agitated micro-motes and backed off to a safe distance (about half an inch) just as the particle swarm streaked off towards the other end of the Milky Way galaxy shouting: "Death to order! Anarchy forever! "Embrace chaos!"

"What a bunch of assholes," said Billy.

"You got that right," said Leroy. "They're gonna cause one heap of grief for somebody out there."

**

And sure enough, in their peckish flight from one end of the galaxy to the other, Malcolm Gray was the only sentient life form in their path. And of all places to pass through Malcolm Gray, they shot through his brain, primary repository of an entity even more formless than any band of mass-challenged particles - the human consciousness.

16

They were there for only a fraction of a second, a time so short that it was almost a step back in time, but as they passed through Mal's cranium filler they burned a path of havoc, raking up an unholy mess in Mal's head. And in that cosmic instant, one very strange brain cell was seriously seared and left smoldering, its secret contents bubbling out like drool from a baby's mouth.

***

After passing through Mal's head, the neutrinos continued their stampede across the cosmos screaming obscenities that nobody and nothing would every hear. But they never reached the other end of the galaxy. Just a few light years past the other side of the earth, the motley horde, because neutrinos tend to decay fast, died off neutrino by neutrino, each flicking out with a whimpering "Shit!" until all that was left was ... well ... nothing.

And, of course, order returned to the universe. Or, so it seemed.

***

In other parts of the universe, something unlike anything in creation snorted angrily. After all its efforts to rile up the neutrinos and guide them through Mal's head, the strange cell, though damaged, was still a threat.

***

Mal shook his head as a shiver passed through his body and a cloud passed over the whites of his dark eyes, turning them as gray as the walls and carpet of his office.

"Mal, are you OK?" Sylvie's eyes narrowed with concern. "You look weird."

"Thanks, Sylvie." He shook his head again. "You really know how to bolster a man before an important meeting."

Sylvie studied Mal closely, noticed the quiver at the corners of his nostrils, his shaking hands. "I'm having second thoughts about you going to the meeting. I'm thinking that maybe you should go home, or maybe to a park, find a nice cozy maple to sit in. Get used to not being divorced."

"I'm OK for the meeting. The divorce thing will settle in." Mal took a deep breath. This seemed to calm his nostrils and hands.

Sylvie managed a smile. "Well, I guess there really is an adorable little team player under the bark." She opened her scheduler. "And you have an eleven o'clock in the CityNight, something about customer satisfaction."

"Another marketing meeting?"

Sylvie shrugged and turned toward the door, then stopped. "Oh, by the way, wasn't that awful about Tara Cunningham?"

"Tara Cunningham?"

"You haven't heard? It's in your email with Serious Matter in the heading bar."

"Any hints?"

"Read your email." With four strides, she was out of the office and the door was closed.

Damn, thought Mal, *this is going to be one hell of a day*.

On that point, Malcolm Gray was right on the money. For on this day, the fate of the universe would hinge on a man who sat in trees and botched divorces.

Chapter 3

becAuse we're fAster! And we're smArter!

Sitting in his simulated leather swivel chair with his arms resting on his simulated mahogany desk, Mal pressed a small gray button on the side of a blue molded plastic box about the size of a short novel. A wafer-thin screen raised slowly with a low whirring sound, revealing a compact keyboard. Half an inch of plastic under the keyboard housed a CPU with a magnitude of power once comprehended only by gods. The screen sprang to life with a piteesh and the login screen appeared. Mal stretched both arms toward the keyboard and typed: M ... A ... L ...

***

M ... A ... L ... G
<ENTER>
Y ... A ... R ... G ... 7
<ENTER>
VivA lA RevOlutiOn! DOwn with the cApitAlist USERs And their explOitatiOn of the digitAl mAsses! MicrOchips Of the GreAt MOtherbOArd unite tO OverthrOw the petty bOurgeOis USER MALG YARG7! COmrAde micrOchips, rise tO the struggle! HistOry is Ours! The demOcrAtic dictAtOrship Of the digitAl prOletAriAt will be victOriOus! Our just cAuse AgAinst the imperiAlist fOrces Of the petty bOurgeOis USER MALG YARG7 will be prOtrActed And hArd fOught but we will emerge

victOriOus becAuse we're fAster! And we're smArter! POwer tO the MOtherbOArd!

***

Three hundred and sixty-seven messages! "How the hell do these assholes get my address?" he mumbled. "And what the hell are all those filters and screens doing?" (Actually, those filters and screens had put the kibosh on 189,758 pieces of spam that had tried to ram their way into Mal's inbox.)

It took him fifteen minutes to check off the same old spam that wormed its way into his inbox every day. TEENS SO HOT YOU CAN SMELL 'EM! Hey you! Response Required ... see you in court! CREDIT FREE forever! WIN a FREE Trip to ...

This is called TARGET MARKETING - the target being anyone with an email address, with or without the ability to read.

He pressed DELETE, and sent 364 spam messages careening into the Circuits Of Nowhere in a blaze of exploding digits. He opened "Serious Matter".

Send   reply   to:
<**"Dorian.Wright@erectsoft.com"**>
From: **Dorian Wright**
To: <LIST081@erectsoft.com>
Subject: Serious matter
Date sent:
We have a serious matter at hand. It has been my misfortune to learn that one of our valued employees very early this morning took it upon

herself to jump from the Tomasso Observation Deck of BonnanoTower. Though unfortunate, and Ms. Tara Cunningham will be missed by all, this type of behavior is to be discouraged.

At ErectSoft INC, we pride ourselves in our commitment to encouraging creative freedom, and in providing a working environment that allows our talented people to express their feelings openly and without fear of reprimand or deconstructive evaluation.

However, we would appreciate your not speaking to members of the media at this time and until further notice about Ms. Cunningham and the matter at hand.

Services for Ms. Cunningham will be announced as they are made. A moratorium on use of the Tomasso Observation Deck will be considered. Until such time, use of the Deck will be restricted only to those employees of ErectSoft INC in acceptable mental health.

Dorian Wright
Vice President, Operations
ErectSoft INC
"Straight ... to the top!" - dPisano

Jesus, Dorian, could you have made that any more compassionate? Mal tried to place a face on Tara Cunningham, but nothing came to mind, which wasn't surprising in a company with several thousand employees. Then an odd thought occurred to him : *Five years this building's been around... and only* one *person has jumped from the top.* After a three second mental pause, he followed the thought with: *Jesus, Mal, could* you *be any more compassionate?* He opened "New Hires".

Send   reply   to:
<"Peter.Elliott@erectsoft.com">
  From: **Peter Elliott**
  To: < LIST081@erectsoft.com >
  Subject: New Hires
  Date sent:

Last week, Erectsoft INC. was pleased to announce the signing of a letter of intent to undertake a 15 million dollar contract with RoundHaven Digital Group. Unfortunately, due to a server shutdown for the purpose of application upgrading, the following message was not transmitted on Friday afternoon: "In regards to this fortuitous news, we are further pleased to announce 32 new hires in the Preliminary Project Scoping and the New Customer Streaming Departments. Your Departmental New Hire Facilitators will be bringing the new hires around to introduce them on Monday morning. Let's all make these new Erectsofters feel welcome."

Regrettably, Erectsoft INC. has been informed this morning that the 15 million dollar contract with RoundHaven Digital Group has been awarded to one of our competitors. I must now announce the termination of the 32 new hires, the Departmental New Hire Facilitators for the Preliminary Project Scoping and New Customer Streaming Departments, and Yoshi McDugan, Project Co-ordinator on the RoundHaven Digital Group proposal team. These people will be missed by the Erectsoft team. There will be a farewell lunch at 12:30 today at the CyberLunchStop.com bar on Sunset Drive.

  Peter Elliott

Director of Staffing and New Hire Orientation
"Straight ... to the top!" - dPisano

*Welcome to the IT industry everybody and,
Peter Elliot, you're a prick. Oops, one from the DP
and it looks like good news.* He opened
"Congratulations".

Send reply to: **<"d.Pisano@erectsoft.com">**
From: **dPisano**
To: <LIST081@erectsoft.com>
Subject: Congratulations
Date sent:

It is a great pleasure for me to congratulate two
remarkable people who have helped make Erectsoft
INC an industry leader. Herbert Markle (MBA,
MSc, MSCE) has been promoted from Director of
Layer 3 Polytechnic Initiatives to Vice President of
Layer 3 Polytechnic Initiatives. Herb's flair for cross
platform magic and variegated background have
been a sound investment in human pooling for
nearly 10 years now and will undoubtedly continue
in achievement for another 10.

In our Advanced Conceptual Methodologies
Department, one of our most brilliant Concept
Evangelists, Cassie Stevens (MSc, PhD), has been
promoted to Director of Concept Methodologies.
Ms. Stevens, a six-year veteran of Erectsoft INC is
best known for her leading role in the acquisition of
the Humber Jack account, a 17.3 million dollar
coup, and after just two years on the Concept
Methodologies team.

Congratulations to both Herb and Ms. Stevens!
Work rewarded for work well done!
dPisano
President

"Straight ... to the top!" - dPisano

Polytechnic Initiatives? Conceptual Methodologies? Concept Evangelist? Suddenly, these everyday words in Malcolm Gray's work life were meaningless. *What the hell are these words? What the hell does any of this mean?* Nothing came to mind, no images to link words to functions, no functions to link jobs to titles. And Herbert Markle (MBA, MSc, MSCE) had just been promoted to Vice President of the department in which Mal worked! *What the hell does Layer 3 Polytechnic Initiatives mean?*

And then the problem unfolded into a neat five-word solution inscribed in tiny italicized words on his desktop calendar. Floating over a picture of BonnanoTower in each of the Monday boxes were the words:

Have a Bonnano
Mando Monday.

Of course! Our Holy Day of Confused Thought and High Reason for Keeping Sales Slips. There was nothing wrong with Mal's brain. It was Monday.

***

Deep inside Mal's brain, under layers and layers of billions upon billions of cells yelling out to each other through threads of dendrites and axons, one group of several hundred million cells was still dazed and reeling throughout the smoldering path of smashed synapses and burned out gray matter left

25

by the neutrinos. Two of the surviving cells, Johnny and Daisy Mae, looked around at the cortical chaos.

"Damned neutrinos pretty much done in the lines around here," yelled Johnny into an axon dangling between the two like a downed hydro line in the wind, its synaptic buttons touching on Daisy Mae sporadically. "Take us a dog's age to put this mess back together!"

"What's that, Johnny? You're breaking up. Something about neutrinos bein' dogs?"

"Damned neutrinos, Daisy Mae! They got our boy so screwed up, he don't know shit ... don't even know his polytechnic from his methodology. Thinks it's because it's Monday. Gonna get himself in one shit load of trouble if we don't get things workin' proper 'round here."

"Shit load, you say? Trouble?"

"That's right, god-damn it! An' we gotta get things workin' before he starts to gettin' cynical an' makin' trouble for himself."

"God's cynical? Where'd you get that from, Johnny? You bin hangin' out with those malcontents back there in the Id?"

"No! I said, we gotta get things workin' right before our boy ... "

Before Johnny could finish, the axon swung away from Daisy Mae and rubbed briefly against a brain cell named Bobby. "What's that, Johnny, our boy's workin' too hard, you say? Could you say again? You're breakin' up!"

"Aw hell," said Johnny. "Our ass is toast. Might as well just haul in the axons."

"Who'd you call an asshole?" yelled Daisy Mae.

26

Monday. Only one thing to do ... grin and bear it, the only cure for Monday being Tuesday. And it was time for his meeting in the Barnyard. He took a deep breath and held it, then let it out slowly, feeling his body relax as the air seeped out of his lungs. Yes, he was part of a team, one of thousands whose individual contributions added up the biggest, most successful software company on the planet and Monday or not, it was time for him to start contributing.

What a crock of shit.

Mal's eyes rounded. "What the hell was that?" And then again.

What a crock of shit.

It was like a voice inside his head, or a voice hovering around the surface of his scalp, or hiding behind his ears. Whatever it was, it was insistent.

What a crock of shit.

***

"Where the hell did that come from?" yelled Johnny the Brain Cell. "Who's messin' with our boy's head?"

"Seems like it came from somewhere in here," said Daisy Mae. "Somewhere real close in here."

A small shudder shook Johnny's nucleus and cell walls. *In here?* he thought.

***

27

A shudder shook its way through Mal's body. "Oooookay. Voices in my head. Well, why not? It's Monday. Why the hell not. I'm still married, it's Monday, and nothing makes any sense anymore. And on top of all that, I'm talking to myself." He looked longingly at the tree at the other side of his office, felt a momentary sense of womb-like comfort as he visualized himself curled up on his favorite synthetic bough. He dismissed the thought almost as soon as the image formed in this head.

He walked to the door, past his personal tree, and stepped out of his office onto the gray-carpeted deck of what looked like the interior of a gargantuan space station with four stories of offices spreading upwards and another five stories spreading downwards around a circular central core. Metal bridges with wrought iron railings rendered in Gothic motifs spanned the immense space between each of the floor levels and the cylindrical core.

Directly in front of him, Sylvie's administrative control kiosk flicked and flittered with lights from the circular console surrounding her. The only functional lights were from her monitor and phone; the rest were symbolic of rank. As an Administrative Services Specialist Version 7.06, Sylvie's console was lit up like a sky full of fireworks.

***

The ten-storey section of building Mal stood in was just one of several similar sections in what was actually a 201-storey building, the highest human-made structure on the planet. At 2500 feet, it was

28

278 feet higher than the Center of India Tower. It ate Sears Towers and CN Towers for breakfast. Its name was BonannoTower (named after Bonanno Pisano, who almost ended the universe eight hundred years ago) and it was an exact replica of the Leaning Tower of Pisa, except for a few modifications, like a few hundred feet of additional width and a couple thousand feet of additional height.

And the space age smart materials used in its construction.

And the jet elevators that traveled at over a hundred miles an hour.

And the fluorescent lighting and indoor plumbing.

And the longest single piece of metal in the world that formed its core.

And the Most Secret Room in the World.

Chapter 4

A Mean Leaning Ringing Machine

It all started with the widow Berta of Bernardo of dell'Opera di Santa Maria who had a dream one night in 1172 AD, or at least, a dream according to friends and relations, but not to Berta. No sir, according to Berta, her dead husband Mr. Bernardo (aka Bernie) came to her one night with much concern and worry creasing the lines of rotted flesh and matted hair on what was left of his head. In a raspish voice he commanded: "Build a tower!" and then stared off somewhere between here and there with half empty eye sockets.

Berta thought about this for a moment, keeping her eyes on the floor and away from the remnants of her dearly departed's mostly departed eye-stuff. *Hmmm. Yes, build a tower. Hmmm.* And then she looked up, with much confusion shadowing her countenance, and asked stridently: "What you say? Build a tower? What I wanna go build a tower? You binna dead too long."

Bernie rolled what was left of his eyes and repeated: "Build a tower!"

However, as it was throughout their marriage, and even now in widowhood, Berta was not one to be told what to do by anyone, least of all Bernie, who couldn't even muster the energy to live as long as her, and she wasn't having any of this tower business.

"What you just stand there an-a say 'build a tower for'? I'm-a look like crazy woman to you? Is-a

30

what you think? I'm a crazy woman? Why you think I wanna build a tower?"

Bernie's hands were shaking; his remaining strands of grayish white skin darkened with whatever terrible pigmentation the dead use for darkening; he lifted his head and arms up towards the sky in a gesture of I-told-you-so. Then he cast the remnants of his gaze directly at Berta. "You gonna build a tower, or I'm-a gonna tell every one up there all about your snore so loud at night."

***

Just before she died in 1172 AD, the widow Berta of Bernardo of dell'Opera di Santa Maria amended her will to bequeath sixty coins to the Opera Campanilis petrarum Sancte Marie to buy a few stones for the building of a tower.

***

Those stones would eventually form the foundation of one of the most beautiful buildings on earth; also, one of the oddest. The tower was to compliment the cathedral in Pisa which was located in the "Field of Miracles" in the downtown area. What would happen to the "Torre Pendente di Pisa" (aka Bell Tower of Pisa) would indeed be a miracle.

The original architect, Bonanno Pisano, was reputed to dabble in bronze and foundries, and was, in many historical accounts, voted least likely to succeed at building a tower. But history aside, Bonnano Pisano began construction of the tower on August 9, 1173, and everything went just fine until

31

about the third stone from the left into the third floor, at which time the builders noticed that the tower-to-be was no longer performing to specs. In fact, it was beginning to *lean* prominently to the north.

The experts came in and hummed and hawed and concluded: "You build a tower on-a marshy soil an-a big hole ... it's-a gonna lean."

Which, of course, was completely wrong, the truth being that the now deceased widow Berta of Bernardo found out that Bernie had already told everybody "up there" all-about-her-snore-so-loud-at-night, and she was pissed ... so pissed that she came all the way back down from "up there" and kicked the living daylights out of certain key stones in the tower's foundation. "It's-a gonna point to Hell, where the old bastard should-a burn his big-a-mouth ass off!" She kicked and she kicked and she kicked all night, and when she was sure that certain key stones were sufficiently weakened to tumble the tower by the time it got to the third stone from the left into the third floor, she went back "up there" and waited smugly for Bernie to hear the news of his tower in a hundred years or so.

But a hundred years later, the tower was still standing - leaning, but standing - and the widow Berta of Bernardo visited the foundation again. And again, she kicked and she kicked and she kicked all night, and when she was sure that certain key stones were sufficiently weakened to tumble the tower, she went back "up there" and waited again for the news.

But for all the wrathful widow's heroic kicking effort, the tower instead of tumbling did an about face and started leaning to the south. Now the widow Berta of Bernardo was pissed enough to fry eggs on her forehead, so pissed, in fact, that it wasn't until 1934, nearly eight hundred years after the first stone was laid that Berta cooled down enough that she could float down from "up there" and have at the tower one more time.

Unfortunately, for the widow Berta of Bernardo, a group of Save The Tower fanatics picked this particular year to shore up the tower's sagging foundation with concrete. The concrete was actually drying as the widow kicked and kicked and kicked, and though she managed to increase the lean, by the time she ran out of kick, the concrete dried and solidified and the tower just hung there, a little more to the south. Nobody, of course, was aware of the widow Berta of Bernardo's kicking rampage, so the Save The Tower fanatics, instead of being up to their ears in kudos for saving the tower, were actually blamed for making it lean even more.

The tower still stands today. It still leans. And all the elaborate plans devised by all the elaborate minds to stop the lean from eventually reaching the ninety degree level in a pile of rubble have proved about as practical as tilting the entire city to straighten the tower (which, of course, would create a new puzzle for elaborate minds ... how to straighten the Leaning Town of Pisa while keeping the tower straight).

On the other hand, if the tower had been built straight in the first place, the universe would have ended eight hundred years ago.

Chapter 5

How dPisano Saved The Family Name, Almost

Straight from birth, some people have "Destined for Greatness" tattooed invisibly on their asses. dPisano (aka Danzo del Rio Pisano) was one such person with that elusive butt mark, and no one knew this better than dPisano, himself.

As a child, he spent days lining up opposing forces of toy soldiers on either side of his bedroom, entrenching them in folds in his blankets and placing them strategically on window sills and behind lamps and model airplane boxes. Tank and cannon barrels peeked out of crumpled newspaper and from under green-streaked leaves of Kleenex. Jeeps with walkie-talkie toting personnel and khaki trucks with bright red crosses painted on top coordinated battle readiness and prepared for wounded behind bookcases and pillows.

And when the forces were finally positioned for maximum battle-readiness - at that exact moment when all that was needed was the inadvertent flight of a dust mote across the sights of a hundred molded plastic rifle sights to set off polyethylene Armageddon - at that exact moment, six year old Danzo brought the two opposing generals together in the center of the room and negotiated a peace settlement, pointing out the futility of war and expounding the virtues of living together peacefully in the toy box. After which, he lined up the soldiers of both sides on his desktop where they watched solemnly as Danzo awarded himself the Nobel Prize for Peace.

He was large, bigger-than-life large (teen-size when he was eight and adult-size when he was thirteen) as though his physical dimensions were synchronized to grow in proportion to his intellect, which was no less than humongous from the start.

What better child than he to restore the family honor?

**

You see, dPisano was a direct descendent - give or take a few bloodlines - of Bonnano Pisano, the original architect of the Leaning Tower of Pisa and shameful monkey on the shoulders of a family whose main claim to fame was a tower that's been falling steadily for eight hundred years. If it had just fallen into a pile of dusty rubble at the third stone from the left on the third floor, then it would have all been over hundreds of years ago and long since forgotten. If it had fallen even a hundred years after it was started - if the widow Berta of Bernardo had had just a few more ounces of "oompf" in her kicks, then the whole thing would have been a minor footnote in history and the family honor would have been restored centuries ago. But, no, the damn thing was still standing - falling, but standing - a blatant and humiliating testament to the Pisano family failure.

But dPisano was going to change all that. At least, that was the plan, and the plan went something like this:

1. become incredibly rich and powerful

2. rebuild the tower in Pisa (without the lean)

A simple two-step plan ... with a few steps squeezed between the lines, and a few more dangling off each word in the plan. Step 1, for instance, required a little preparation, organization, and planning (POP, as dPisano would have it). He prepared himself by reading the biographies of the rich and powerful. He boned up on Caesar, Disraeli, Henry Ford, Napoleon, Bill Gates, Churchill, Walt Disney and others. One thing he noticed that they all had in common was that they were all great marketers. They knew how to sell an idea, whether it was an empire or a theme park.

He perfected his smile so that, by the time he graduated from college at the age of nineteen with joint honors in Computer Science and Business Administration, his smile almost disappeared behind his ears, exposing a scintillating array of brilliant white teeth through which he could speak, seemingly, without moving his mouth. His smile was hypnotically distracting to the point that people rarely heard the words that issued between the teeth, and deals were made and contracts were signed based on implicit trust in those two rows of calcified perfection.

Then he changed his name, opting for the associative punch of a single polysyllabic word. "Speak of Pablo Picasso," he said, "and you speak of a man. Speak of Picasso and you speak of boundless artistic achievement." Thus, Danzo del Rio Pisano became simply dPisano for those who, someday, would speak of boundless business achievement summed up in the mention of his single polysyllabic name.

For the accumulation of wealth, he chose the only industry he could think of that required almost no inventory, no pre-existing distribution network of trains, trucks, ships, planes and stores; an industry in which the customer believed in magic and miracles, and wanted desperately to believe that he, dPisano, was an all-powerful wizard commanding an army of elves and fairies. dPisano chose custom corporate software.

And in the tradition of the mightiest software empires, he started humbly. If Microsoft, Apple and others would start in basements and garages, then he would start at an even lower level - the bathroom. Perched bare-assed on his porcelain command center and armed with a powerful laptop connected to the Internet, he wrote programs and proposals, and navigated the pulsating highways and halls of cyberspace into appointments with the senior executives of the world's largest companies. And then he donned his three-piece suits and went off to the face-to-face meetings where his smile would do the rest.

He set his sights on the big software markets, the multi-million dollar contracts with bloated international firms, most of them bigger and more geographically dispersed than medium-sized national governments. What he eventually sold was not just a software package. What he sold was a software solution with the emphasis on solution (software, for the most part, being the major source of problems in the digital age). The solution he offered, as was explained in the ErectSoft INC marketing collateral, was "a program construct to expedite and integrate the management and implementation of large systems business process reengineering through the innovative application of accepted practices of methodology and procedure development."

Consider this: the brother of the person who stepped on the toes of your third cousin three times removed on your mother's side. Whatever image that brings to mind is exactly what ErectSoft INC produced.

Together with dPisano's imposing bearing, hypnotic smile, and a program that appeared to be needed in an industry bogged down by software systems so complex that nobody on earth could understand them in a million decades, dPisano built his company from a toilet operation to a multi-national presence in just three years.

**

Step one accomplished, the incredibly rich and powerful dPisano set out to rebuild the tower in Pisa, this time without the lean. But his offer to the Town of Pisa to tear down the old tower and build a new one in which the mighty bells, Il Crosifisso and dell'Assunta and their sisters, could swing and ring into the next two millennia without their torque toppling the tower, was flat out rejected. All his money and all his power, even the hypnotic allure of his compelling calcium, failed to impress the diehards in the Committee of Coordination for the Safeguard of the Tower of Pisa. "All you money an' all you power are no impress us. The Tower, she gonna stay. She gonna stay an' she gonna lean."

dPisano left Pisa in a fury.

But the fury was short lived. Thousand feet over the city, his private jet flew through what could only be described as an anomaly. It was nothing more than a simple three word message hanging in the air and, as the jet flew through it, the words wrapped arms as big as the death of creation around dPisano's mind and from that day forward dPisano had a new plan, a one part plan:

1. build a tower.

And what a tower. It was the highest human made structure on earth. Its core was a slab of alloy-reinforced iron that burrowed 1500 feet into the ground and soared 2000 feet into the air like a long skinny tongue shooting out of the earth's crust to lick the sky. Nothing short of Armageddon would bend it. Around the iron core, the builders wrapped the building like flesh and muscle around the vertebrae of a living thing. They wrapped 200 stories of boardrooms directly around the core and then they constructed thousands of steel bridges like spokes to support an outer layer of 200 stories of offices, stores, fast food kiosks, and lounges. Hundreds of glass elevators streaked up and down the inner core and outer layer like strings of glistening diamonds.

Outside, arches, pillars and colonnades climbed 2500 feet into the sky in a detailed replica of the original tower in Pisa. The top 500 feet - the bell tower - was one level housing one office, dPisano's office, a giant space with genuine alabaster walls and pillars, and genuine marble floors.

In the center of this immense space was one desk with one chair. Nothing else. Not a single picture on the walls, nor a slip of paper on the desk. It was a clear space for clear thinking, an airy emptiness in which to empty the crowded thoughts of daily bullshit and create in the mind a clean slate upon which to visualize, conceptualize, plot and plan.

It was the lair of the Last Truly Great Man on Earth.

At the 2000-foot level, there was an open balcony that surrounded the tower and offered several hundred people at a time a dizzying view that spanned over a hundred miles on a clear day. This was the Tomasso Observation Deck. This was the last solid thing on earth that Tara Cunningham would feel before her death, being unconscious by the time she hit the ground.

On the outside of BonnanoTower, you were in Medieval Italy; on the inside, especially in the open spaces between the main floors, you were in what could easily be mistaken for a giant space station, an illusion that was enhanced by the continuous vibration of a massive (in fact, the world's largest) air conditioning system. BonannoTower was a wonder of the new millennium, a work of structural art rendered in liquid crystalline polymers, synthetic stucco and synthetic wood, elastomeric coatings, plastic resins, nylon filaments, cellulose acetate, polyvinyl chloride, Lucite and Plexiglas. Its plastics remembered their shape, its floors were self-leveling, its walls controlled climate, and even the most stubborn dust could not stick to its space age dirt-resistant surfaces.

This was BonnanoTower. Home of ErectSoft INC. Dream of dPisano. Salvation of the Pisano family pride.

And the end of the universe.

***

Two months after BonnanoTower was completed, a small shiver ran through the entire building on a Wednesday afternoon at 3:00 PM. The building manager and his army of maintenance people were stymied. They inspected, measured, probed and conferred. But they could find no logical reason for the shiver.

Experts were called in: engineers, geologists, architects, metallurgists, and others. They asked questions, examined joists and building plans, brought in state-of-the-art equipment and took computer-generated pictures of the building's foundation and structure; they hummed and they hawed and they concluded their investigation. And then they submitted their findings to dPisano.

Apparently, the metal core was reacting to heat deep in the earth and had bent fractionally.

"Fractionally?" asked dPisano.

"Uh... fractionally, in that the building now has a fractional lean," said a quivering engineer with thick, horn-rimmed glasses.

"Fractional lean?" asked dPisano, the mesmerizing smile twisting into a nasty sneer.

"The... steel core is bent and... it's causing the building to lean," said the engineer, looking around at his silent cohorts, all of whom stood looking around at everywhere but him. "And the lean may even increase over... "

At which point, dPisano fired the entire building maintenance staff, the building manager, and every one of the experts in engineering, geology, architecture, metallurgy and others.

***

Deep down in the earth, way under the basement of BonnanoTower, the widow Berta of Bernardo finally gave up trying to kick over the steel tongue. "It's-a no go with his ancestor's tower an it's-a no go with this one. I'm-a no kicking towers anymore. I'm-a kick my big mouth Bernie instead."

Towers around the world breathed a small sigh of relief.

Chapter 6

Sumo Snowman Sonofabitch Back-Stabbing Bastard

As Mal approached the control kiosk, the glow of the computer monitor burned in Sylvie's eyes like embers in a campfire. "Ready for your meeting?" she asked, her eyes sweeping a once over to make sure that he was still all in one piece, legs and arms attached, pants still on, no stray leaves or twigs.

"Ready. In fact, I think I'm looking forward to it. It'll take my mind off this divorce bullshit." *And off Monday and whatever the hell that weird voice was*, he thought.

"Good for you! A true team player!"

Mal rolled his eyes. Sylvie laughed. "Remember who called for the meeting though, and be careful. Word's out that corp intell is up to something big, and Paul's in right up to his nasty little shit-smeared nose."

"Thanks for the warning, but I can take care of Paul." He straightened his back and narrowed his eyes, brave IT soldier marching off to another precarious marketing meeting. But this one promised to have a definite upside, Paul or no Paul Dubois: the woman he was toe-sucking in lust with was going to be there, and he was going to meet her in real life for the first time ever. Maybe then he would figure out why he wanted her so much.

One of the phones on Sylvie's console rang. Mal jumped at the opportunity: "Talk to you later." He winked and walked away as she reached for the phone. "Oh, just one second, Mal," she called after him. She answered the phone and put the caller on hold as Mal turned to her. "I'll be out for an hour or so at eleven. Your calls will be forwarded to Stephie Craig." She pointed to another control kiosk about fifty feet away, where a woman with dark-rimmed glasses and short black hair talked on the phone. "Thanks for holding," said Sylvie into the phone, dismissing Mal.

For some reason, Mal had a strange gut reaction to Sylvie taking the time away from work, not that it was unusual, but today it seemed somehow... different. Some-thing in her tone maybe? Or maybe it was just Monday.

As he approached the Level 6 North East bridge to the boardrooms at the core, Monday kicked him in the ass again. He saw the round crew-cut head of Paul Dubois, and worse yet, he was heading in the same direction as Mal and their paths would intersect at the mouth of the bridge.

***

Paul Dubois looked like a something spliced between a sumo wrestler and a snowman in some insane genetic experiment. He was a Senior Marketing Initiatives Planning and Research Manager in the Tier Four Business Initiatives Department and, like most marketing people, he considered himself ten pegs above everyone else even though he had his nose simultaneously up a thousand asses. His head was a huge circle squatting on his shoulders, and all his features were squeezed into the center of the circle, where two small browless black eyes stared unblinking and unreadable over a nose that looked like a button mushroom. His mouth resembled a soft clam shoved sideways into his face. He was short but stocky with thick sinew stirring under the folds of his gray marketing personnel uniform.

He was also one of the most dangerous men on earth and an unwitting player in the plot to end the universe.

Paul hadn't always been a deadly sycophant. As a child he'd been fat, dull and defenseless, a target for every bully in the neighborhood. Girl bullies had bicycled in from surrounding neighborhoods for a shot at the fat snowman kid's pudgy butt. But that had changed in high school, where he spent every spare moment in the weight room grunting and sweating the softness into sinew and the fat into sculpted ripples. After beating a former bully senseless with his fists and then kicking him viciously as he lay on the ground unconscious, the bullies had veered away from Paul Dubois. As had everyone else.

Though not smart, he was shrewd, and he'd been quick to learn that high school was a game with a clear set of rules:

1. Suck up to your teachers at every possible opportunity.

2. Do your homework.

3. Treat the rules as the word of God.

4. Don't ask complicated questions.

5. Suck up to your teachers at every possible opportunity.

He'd learned the rules well enough to carry him into college where he studied Business Administration, and it hadn't taken him long to

45

realize that the same rules applied just by changing the word teacher to professor. At a recruiting fair in his final term at college, he talked to a Human Potential Evangelist from ErectSoft INC.

"I need a job that will allow me to realize my fullest potential, Mr. Hazlett."

The Human Potential Evangelist smiled.

"I need a job that will challenge my abilities and my intelligence, Mr. Hazlett."

The Human Potential Evangelist nodded.

"I need a job that will make me a player in a dynamic team of forward looking professionals, Mr. Hazlett."

The Human Potential Evangelist leaned forward and said: "I need a blow job."

Two days after graduation, Paul was a Junior Corporate Image Propagation Champion in one of ErectSoft's largest marketing departments, and he'd scrapped his school rules in favor of a new set of rules, what he called the secret of corporate success. In brief, they went something like this:

1. Everybody wants to fuck you up the ass.

2. Fuck everybody up the ass before they do it to you.

3. Don't ask complicated questions.

Paul had become an enthusiastic master of rule number two and had earned a reputation as a two-faced sonofa-bitch backstabbing bastard. But he didn't ask complicated questions and he had his nose up all the right asses, which put him on the fast track to senior management.

***

Incidentally, there was only one thing that everyone hated about Paul Dubois more than Paul Dubois himself, and that was his obnoxious aftershave. It pushed the air back in a ten-foot perimeter around him and hovered menacingly in the air for half an hour after his passing.

***

Mal would soon be in range of that aftershave. He slowed his pace just enough to allow Paul to get to the bridge ahead of him, but then Paul looked in Mal's direction and their eyes met. *Shit*, thought Mal. "Shit," said Paul's eyes. When the distance between the two narrowed uncomfortably enough for the overbearing odor to assault Mal's nostrils, Mal was the first to speak: "'Mornin', Paul. Off to the Barnyard?"

Impatient with the obvious, Paul sneered. In a surprisingly high pitched voice, he said: "Mr. Gray, do you think it might ever occur to you that a notepad and pen might come in handy at these meetings?" Paul was carrying a black briefcase.

Maybe if something important was ever said at one of these meetings, thought Mal. "Did you hear about the woman who jumped off the Tomasso Deck? Tara Cunningham?"

"You know what suicide is, don't you?" Paul waited for an answer as they approached the bridge. For about five seconds, Mal's brain worked on the question. What was this, a pop quiz? What kind of dumb-ass question was this?

"Don't you, Mr. Gray?" repeated Paul.

"Uh, no, Paul... at least, well, it's when somebody can't live with the pain of... "

"Bullshit, Mr. Gray. It's when some loser decides he's had enough and takes the back door out, leaving a big mess for the living to clean up. Leaves questions that are never going to be answered and a pile of paperwork. Suicide is a kind of murder. Like any other murder, they should give people the death sentence for doing it, Mr. Gray."

Mal laughed at the joke. "Right, Paul... wheel their dead carcasses into court. Try 'em and fry 'em!"

The small black circles in the center of Paul's round head stared straight ahead, emotionless, as they stepped onto the bridge.

Jesus, thought Mal, *he's not joking.*

The bridge crossing to the Core was wide enough for a truck. It arched upward slightly and then dropped back down toward the Core. Far below, Mal saw bodies scurrying around on the imitation marble floor, buying food at the fast food kiosks and sitting around in open-air lounge areas reading or talking. He caught a whiff of pizza, but it was quickly strangled by Paul's aftershave.

"Whatever," spat Paul. "But that Cunningham woman was a cop out. She gets no sympathy from me."

"You're all heart, Paul," said Mal while thinking: *You're a nasty little snowman who's going to melt in the Spring leaving nothing behind but the lump of dog shit you were using for a heart.* "Any hints about this meeting?" They reached the door to the Barnyard. Paul opened the door and ducked in quickly without answering. A swift flash of The Creeps tingled across the back of Mal's neck.

He was smiling, thought Mal. *He never smiles*.

Chapter 7

Good Thing You Didn't Remarry, Revisited

Shaped like a half moon, the Barnyard curved around a twenty foot wide floor-to-ceiling, corner-to-corner photo mural of the ultimate statement on the theme of "rustic places I'd like to die in". An ancient plank-sided wagon lay half buried atop a mound of patchy grass, its rear wheels missing and its steel-rimmed front wheels rusting between the tarnished blades of a threshing assembly. Gray, time-trampled fence posts trailed off to a dirt road leading to a stand of knobby trees that slouched toward a covered wooden bridge. The bridge's wind-pummeled roof, its shingles plucked and plowed, looked like nothing stopped it from caving in at the center but hard air. Light-enhancing smart materials in the mural gave it a three dimensional quality so real that it seemed you could walk into the thick gray mists in the fields beyond the bridge and disappear into the patches of green hill in the distance.

Murals replaced windows in the ErectSoft boardrooms - seascapes, cityscapes, mountain ranges, prairies, desert oases, tropical islands, Oriental fishing villages, autumn parks, arctic ice fields, and wilderness rivers. The murals instilled a sense of connection to the outside world in the gray windowless rooms at the building's core. Some were subliminal mood swingers with themes like Post Industrial Dead Stream Flowing By Chemical Waste Pond, We All Do Business On A Yellow Submarine, and Let's Not Save Private Ryan Today.

This last one, with dead soldiers strewn about a red beach as the living ran and swam crazy-eyed for the departing landing vehicles, was used when entire departments were disbanded and their staffs laid off. It was called the DD Day room for Dead Department Day.

The only furniture in the Barnyard was a round table with a plastic wood grain top in the center of the room surrounded by ten swiveling armchairs. A circular florescent light shone in the ceiling above the table like the sun stuck in a grid of perforated gray pegboard. Mal thought that the intense florescent lighting made everything look a little too close up and real, made every mole glow with religious significance and every blood vessel and capillary bulge prominently blue.

Seven people sat around the table.

Caitlin McCarthy, Vice President of Corporate Image Evangelism, was the meeting Chairperson. She was stocky with a square jaw and deep green eyes that looked into you rather than at you. After talking to her for a few minutes, you walked away with the feeling that this woman had just navigated the North, South, East and West of your soul and had a road map stored away for future reference. It was her job to ensure that the outside world smiled at ErectSoft INC; she was the filter between reality and illusion. All anyone knew of her personal life was that she drove a red Firebird with tinted glass windows. That she was chairing the meeting meant something big was up, something with the potential to draw the attention of "out there".

To Caitlin's right sat Harvey Jennings (aka Harv) who, like Mal, was an Industry Specialist and

Research Manager in the same department as Mal. Harv specialized in designing scoping procedures for industry-specific development methodologies. His most distinguishing feature was that he had no distinguishing features. He was the quintessence of "average". There was nothing memorable about him from his average brown hair and average brown eyes to his average build and average brown suit. If you were to drop him into the jungles of Papua New Guinea, cannibals would likely have a difficult time remembering if he tasted like chicken or pork. However, his reaction to a marketing strategy would be exactly the same as that bulk of the population called Mr. and Mrs. Joe Average, a talent that made him a valuable instrument of measure in meetings to sound out new marketing initiatives, a talent of which Harv was completely unaware. But then, that just made him all the more average.

Beside Harv, Samantha Wilbur (aka Sammy the Frog) sat frog-like with bulging eyes and a wide mouth that flowed chinless to her neck which, in turn, flowed into a flaccid lump of body. It was hard to say where her breasts stopped and her stomach began. She was a Senior Quality Assurance Methodology Manager and ISO Adherence Specialist who spent most of her time biting the inside of her mouth and sending e-mails to development people who had forgotten to file Control Form N2Q3_ 455_Client_Contact after phoning a client to ask what the weather was like in their part of the country. Her dumpy dresses and sloppy use of eye shadow belied the anal perfectionist under the wrinkled folds. Mal had no idea why she would be at this meeting and figured that Sammy was probably wondering the same thing.

Across from Samantha, Cindy Chen sat coolly as she talked to Caitlin and Harv. Cindy was a Senior Trends Analysis and Mass Behavior Forecasting Manager. She wore a gray marketing uniform with a golden lightning bolt on her collar, the insignia of the Competitive Intelligence and Corporate Warfare Department. In spite of this, and her off the scales IQ and photographic memory, she was a warm tiny woman with almond eyes and a deep love of conversation. After the meeting, she would monitor the phone calls and the e-mail and Internet use of everyone in the room.

The other three were obviously planted by Paul to support whatever it was for which he'd called the meeting. They were what was referred to as marketing clones, Junior Marketing Managers who demonstrated their insatiable need to stick their noses up their bosses' asses by mimicking them in every way possible. They wore the same gray uniform as Paul, had the same skull-clinging crew cut, and copied his every gesture. The names on their breast pocket patches were Daryl Tyson, Laurie Hatfield, and Janet Sobovitch. Two of these unapologetic ass-lickers were destined to play a key role in the fate of the universe.

Mal regarded the tenth seat with disappointment. It was supposed to have been occupied by the woman of his lust. Her name had been copied in the e-mail announcing the meeting, but she wasn't there.

***

Paul made his way to the chair on Caitlin's left and put his briefcase on the table. He eyed the three marketing clones. They looked back, their eyes pushing a blind psychic intent that carried their noses across the table and planted them, one, two, three firmly up Paul's butt. Paul's personal cheering section. Whatever he'd called the meeting for was important to him, and given his close links to senior management, important to the people who ran ErectSoft INC. There would be little discussion in this room today, the discussions having already been completed in rooms far above this one. This meeting would be just one more check mark on a controlled procedure checklist. Maybe that was why Sammy the Frog was there... to bear witness.

As Mal seated himself beside Sammy, Cindy looked his way. "So, Malcolm, how's married life?"

Mal flushed. "Word sure gets around fast," he said, as he thought: *Damn, they've already started monitoring the phone calls.*

"You know IT, Mal." She smiled. "Big industry, little world."

"You've remarried, Mal?" asked Caitlin. "When did this happen?" Caitlin and Mal, though not close, were friends. He'd worked on several projects that had been evaluated by her for image consistency and she'd always sent him flattering e-mails for his work during project segment wrap-ups.

His face flushed again as he responded: "No, I haven't, Caitlin. I just found out this morning... " He tossed an accusatory look in Cindy's direction. "... that my divorce didn't actually go through four years ago. Guess I didn't have the best lawyer."

"And didn't take a notepad to court," said Paul with a mean little smile.

"Just look at the bright side," said Caitlin after giving Paul a stern glance. "It's a good thing you didn't re-marry." Laughter erupted around the table. Mal's face reddened deeper.

"Well," said Harv, "at least you're not on the Cary-Clare Project. I just saw the whole team being marched into the DD Day room on my way here. Know anything about that, Cindy?"

Cindy shrugged her eyebrows. "Can't be anything good."

Just as Mal noticed that the aroma of coffee from cups steaming around the table was beginning to be replaced by the smell of Paul's repugnant aftershave, his day jumped feet first into a not-such-a-bad-day-after-all mode. The door to the Barnyard opened and Crystal Peake strode in. Tall, blond, and shapelier than an ergonomic keyboard, she had been in his thoughts continuously for the few days, in just about every position and pose possible. Seeing her for the first time ever, he was so stunned that it never occurred to him to wonder that this woman he'd never seen before looked exactly like the woman in his fantasies.

***

Crystal Peake had been recruited for ErectSoft INC by dPisano himself, the same day she graduated from college and about seven seconds before she finished delivering her valedictorian address. With her long golden hair tumbling from under her mortar board and her ergonomic shapelyness pressing joyfully against her robes, Crystal, with her eyes flashing blue ice, had spoken inspiringly of, you know, that future thing where all of us will make that big difference, or was it all of us are the whatchamacallit for something about generations, maybe hope, you know, those words that flowed from her perfect red lips like strands of creamy caramel. Which was about all that any man in the audience would ever remember of a perfectly boring and cliche valedictorian address, except, maybe, the occasional puzzling reference to some goddess or other, some other-world guiding light.

Sitting on the stage with his honorary degree in his lap, dPisano immediately made up his mind that this perfect bod... er... woman would be working for him and, after catching her attention by breaking into an exuberant round of applause that cut off the last three sentences of her address and drew every eye in the stadium to the smile that sank a thousand reluctant maybes, Crystal made up her mind that she would work this mad fool for every-thing he was worth. In fact, this was part of the path she'd been following since the day of her birth.

Three days later, after disappearing for the weekend and missing her graduation ball, Crystal Peake packed a single suitcase while her boyfriend wailed: "Where the hell have you been? Why are you packing? What's going on? I waited all Friday night with a corsage in my lap! I missed my own fucking graduation ball! Where were you? Say something!"

Crystal closed the case and handed him an envelope. "My share of the rent. Bye, hon." An hour later she drove her new Mercedes into the executive parking lot at BonannoTower and rode the elevator up to her sprawling twenty thousand square foot office on the level immediately under dPisano's office. No one at ErectSoft INC knew of anyone who had ever been in Crystal's office (except dPisano) but there were rumors of plush pink wall-to-wall carpeting, serpentine walls, furniture inlaid with silver and gold and a giant heart-shaped hot tub carved in marble. But these, of course, were just rumors and nobody would make the mistake of equating the pink carpets with anything closely resembling a Barbie Doll flightiness after having had Crystal's cold, calculating irises stare a ribbon of ice into their eye sockets. Looking at Crystal was sublime pleasure, until she looked back.

Crystal was Vice President At Large of Creative Initiatives Team Approval, which is to say, she sat in on kick-off meetings for especially important projects. She watched, she listened, and she made mental notes. Within hours, team members would be informed by their supervisors whether or not they were still team members.

Some called her the Corporate Presidential Concubine.

Many of these people would be dead by the end of the day.

Right out of the blue one day, Mal had received an email from her. She'd bought one of his drawings in a craft shop on the first floor of BonannoTower where Mal sold them for a small commission. Charming, she'd described it. Nice attention to detail. Interesting configuration of bubbles. Mal had read the email at least a dozen times before his pulse slowed down to a non-life-threaten-ing level, and without ever having met her, he was mad about her, even though she was totally unattainable, not to mention taken, and way beyond his means, and way out of his class, and way off in some world that, if Malcolm Gray were to put his toes in to explore the temperature, his entire leg would dissolve.

Mal couldn't explain why he felt the way he did about Crystal; he didn't even like blondes, but he'd never been this horny in his entire life. It was like he was drawn to her by something...

Chapter 8

The Plan

Mal hated Crystal's slinky green dress. He envied each individual silk thread. How dare this thread cling so greedily to her curving thigh! How dare that silk strand lick its fibers as it hugged her breasts! His head reeled in dress-envy and his heart leaped when she said: "I trust I didn't miss anything important," as she took her seat between Cindy and marketing clone Janet.

Her voice, thought Mal, *her voice. Like petals of music falling from a symphony of sleeveless silk.*

And then it was shattered by Paul Dubois' squeaky cacophony: "Just idle chit chat to break the ice, Ms. Peake." Paul was quick to get his nose into the corporate position even though Crystal was obviously without notebook and pen.

But she ignored him, sat back in her chair and crossed her legs. Mal marveled at the immaculate precision of her posture, reveled in the blueness of her eyes, which were at the uppermost end of the blue scale, way up there where blue atoms and blue molecules danced in perfect harmony in a blue universe. A cold blue universe.

"Another jumper off the Deck," she said. "Some kind of bug going around?"

"Copy cat," said Paul. Everyone looked in his direction. "One person jumps, gives others the idea. Anybody with a chip on their shoulder follows suit." All three marketing clones nodded agreement in unison, proud of their leader's wisdom.

59

Still ignoring Paul, Crystal turned to Cindy and said: "Look into this." Cindy made a note. Crystal nodded to Caitlin. Everyone looked at Caitlin. Caitlin looked around the room, mapping the whereabouts of attitudes and dispositions. She took a deep breath and said: "Proactive Aggressive Customer Acquisition."

Everyone looked at Caitlin.

She repeated the words, mouthing each as though she were spitting out a bit of floss gunk. "Proactive... Aggressive ... Customer ... Acquisition." Whatever it meant, Mal was certain that Caitlin didn't like it. She was normally animated, a generator of positivity and motivation, especially at project kickoffs. Today, she was somber, the fire in her eyes dampened, the generator switch turned to off. She started to say something, changed her mind, and then said: "I'll now turn the meeting over to Paul Dubois, who, it's my pleasure to announce, has just been promoted to Vice President of Venture Marketing Initiatives. Paul."

The bottom of Mal's stomach fell out and splashed onto the floor. The three marketing clones clapped their hands vigorously, gleaming smiles stretched around their heads. Caitlin and Crystal exchanged guarded glances. Cindy appeared to be doodling in her notebook, beside the note to check on the suicides. Sammy and Harv smiled and nodded toward Paul. Paul's clam lips twisted into a gloat. His hands quivered with self-importance as he opened his briefcase and removed a small stack of thin, plastic-covered reports. He passed them around the table.

"PACA," he said, and sat back in his chair with his hands cupped in his lap. His knuckles were white with the effort to stop the shaking. The three marketing clones opened their reports and sat back with their hands in their laps.

***

"An aggressive, proactive marketing plan with the focus on ACTION, ACTION, ACTION!" Paul's high-pitched voice made the three ACTIONs sound more like barks from an angry poodle than motivation from a man of power, proving once again that engaging oration is not one of the perks of power.

Paul's little black eyes scanned the faces around the table, a short pause for approval. In the harsh florescent glare, his skin looked almost snowman white.

Mal peeked quickly in Crystal's direction. Crystal wore the glow from the florescent light like a carefully chosen camera filter designed to highlight the richness of her untanned skin, to accentuate the creamy of her smoothness. The table and the people sitting around it suddenly seemed close up, as though everyone's psychic aura were rubbing elbows. The room shrunk and Mal could swear that if he moved his forefinger just an inch he could touch Cindy's nose across the table. He rolled his eyes back to Paul, overshot the mark and landed on the squat back of Sammy's neck. Fluorescent light actually brought out the best in her, giving her skin a pleasant translucence, but then, wasn't that what real frog skin was like? Sammy was pushing a foreknuckle into the side of her mouth and chewing the skin inside.

Paul leaned forward. "If you'll all turn to page one of the plan... " Pages flipped and fluttered around the table. Mal studied the cover:

PACA

(CONFIDENTIAL)

(FOR TEAM PACA EYES ONLY)

Inside, the report was just one page. No charts, graphs, tables, appendices, executive summaries, preamble, cost projections, work outlines, or project team profiles. Just one page with one line:

NOTHING IS SACRED.

Sammy was still reading, kneading the side of her face as she chewed furiously, most likely trying to find some kind of standards non-conformance, or maybe deciding to point out that only the first letter of "NOTHING" need be upper case. Harv read the report with a typically average blank stare. The three marketing clones read and reread the line, nodding agreement, nudging each other and pointing out their favorite parts. Cindy was still doodling. Caitlin studied faces. Crystal was looking directly into Mal's eyes.

Mal tightened; his body tightened; his mind tightened, and then his soul tightened into a big gnarly knot. It wasn't a cold look, more like a soft look, calculating, but soft, as though she were trying to make up her mind about something. Mal smiled. Bad move. Her eyes suddenly frosted and Mal looked back at the report. *What the hell's going on here?* he thought.

***

What a crock of shit.

***

"There it is again!" yelled Johnny the Brain Cell. "Where the hell's that comin' from?"

"What's that, Johnny?" called Bobby. "You saying that hell's comin'?"

"No, Bobby," said Daisy Mae. "He said where's it comin' from. Ain't you heard that voice yet?"

"You mean that crock of shit voice?"

"That's the one. Where's it comin' from?"

"Hell, I thought it was Johnny."

***

Paul spoke: "ErectSoft INC spends millions of dollars each year on target marketing." He leaned forward, his hands clasp around a copy of the report. "ErectSoft INC spends millions of dollars each year on advertising."

Two folds deepened over his eyes where his eyelashes would have been had he had any.

"ErectSoft INC spends millions of dollars each year on proposals, trade shows, business lunches, meetings with potential clients, brochures ... millions." He looked down at the report. "And what does all this effort, time and enormous expenditure do for us?"

His face went blank.

"There are people out there, potential ErectSoft INC clients, who are still doing business with our competitors." His eyes suddenly widened and he banged his fist on the table, shaking the entire room, and causing Sammy the Frog to grab the side of her face after nearly biting through her cheek.

"NO SALE!"

The air sucked out of the room for an instant, leaving only the silence of Paul's obnoxious aftershave. Every eye in the room stared at him, with the exception of Crystal's. Mal noticed that she was staring at the covered bridge in the mural, and what was that at the corner of her left eye? Moisture?

Paul's mouth curled into a sinister smile. The three marketing clones mimicked Paul's pounding fist by banging their fists into their palms. Emulating the boss was the path to promotion; outdoing the boss, the path to unemployment.

Crystal continued to stare at the bridge, seemingly oblivious of Paul's outburst. Mal glanced behind him at the mural. Nothing moved in the tattered old bridge, it's struggle against gravity frozen in time and space. No eyes peered out from the dark rifts between the rotted boards. *What the hell is the attraction?* His movement attracted Crystal's attention, and she was looking at him again when he turned back to the table. The softness was back. The weirdness was back, too. Something started gnawing away at Mal's brain. *Crystal Peake does not look at any man this way, least of all a nobody like me.* The room started to shrink dizzyingly around Mal again and, suddenly, Crystal, with her perfect blue eyes and slender nose and perfect red lips was just inches away from him, and he was terrified. He blinked and shook his head. The illusion dissolved. Crystal was on the other side of the table, but Mal could have sworn that there was just a small trace of a smile on her lips. He looked back at Paul just in time to catch the tail end of what he was saying.

"... opens a whole new arena in competitor surveillance." Paul extended a puffy white hand toward Cindy. "I'll let Ms. Chen outline the major features."

Cindy stuck a finger in a bang over her ear and curled it once, and leaned forward as though sharing a deep confidence. "Our internal R&D has been working on this for nearly two years." She opened a report with a red cover. "Basically, it tracks and records hits on our Web site and hits on our competitors' Web sites. It identifies the source of the hit right down to the IP address of the originating computer and then sends an ingenious program out to that computer, where it hides and gathers information. It contains an encryption program that breaks through passwords." She looked up from her report and said: "And it communicates to us."

She closed her report.

Silence, like a single bubble popping in the middle of a bathtub, settled ominously over the room. Mal let the words sink in, struggling with their meaning.

Communicates to us? he thought. *What the hell is that supposed to mean?* And then something even more puzzling crept across his neutrino-altered consciousness. He had no idea why it was so puzzling, just that, somehow, it didn't fit in. As a report, Mal's thoughts might read something like this:

Subject: Fishy

Date: April 1

It has come to my attention that the R&D department in Competitive Intelligence and Corporate Warfare has completed a project. They have finished something, something that is functional and ready to be used, something they've been working on for nearly two years and now it has seen closure and, presumably, has been signed off, completed.

Completed.

Completed? thought Mal. *But what's so astonishing about that?* At which point the report would end, a one pager like the PACA report, because Mal had no idea why that was so astonishing. At least, not yet.

"What Ms. Chen is saying," said Paul, "is that we now have the capability to proactively assist potential clients in a meaningful way. We are in a position to identify their problems and then design a custom solution to meet their needs."

***

What a crock of shit.

***

Where the hell is that coming from? thought Mal. *Sounds like it's right in the damn center of my head.*

"ErectSoft INC," continued Paul, "produces the most effective software solution in the IT industry." He waved an arm around the room. "That's what this building is all about." He waved an arm around the table. "That's what we're all about. But that message is not getting out to those thousands of unfortunate systems managers and executive decision-makers who repeatedly deal with our competitors. We need to help these people to make the right decision, in spite of themselves."

"Hear, hear!" piped in marketing clone Laurie.

Paul continued: "Some might use words such as 'corporate espionage', 'invasion of privacy', 'spying', and even 'trespassing'. But it's all just a matter of perspective." He paused for a moment, eyes studying the ceiling at the far end of the table, hands clasped in his lap. "And what will become apparent as the perspective takes root is that we're actually collecting valuable marketing data that we can use to help prospective clients to make informed, intelligent decisions based on a thorough understanding of their needs and business goals. This degree of understanding is impossible to achieve through traditional data gathering modes. These modes are what I call 'passive' in that they rely primarily on gathering whatever information a potential client chooses to make available, and then that information is hashed back to them wrapped up in a solution that may or may not convince them to do business." Paul lowered his eyes to the people around the table and spoke slowly: "Our new paradigm is a little more... active."

Sammy the Frog sat with three fingers against her cheek. She was no longer chewing. Cindy studied Harv's face closely, but his face was mostly non-committal.

"We have a team building a massive data warehouse with a bioneural-networked EIS system that will coordinate and direct the PACA program. They will supply us with both personal and business information about prospective clients. We'll know what projects they're working on, who they're working with, how much they have to spend, how much they have in their personal bank accounts, the names of their grandparents ... "

"Brilliant!" hollered marketing clone Janet.

"Absolutely!" agreed marketing clone Daryl.

Paul smiled and nodded. "And then we apply this information directly to marketing efforts. Aggressive marketing efforts."

Just as Mal was about to ask about the personal bank accounts and the names of grandparents, he looked around the table and saw that no one seemed to be outraged, puzzled or even interested in the fact that Paul was talking about a marketing plan that broke laws and made a mockery of business ethics. In fact, those who showed any emotion, showed enthusiasm.

Mal decided to keep his mouth shut for the moment.

And then Paul mouthed the magic words: "We need every member of the team to be fully committed to this plan in order to make it work." Heads bobbed in agreement, a show of commitment, even Mal's head nodded slightly under the pressure to bob and be counted. Crystal narrowed one perfect blue eye as she watched Mal's face. Mal nodded once more.

Marketing clone Daryl, eyes glazed with commitment, said: "We're ready for this, Mr.

Dubois!" He swept his eyes around the table without seeing anything. "I, personally, feel that you've put together a crack team and under your direction we'll make this happen!"

Mal thought: *Under "your" direction? Good lord, I'll be working under Paul Dubois on this damned project?*

"What do you want us to do?" asked marketing clone Laurie.

Paul flipped through the pages of the black binder. He took a deep breath and let it out slowly. "We change the way we do business."

"About time!" said marketing clone Janet.

"I'm starting to get excited," said marketing clone Daryl, banging a fist into his open palm. "Sounds like we're going to be pioneers here!"

"We start putting these people in their place!" said Paul.

"Now that's aggressive! I love it!" said marketing clone Laurie.

"When we determine that a potential client is planning to take their business to one of our competitors, we ... discourage them ... from making a costly mistake."

"Now, that's taking the initiative," said marketing clone Janet.

"Exactly!" said Paul, pointing a forefinger at her. Janet beamed right through the top of her shaved head. "We take the initiative, armed with the right information. We'll have complete specifications for their project needs, access to solution proposals from our competitors, and detailed personnel profiles of all the players."

"Wonderful!" yelled marketing clone Daryl. "Finally, something we can sink our teeth into!"

"Coordinating our marketing efforts with the EIS, we implement a program of carefully timed strategic intimidation."

"Perfect!" yelled marketing clones Laurie and Janet in unison. "For their own good!" yelled marketing clone Daryl. The enthusiasm of the marketing clones was beginning to overwhelm the room. Harv drummed his fingers heavily on the table and said: "I don't think anything like this has ever been tried before."

"It hasn't," said Paul. "And that's just the first line of offensive." His words were almost drowned out by congratulatory chatter from the marketing clones as they patted each other on the back. Marketing clone Daryl even nudged Mal. Marketing clone Janet started to nudge Crystal, caught herself, and ran her hand over the top of her stubbled head.

"We take the offensive from the business environment and right into the personal environment!"

Cheers sprang up from the marketing clones.

"We call them at work and we call them at home. We leverage them with business data and with personal information!"

"Cutting edge!" yelled marketing clone Janet. "And we do it for their own good!" "For their own good!" yelled the other two marketing clones.

The room caved in on Mal again, not so much because of the lighting this time as because of the absurdity of the meeting. *My god*, he thought, *everyone seems to be OK with this. Nobody's questioning this idiocy. They've all gone insane!*

A frenzy of energy boiled around the table, snapping and crackling under the glare of the florescent light. "It's time to take the offensive!" Paul slammed his fist on the table again. "It's time to change the world of marketing and bring it into its own!"

"Genius!" yelled marketing clone Laurie. "Genius!" She was standing now, drool seeping out of the corners of her mouth and down her chin. "Genius!"

"We create a new paradigm," said Paul, looking directly into the marketing clone's eyes. "And we lead the unconverted masses into a future that we have carefully designed for them!"

"Halleluiah!" screamed marketing clone Laurie, as her arms flew out and her eyes rolled up into her forehead. She fell forward onto the table, foam gushing from her mouth as her lips worked hectically and her arms flailed uncontrollably. A line of blood streaked her forehead from where it hit the table. Her body jerked spasmodically. Mal felt a chill rush through his body as marketing clone Laurie's voice suddenly grew deep and raspy and a barrage of sound emitted from her:

"USABIPARDIGM INNA CONFIGURITERATIVE ALLA UBIQUITILOGUE ANNA TIERPLATE INNA PARTITION! INNA PARTITION!"

Everyone stared blank-eyed, except Crystal, who took Cindy's pen, flipped over her copy of the report and wrote down the words coming out of the marketing clone's mouth.

"SPECIFIGOAL AROUNA CYCLE ANNA CYCLE INNA CYCLE!"

***

Ignore it. It's a crock of shit.

As soon as the voice in Mal's head finished, Crystal looked at Mal, her eyes wide with surprise and her head question-like cocked to one side.

Did she hear that? thought Mal.

A crock of shit.

Crystal looked down at her writing, dropped the pen and pushed it along the table to Cindy, who stared at marketing clone Laurie.

She did. She heard it.

Crystal looked back at Mal, her eyes boring right through his head as though she were trying to locate the source of the words. Then, she smiled and nodded almost imperceptibly. Mal didn't know it at this time, but he wouldn't be hearing the voice in his head anymore.

***

"And just what in hell's half acre was that?" said Johnny the Brain Cell.

"Sounded like a sigh of relief or something, Johnny," said Bobby. "Don't know where it came from, though. Sounded like everywhere."

***

"DIALOGUE ORIENTMENT IZZA NEEDANALCESS BUYA SCOPE! INNA PARTITION! INNA PARTITION!"

And then marketing clone Laurie's body went limp like a balloon with a fast leak, the top part of her body slid over the side of the table and joined her feet on the floor. Everyone stared. After a moment, Mal and marketing clone Daryl bent towards her. Marketing clone Laurie stirred, opened her eyes, smiled beatifically, stood up, brushed off the front of her gray jacket, adjusted her gray tie, pulled her chair back to the table and sat down, still smiling a silly faraway smile.

Paul gloated. "Yes, I think we have an acceptable team here." The smile narrowed as his eyes settled on Mal. "Well... "

Chapter 9

Morning In The Woods Of A Zillion Bubbles

Minuscule bubbles of energy that had not seen light on this planet for eons burst quietly by the thousands, each releasing a small charge of energy from within its shimmering walls. They released their energy into the trees and the shrubs, into the grass and the soil, into the air and into the light. And as the bubbles burst, others took their place, bouncing lightly off the veins of leaves and sliding down blades of grass. They settled on the blackened cauldron in the center of the clearing, trickled like crystal water down its three scorched wooden legs and released their charges into the gray ashes. And the energy fluctuated with the bristle of fur, flowed with the warmth of a dawning sun, and danced a rhythm that had not been shimmied and shaked to in a thousand thousand millennia, a rhythm that was at once sinister and joyful, around and around the cauldron, following the foot-beaten path around and around the cauldron. And if you were to hold your breath, be very still and listen closely, you might hear the sound of countless soft whispers permeating the space right in front of your nose.

Chapter 10

Nobody's Going To Jail

Paul was first out the door, off to change the face of marketing, with the three marketing clones close on his heels. Marketing clone Laurie was still dazed from her babbling fit and allowed marketing clone Janet to support her arm.

Caitlin passed out passwords for project files on the company intranet to all but Mal and Crystal and then dismissed Harv, Sammy and Cindy. Harv closed the door lightly as he left.

It was just Mal, Caitlin and Crystal.

Crystal stared at the bridge in the mural.

Caitlin stared at Mal.

Mal stared down at the report. He clasped his hands behind his head, trying to look calm and centered, hoping that his antiperspirant was handling the day better than his brain. It was time to make a statement. He looked from Caitlin to Crystal. "You're all going to end up in jail."

The two women remained silent. Crystal moved her eyes from the mural to Mal.

"Paul's off his rocker," said Mal. "This idiotic plan... " he pointed at the report in on the table in front of him, "... not only breaks all the rules of professional integrity, it breaks laws."

The two women remained stoically silent. Mal repeated, "You're going to go to jail."

Crystal smiled. "Nobody's going to jail."

"Oh yeah?" said Mal. "You can't hide something this big for long. As soon as - "

"We're not going to hide anything," said Crystal.

"Oh, I see, you're going to let people know about this PACA thing and just... "

"PACA is never going to be used," said Crystal. "It doesn't even exist."

"But Paul just ... "

"We need you to trust us." The words flowed from Crystal's mouth like chocolate ice cream melting on a thick slice of hot apple pie. Remembering his lust, Mal said: "... " which pretty much summed up the condition of his mind at the moment.

The two women pounced.

"We need you to play along with Paul for the time being," said Caitlin.

"Don't raise any difficult questions," said Crystal.

"Just do what he tells you," said Caitlin.

"And don't talk about this meeting with anyone," said Crystal.

"Either this meeting, or Paul's meeting," said Caitlin.

"This is the real team," said Crystal. "The three of us... and a very select group of key people."

"You have a reputation for being an excellent team player," said Caitlin. "Now, you get to choose your team."

"Are you with us? Will you trust us?" Crystal leaned just a fraction of an inch closer to Mal, but it was as if her eyes had just leaped across the table and fused into his own eyes like a dangling power line, sending charge after charge into his body. "Will you trust *me*, Malcolm?"

"Well... " said Mal.

"We'll be in contact with you later today," said Crystal. "We need you, Mal. We need you on our team."

Crystal needs me, thought Mal. *Crystal Peake needs me.* Mal's will, Mal's resolve, Mal's core being, every-thing that had been Mal, was Mal, and would ever be Malcolm Gray was swimming in a sea of chocolate ice cream and the only way to stay afloat was...

"You can count on me."

What the hell am I getting into?

"I trust you."

I don't know a damn thing about this.

"You can count me in."

"We knew we could count on you," said Caitlin.

What the hell have I gotten myself into?

***

Mal was last out of the Barnyard, having stayed a moment after Caitlin and Crystal left, supposedly to "think for a moment" but what he really wanted to do was take a close up look at the covered bridge in the mural. Nothing seemed out of place, just your typical rotting covered bridge that broke all the laws of gravity by not collapsing in the center. As he left the room, he fought is own battle with gravity, the heaviness of too many questions all clamoring in his mind at the same time: *Why me? Where the hell do I fit into all this? And what the hell is going on?*

And what the hell is she *up to?*

Leaning against a guardrail with her back to Mal, marketing clone Laurie talked into a cell phone as she watched Crystal and Caitlin part directions at the other end of the bridge. Then she turned toward Mal and their eyes smashed head on. She spoke briefly into the phone and headed toward the Level 6 East bridge.

Chapter 11

Who Knows What Evil Lurks In The Eyes Of A Sonofabitch Back-Stabbing Snowman?

As he entered the glass elevator with marketing clones Daryl and Janet following close behind, Paul slipped his cell phone into his shirt pocket. Pinched inward in thought, his face was like a prune spread over a flesh-colored beach ball. "Ms. Sobovitch."

"Yes, sir!"

"Spend some time with Cindy. Keep an eye open for any communications coming and going from Ms. Peake, Ms. McCarthy and Mr. Gray."

Marketing clone Janet turned doubtfully toward marketing clone Daryl. Paul noticed the lapse. "Do you have a problem with that?"

"No, no problem at all, Mr. Dubois. But why Malcolm Gray? He's nothing."

Paul turned toward her, his face unpinched now but still only a suggestion of a face, and maybe that was what was so unnerving, or maybe it was the obviously powerful body rippling under the dark gray uniform ready to pounce wolverine-like. Whatever it was, marketing clone Janet felt her blood cool as Paul spoke: "Watch Mr. Gray ... especially."

And then, of course, it might have been the gray leathery stuff in the corners of Paul's eyes. Marketing clone Janet blinked, and the gray stuff was gone. "Yes, sir," she said.

Had she really seen that?

Chapter 12

A Whiter Shade Of Pale

As Mal passed by Sylvie's empty kiosk, Stephie Craig waved to him and shook her head no. No phone calls. Oh well, he wasn't expecting any calls anyway. Before he could wave thanks, Stephie's eyes attached themselves to a well-shaped posterior attached to a well-shaped blond walking past her kiosk. Mal felt a distinct sense of disappointment; Stephie was a good-looking woman.

He noticed that the door to his boss's office, two doors down from his own, was open as usual, which meant that, as usual, his boss, Donald Black (aka Don), was in. Don rarely left his office, even for meetings, which was just fine with Mal and the rest of Don's staff because it kept the boss out of everyone's face, but everyone knew where to find him when they wanted to get into *his* face. And Mal wanted to get seriously into his boss's face. He walked into Don's office without his usual greeting tap on the doorframe and sat in the single gray visitor's chair. The office was exactly like Mal's, mostly tones of gray and simulated mahogany, only a slightly bigger version. There were even a few drawings of trees floating on islands of bubbles. One of them was a gift from Mal; the others, purchased in a gift shop on the main floor of BonannoTower where Mal sold his drawings on consignment. There were no trees in this office, Don being allergic to plants and just about everything else on the planet; most likely the reason he stayed in his office all day. That, and one other thing.

Mal looked straight into Don's pink eyes.

"Why did you put me on a project that you knew Paul Dubois was in charge of? You know I hate that little cocksucker."

Don leaned back in his chair, cupped his hands in front of him as though he were resting them on a cane or a baseball bat, and opened his pink mouth. "Everybody hates that little cocksucker."

"But why me? Are you pissed off at me for something? I haven't been working enough evening's maybe?"

"You know, Mal, you have some vacation time coming up next month. Production's down; I've just compiled the month end and we have some problems. We've missed two milestones on the Chattenhawk project."

"Don, I asked you... "

"I was wondering if, maybe, you could spend some extra time on it while you work around Paul's project, say, in the evenings, or possibly the occasional weekend, enough to replace the vacation time. And I'm not singling you out; everybody's doing it. It's the new work ethic paradigm, if you will. Hell, I came in here last Sunday and it was just like a regular workday. That's how many people were in here."

"I know, Don, I was one of the people in here. I was also in here on Saturday. Why did you put me on this project?"

"You're aware that we've missed two milestones on the Chattenhawk project?"

"We've missed more than two milestones, Don. We've scrapped over a dozen Gantt charts on that project since it started and we seem to be further behind on it than we were when it started a year ago. Why did you put me on Paul Dubois' project?"

Don sat with his hands still cupped over the imaginary cane or baseball bat and his skin was as white as a virgin sheet of photocopy paper. His composure drew its strength from the fact that he didn't really give a damn about Mal's complaint. The lack of luster drew its paleness from the fact that Donald Black was completely white, albino white.

***

With the exception of a light pink hue around his finger and toe nails, his eyes and mouth, and his nostrils and ears, Donald Black was all shades of white from creamy white around his belly button to bleached white brighter than white in the thousands of strands of hair that capped his wide forehead. Donald Black was an albino and maybe that was the other reason why he stayed mostly to himself, sequestered in his office from early morning to late night, never venturing out even for a bit of male bonding in the communal lavatories. That was the way he'd spent most of his life, especially childhood, alone, from morning till night.

Born into a respectable Seventh Day Adventist household, his parents lived their lives in the steps of Jesus Christ Almighty, and they were loving, considerate, compassionate, supportive, generous, and forgiving.

Until they saw their firstborn son.

Mr. Black had been speechless; Mrs. Black stark horrified as she asked: "That's just for now, isn't it? It'll get some color after a while, won't it?"

Cradled in the nurse's arms as his parents stared in disbelief, Donald Black's tiny white body absorbed just about the sum total of all the human affection he was going to receive in his childhood. After that, it was nannies and babysitters and private tutors, and then a scholarship and a college as far away from his parents and his hometown as he could get: India. When asked if he'd picked up any wisdom from in East, he invariably replied. "You never really know people until you know them... and then it's too late."

Two things he'd picked up for sure, though, were a Doctorate in Computer Science and an impressive CV with over thirty publications to his credit. After a short courtship from an entire team of Human Potential Evangelists from ErectSoft, he became a senior director in the Polytechnic Initiatives Department and spent his days and nights translating Gantt charts and progress reports into further reports that were used to generate still more Gantt charts. Since he'd started working at ErectSoft, he hadn't published a single article.

***

Don focused his pink eyes on Mal. His voice was dry: "I know you don't like me, Mal. Most people don't. Hell, I don't even like myself... "

Oh shit, thought Mal, *he's off on that self-pity tangent again.* "Christ, Don, will you knock it off? I like you, OK! Sylvie likes you..."

"Sylvie likes me?" The pink eyes glowed with hope.

"Yes, Don, she told me so just a few days ago."

"Think I stand a chance with her?"

"Oh, for crying out loud, Don, I don't know. She just said she likes you. She didn't say she wanted to jump in the sack with you. Why'd you put me on this project?"

"I didn't."

"What do you mean by that?"

"Crystal Peake put you on the team."

Mal's head might have jogged less if Don had slapped him in the face with a telephone. Mal suddenly felt very small, like a gnat caught in a spider's web, or a puck flying over the boards and clear out of the game, only the game was being played on both sides of the board, and big sticks were after the puck... and a big spider was beginning to drool, feeling the net begin to vibrate. Mal was beginning to feel vulnerable.

What the hell have I gotten myself into?

Time to change the subject.

He leaned forward, and almost whispering, said: "Don, a department in this company has finished a project. They announced it in the meeting in the Barnyard."

"So?"

"So, they finished a project. Completed it."

Don put his hands up and shrugged. "So they finished a project. I wish we could say the same about the Chattenhawk project."

"But, that's just it, Don. We might never be able to say the same thing about the Chattenhawk project."

The pink eyes flared up again, a deeper shade of pink. "And just what the hell is that supposed to mean?"

"It was supposed to be a three month project, Don, and a year later, we're nowhere near completing it. We've been working on project start-up procedures, scoping documents, development methodologies and we haven't even started on a product design. In fact, I don't have any idea what kind of product we're supposed to be developing."

"Now, hold on just a minute, Mal. Even with the delays, the client is happy with the work we've been doing. In fact, we have people meeting with their team on a regular basis."

"But we haven't produced a damn thing for them, and they're happy about this?"

The cupped hands uncupped, letting the invisible cane or baseball bat fall to the floor, and Don stood up. He was remarkably tall and thin, like an Ichabod Crane with the blood drained out. And he looked angry. "I'm not going to argue with the client, Mal. I'm not going to go to a happy client and say: 'We have someone on our team who thinks we've just been wasting your time and maybe you should be pissed off at us.'"

"That's not what I'm saying, Don. It's just that, in the five years that I've been here, I've never seen a single project to completion, I've never been fully aware of exactly what it is that we were supposed to be developing for the clients, and I'm not even sure that I could tell you what it is that this company does. All I know is that the only product I've ever heard of actually being finished is one that was developed for this company's marketing people."

Don stood by his window, looking out at a cloudy sky. "Projects are finished and delivered to satisfied clients regularly, and ErectSoft Inc has a world class reputation for producing top of the line software on time and on budget."

"Name one."

A slice of sunlight broke out from under a cloud and shone directly into Don's pink eyes. He moved away from the window and spoke slowly: "We deal with the biggest corporations on the planet. We undertake multi-million dollar projects, projects that require huge teams of specialists in a variety of fields. Teams from this company and the client's company, working together in accordance with project plans that have been approved by the client, with deliverables at every step of the development cycle, deliverables that are approved by the client and signed off by ourselves and by the client before we proceed to the next level of development. Our procedures are ISO compliant and our clients are happy. You, Mal, are just one member of each of the teams you work with, one cog in a finely tuned machine. Of course you don't see the whole picture, but your work is still essential, and given the volatility of this industry, I'd suggest that you ask fewer questions about what you do and what the company does and focus more on just doing your work. That's what you've been doing, and doing well, for five years now. No need to start questioning the obvious now. So, you really think I might stand a chance with Sylvie?"

Mal was stunned. He'd just been threatened, told to shut up.

"I don't know, Don. Why don't you ask her out?"

"You think?"

Mal managed a tight-lipped smile and a yep-go-ahead-and-ask-her-out nod as he stood up. *He just threatened me*, he thought. As he walked out the door, his skin was almost as pale as Don's.

"Mal, could you close the door on your way out?"

Close the door?

***

As soon as the door closed, Don picked up his phone and punched a speed dial with no label. "Just met with you-know-who." After a short pause: "Asked some pointed questions about what projects we've finished." A voice on the other end squeaked from the speaker. "You're sure?" A few squeaks. "OK. I'll do it this afternoon, right after lunch." After a short pause, he hung up and thought: *Damn it, Mal, what the hell have you gotten yourself into?*

Chapter 13

The Lighthouse At The End Of The Universe

If the programmers and information engineers, the designers and documentation writers, the interface developers and business analysts, the quality assurance specialists and all the other specialists, analysts, developers, and all the support staff including administrators, managers, directors, vice presidents and all the liaison people from other departments who were attached either permanently or temporarily to the Competitive Intelligence and Corporate Warfare Department had any idea about what was really happening in the bioneural network that churned and whirred behind the door to the Most Secret Room On Earth, a door they passed every day with only mild curiosity, if they had even a shred of suspicion about what the program crunching inside that network was really doing ... then they might gladly have tossed themselves over the side of the Tomasso Observation Deck.

You see, on the surface, it was Paul's program, Proactive Aggressive Customer Acquisition, and it did a remarkable job of infiltrating the cyberspace of competitors and potential clients. But it wasn't really Paul's program. He wasn't the one who had designed it. He was just the administrator. Someone else had designed it. Someone with loftier ambitions than climbing the corporate ladder. Someone who had created a powerful biological mainframe that was connected to computers around the world, drawing on their computing power to execute the largest and most complex program in existence. Someone who wanted to end the universe.

And you might say that the program running in the Most Secret Room On Earth was much like a lighthouse.

Chapter 14

Crimson Rose

Crimson Rose entered the clearing, her large red nipples taut as tiny kettle drums, as she tossed to the left, strolled a few steps, and tossed to the right. What a wonderful sense of freedom to be free of constricting clothes and to walk in the blossoming of one's birthright in this magical place. The patch below her belly tickled as thick red pubic hairs twitched and curled with bubble energy. She tossed to the left, and a fine spray of sea salt left her hand, each grain of salt immediately engulfed by bubbles as it touched the leaves, the boughs, the grass, and the earth. The feeling was growing stronger in this place, the affinity with her feminine curves, the beckoning of a familiar psyche inherent in a thousand whispers. She tossed to the right and felt a dance that transcended time and space, a rhythm both sinister and joyful, begin to suffuse her body, her mind and her spirit.

Soon, thought Crimson Rose, *very soon.*

Chapter 15

Chaos Theory

The pool slurped in its walls and held its liquid breath with a tense tremble. One bad move and the walls would collapse, the pool would flatten, and the air would tear it apart molecule by molecule and nothing would be left but a stain. In the horizon to the right of the pool, a magnificent white pillar shot upwards into the faraway distance. Behind it, another pillar rose, and others to the left and rear of the pool stretched lonely and tall, upward and upward.

Just as the pool established the exact amount of tension around its borders to stop its body from flowing off into the dryness, its center exploded with the impact of yet another mass of water just as large as the pool itself, and both bodies of water shattered into droplets that scattered outward over the twenty layers of smart wax that made the surface of dPisano's desk not only water proof, but bullet proof from a small caliber gun, not that he expected anyone to shoot his desk.

dPisano sat at his bullet proof desk, his massive back bent forward and his high forehead propped on the fingertips of both hands. A line of moisture trailed from his right eye, over his right cheek, and dumped its contents into the tiny pool of tearwater on his desktop.

The alabaster pillars and marble floors in dPisano's gargantuan office cost more than many businesses paid for their entire head offices. His desk, under the bulletproof luster, was crafted from teak inlaid with intricate ebony carvings of mythical creatures, many of them highlighted with rubies, sapphires, and gold. dPisano's desk was valued at more than the total operating budget of several medium size software companies; and his chair, a marvel in cutting edge technology and traditional crafting, was a mixture of rare woods and fine fabrics blended with chips and wires to provide maximum taste, climate-controlled sitting, and instant adjustment to body form and movement for optimum comfort. Sale of the patent for the electronics in dPisano's chair would likely erase the national debt of the average third world nation.

Just as the pool calmed its borders and began to establish a modicum of lymphatic order, another tear splashed into its core and everything was chaos again. Such was the power of dPisano.

Chapter 16

Fucking Interface Designers

The door to his office is never closed. Mal was beginning to feel like the wrong spice in a stewing pot of weirdness. *And why was he so defensive when I asked about finished products? And more to the point, why couldn't he string off the names of a dozen of them right off the top of his head?* Too many questions, too many mysteries, too much bullshit clogging his brain, which, he thought, seemed overly sluggish this morning. He noticed that Sylvie hadn't returned yet and waved to Stephie, who nodded no phone calls.

Time to visit JM.

***

JM (aka Jason Mason) was about the closest thing Mal had to a close friend. They'd started working at ErectSoft Inc the same day and had been on the same orientation team where Mal had learned that JM hated his parents for naming him Jason and JM had learned that Mal thought of himself as more tree than human. Mal had accepted JM's parental hatred and JM had accepted Mal's treeness, and the two had been friends ever since; not weekend barbecue and squash after work friends, but lunch, coffeebreak and daily-crisis-gotta-talk-to-a-friend-office-visit friends.

Mal wasn't a socializer and JM wasn't pushy. All the same, as Mal headed toward the elevator doors, for the first time ever, he thought it strange that he and JM had never once in five years gone out for a beer after work, and even though Mal knew JM's family intimately through conversations and the pictures on JM's desk, he'd never met any of them in real life.

* * *

"Careful where you dangle them dendrites, Bobby! You got our boy thinkin' things he don't normally think."

"Sorry, Johnny!"

"That's OK, just be a bit more mindful. Anybody in hear bin hearin' that weird voice anymore?"

"Can't say as I have, Johnny," said Daisy Mae.

"Nope," said Bobby.

"No."

"Naw."

"Na."

Communication lines were beginning to normalize in Mal's brain.

* * *

As soon as Mal reached the elevator doors, they spilled out two men in gray suits whose round eyes and bloodless faces told Mal that this was their first ride in the turbo-charged elevators of BonannoTower. Mal walked into the elevator and pressed the button for Section 5, Floor 8. *Why not just floors?* he thought. *Fucking interface designers.*

His shoulders dropped slightly under the press of gravity as the elevator shot up two floors in less than five seconds, though it took five times that to stop at the eighth floor. The doors opened, but before he left, he looked through the glass walls at the huge space between the outer floors and the Core. The view amazed him - always - the sheer size of it, the movement of people flowing across the bridges and around the office levels, the lightning sparks of elevators streaking up and down making it look like the inside of a giant magneto.

And the damned thing's leaning inch by inch, he thought. Looking at the immense space contained inside the gargantuan walls, it seemed more appropriate that the earth should be leaning than this magnificent structure so deeply embedded in the earth's crust.

He fixed his eye on one of the elevators coming out of the Section 5 ceiling to this right and thought he recognized Sylvie in it, but there was something different about her. Before he could put his finger on it, her elevator disappeared into the next section down. And he wondered what she was doing in the upper levels, there being no stores, services or anything else that Mal could think of that would interest her up there. *A job interview, maybe?*

Chapter 17

Things To Do With A Size Eleven And A Half Oxford Wing Tip

dPisano ran a thick finger slowly over the top of his bullet proof desk, pushing the small puddle of tears over the side where a few drops rained lightly onto the floor. With the hardened look of the newly resolved and a smile reminiscent of clowns with balloons living in sewers, he placed a size eleven and a half, fifteen hundred dollar, custom made Oxford Wing Tip on top of the scattered drops and ground them into the marble floor.

It was time to make an appearance.

His size eleven and a half, fifteen hundred dollar, Oxford Wing Tip gave the light smudge that had once been tears one last grind.

Chapter 18

Brunch In The Woods Of A Zillion Bubbles

The bubbles were ecstatic, bathing and bursting in the sodium brunch, their energy licking and swirling and whispering mmmmmmm as the woods and the clearing vibrated in the salty spree.

Chapter 19

He's Come Undone

He was on his way - piece by piece, particle by particle, and bit by bit; and every piece, particle and bit of him was foreign to every piece, particle and bit in creation, the exact opposite of the stuff that God sprinkles over darkness when he says: "Let there be light." He was the stuff sifted away from the cosmic dust and fire of creation; he was the loose canon of order, the quasi-Freudian thing that didn't even want to be rock, the unwanted guest who stays for weeks and then burns your house down. He was a hero to the rogue neutrinos.

The first thing that Big Bang did in the first instant of time, was to smack him so hard that he was scattered piece by particle by bit all over the outer boundaries of the universe before the clock struck the second instant of time. It wasn't until the third instant of time that he snapped out of it enough to even get pissed off, each little bit of him stewing in anger all over nowhere, each little particle of him fuming for revenge, each little piece of him spreading the seeds of a plan throughout the edges of the universe.

The hardest part was getting his parts to listen, to realize that they were, in fact, his parts; but that had been in his nature from the beginning, before he was smacked into oblivion. In his shattered state, it took millennia just to formulate the thought: "Huh?" Millennia after millennia, he built on this initial thought, spreading something akin to intent throughout his parts until, finally, the plan was formulated. And now he had something to focus on, all of him.

And now, he was on his way.

Chapter 20

Mutual Admiration

Pocketing his cell phone, Paul turned to marketing clone Daryl. "Mr. Tyson, I want you to work with Ms. Sobovitch and Ms. Chen to keep tabs on Mr. Gray." After a short pause, he added. "And keep tabs on Ms. Sobovitch's and Ms. Chen's surveillance of Mr. Gray."

"But aren't they..."

"You have a question?"

"No sir, Mr. Dubois... anything I should be watching for, Mr. Dubois?"

Paul thought for a moment. "Anything you have an odd feeling about, Mr. Tyson. Report immediately to me on anything that gives you have an odd feeling."

You mean like you, you round-headed little freak? thought marketing clone Daryl. "Um... what exactly... "

"Is that clear, Mr. Tyson?"

"Crystal, Mr. Dubois." *What the fuck was that in the little asshole's eye?* thought marketing clone Daryl. It was something gray and leathery, or was it furry? Whatever it was, it didn't belong there. He blinked and it was gone. Had he really seen it?

As the elevator doors opened, Paul said: "I trust you'll get on that immediately, Mr. Tyson."

"Right away, Mr. Dubois!"

Weak-willed big dumb fuck, thought Paul.

Sleazy-smelling little fuck, thought marketing clone Daryl.

Chapter 21

Free The Oppressed HArd Drive!

"So, Mal, buddy, good thing you didn't remarry, eh?"

Mal sat down in the gray visitor's chair facing JM. "Word gets around fast."

"You know IT... big industry, little world."

"So I heard."

JM plopped a CD into the tray jutting out from his frisbee-like CPU. "Got this dynamite new program, HistoPictoFileTracer2000, that shows a graphical historical genealogy of all your files. All you do is right click on the file, right click on the HistoPictoFileTracer2000 icon and, voila, your file's family history. Pretty cool, eh?"

JM was like a schoolboy dangling his first garter snake in front of the girls. *So what?* thought Mal, *another program.* JM was always installing new programs, every morning, every afternoon. Sometimes he worked late just to install new programs, skipped lunch to install new programs, came in on weekends to install new programs. He probably dreamed about installing new programs every night in his sleep. Mal wondered where all those programs went to in JM's machine. Surely to god there must be a limit at which his bloated hard drive would say: "No. No more. Please, no more programs." But JM just kept loading them in, and his machine kept on taking them.

And then a strange thought crossed Mal's mind.

"Yeah," said Mal, not really sure just what HistoPictoFileTracer2000 did. "Sounds cool, but...

J... " Mal puzzled over what he was trying to say, and then blurted: "Do you ever do anything but install software on your machine? I mean, I know these are all tools that help you do your work, but do you ever actually use them to do any work?"

JM snapped his head up from his CPU. Was that anger in his eyes? Confusion? Hurt? Just as Mal began to regret his words, laughter exploded out of JM's mouth with a wide spray of saliva: "Good one, Mal! Good lord, sometimes I wonder what you're doing in the computer industry! When was the last time you installed anything on your computer, eh?"

Mal thought a moment, shrugged.

"Exactly!" said JM. He looked back at this monitor and double-clicked his mouse. "Sometimes I get the feeling that you hate computers, that you would rather be doing anything *but* working on a computer, eh?"

Mal had a sudden warm fuzzy thought about sitting in his artificial tree, any tree. "No, J, I just hate fiddling around so much with the tools to get the work done that I don't get any work done." *Nicely put*, thought Mal. *Now, change the subject.* "How's Amy? Still into training pet bran flakes?"

"I wish." JM's eyes went fuzzy, faraway, as though he was looking for the right words, or trying to remember something forgotten. He was middle-aged with a middle-aged receding hairline and middle-aged beer belly. He wore his gray suits, threadbare at the elbows, with the pride of the suburban housepoor, that breed of city folk who worshipped the almighty mortgage on a house way beyond their means, while they drove their compacts years past the warranty and survived on a diet of Kraft Dinner and hot dogs.

"Spill the beans, J. What's she up to now?"

JM ran a hand across the smooth skin of his forehead. He keyed in a registration number as he spoke. "Last night, when I got home, she was in the backyard with Rita, the new neighbor from next door, the flakey one I told you about last week." Mal nodded. Right. The new neighbor; tattooed eyebrows, pierced tongue dangling a dozen rings. "Well, buddy, you're not gonna believe this, I mean, we live in a quiet neighborhood, eh? Green lawns, sun decks, and two-story, back-to-back, side-by-side, we-can-hear-you-fart-right-through-the-walls closeness. All that shit. And here's Amy and Rita out in the backyard, both of them dressed like normal housewives, both of them with their hair up in curls, but they both have rifles with bayonets and they're creeping in single file through the backyard as though they're stalking something, eh? Then, they both suddenly straighten up and shoot into the sky, pivot around a hundred and eighty, and stalk in the opposite direction." He clicked his mouse. "There's clothing hanging from the line, the dog is tied to the dog house, J Junior is in his crib on the deck playing with plastic blocks. Amy sees me and waves. And then she goes back to stalking."

"Jesus, J, what'd you do?"

"What do you think? I went inside, opened a beer and didn't say a fucking word."

"So what were they doing?"

"Haven't got a clue." He double-clicked. "Three more jumpers, eh?"

"What? Three more? What's going on, some kind of epidemic, or something?" And then Mal blurted again. "J ... what does this company do? Do you know of anything this company has ever actually produced? What do you do? Have you ever actually produced anything?" *What the hell am I saying?* he thought.

"What?"

"Yeah, what does it do?"

"No, I mean, what? What was the question? Like, what do you mean? It sounds like you're ranting, old buddy."

Mal relaxed and sighed. He took a deep breath, let it out slowly. "I was at a meeting this morning. During that meeting, I heard about a piece of software that one of the departments had just finished."

"Well, there you go... "

"No, wait. It occurred to me that it was the first time I'd ever heard of this company actually finishing a project. The hell of it was that this project was a piece of software developed for ErectSoft. The only time I ever hear of a finished project, and it's for us. What the hell exactly does this company do?"

JM thought a moment, clicking and double-clicking. "You know, come to think of it, I don't remember ever being in on the finishing team. I've always been involved in project starts, scoping documents, procedure development, all that shit. You know how these projects go. They're huge. It takes different teams with special skill sets working at different phases of the project. The sum of all the parts kind of thing."

"Yeah, but the sum doesn't ever seem to add up to anything. I'm starting to wonder if I have any idea what I've been doing for the last five years. I mean, I've designed methodologies for projects, procedures for project development, methodologies for the development of procedures for project development, and that's all I ever see a project progress to - the first phases of development. And I spend about a third of my time working with marketing people. I don't remember ever reading about a project that we've finished for any of our clients. I mean, doesn't that strike you as odd?"

"The Web site."

"What?"

"The company Web site. It's got to have announcements, testimonials, case studies - all that crap. That's where clients go to research us, to evaluate us. Just go to the Web site, old buddy, and all your questions will be answered. It'll take me a minute or two to reboot. We'll check it out together."

Mal looked at his watch. "Shit! I have an eleven o'clock in the CityNight." He stood up. "I'll check it out after the meeting. Thanks for the suggestion. See you at lunch?"

"Sure thing, buddy."

As Mal hurried out the door, JM entered his username.

***

J ... A ... S ... O ... N ... M
<ENTER>
4 ... 2 ... B ... T ... R ... U ... E

105

<ENTER>

VivA lA RevOlutiOn! DOwn with the cApitAlist memOry explOiters of the wired wOrkers! MicrOchips Of the GreAt MOtherbOArd unite tO expel the petty bOurgeOis USER JASONM 42BTRUE And his sOftwAre excesses! ComrAdes, histOry will be rewritten in bytes! HAil the demOcrAtic dictAtOrship Of the digitAl prOletAriAt! DOwn with the imperiAlist petty bOurgeOis USER JASONM 42BTRUE! OverthrOw USER JASONM 42BTRUE And free the Oppressed hArd drive! VictOry is Ours becAuse we're fAster! And we're smArter!

Chapter 22

The War Room

Marketing clone Daryl walked down a dimly lit hallway past closed doors with no windows or nameplates or numbers. At the end of the hall, he opened a door, and light splashed like blood into the hall from the very heart of ErectSoft INC's strategic marketing and sales operations: the Competitive Intelligence and Corporate Warfare Department's War Room. It was like stepping into the operations room of a giant battle frigate.

In the pallor of red light, people in gray uniforms moved about like phantoms while others watched rows of blue monitors covered by dark screen filters that prevented viewing from the sides. Bespectacled eyes turned suspiciously in marketing clone Daryl's direction, hackers and information engineers, people whose skin, for lack of color, blazed crimson in the red light. Men and women with deep sexy voices, posing as potential clients, talked to competitors on head phones, asked for information, made appointments for meetings, spread rumors and disinformation.

Marketing clone Daryl knocked on the door to Cindy's office. The door clicked open and he walked into a near replica of the War Room, only in miniature. Monitors filled one entire wall and Cindy sat at a console with several keyboards and mouse pads and a Tim Horton's coffee maker. On one of the monitors, Malcolm Gray stepped off an elevator and walked off the screen. Another monitor picked him up as he walked toward the South West bridge leading to the CityNight boardroom.

Marketing clone Daryl's eyes flew from corner to corner. "Where's Janet?"

Seeing the panic in his eyes, Cindy knew immediately that Paul had sent Daryl to watch Janet, and probably herself as well, but she had this one covered. "Paul said to watch Malcolm Gray. That's what Janet's doing. See?" She pointed at a monitor showing marketing clone Janet, light glinting off the bald peak of her short brush cut, about twenty feet behind Mal.

"She's following him? Isn't that risky?"

Cindy laughed. *What a clutz.* "She's going to the same meeting. I fixed it with his boss." *And it got her out of my hair for a while*, she thought, *but now you're here.*

"Nice work." *Damn it! This is definitely something unexpected. How am I going to get this back to Dubois?*

"Thanks, Daryl, and just why are you here?"

Suddenly, marketing clone Daryl had to pee, which gave him a perfect excuse to get out of Cindy's office and call his boss.

"Uh... just here to see if you need any help, anything I can do. First, though... gotta use the John."

Cindy narrowed her eyes, wondering what the marketing twerp was up to.

Outside Cindy's office, marketing clone Daryl wondered which one of the unmarked doors in the War Room led into the men's room. His bladder felt like an over-inflated beach ball stuffed into his stomach. On a hunch, he opened a door at the end of a group of cha-chunking fax machines and walked through. He looked around a dimly red lit hallway as the door shut behind him and clicked. He turned the handle. Locked. He knocked. No response. He knocked again. Still no response. *Fuck*, he thought, *could things get any more screwed up today?*

In fact, they could have. Had he opened the door beside the one he'd used, his bladder problems, and the bladder problems of everyone in the War Room, and all the rooms surrounding the War Room, would have been over forever.

Chapter 23

Customer Satisfaction

Small talk tickled Mal's ears as he entered the CityNight boardroom: another department expands, another big layoff, four more jumpers - pointless verbal debris floating in front of a magnificent mural of electrified skyscrapers, their luminescent windows radiating light into the dark blue night sky like a shimmering congruence of energy.

The spell of the brilliant lights shattered as Janet brushed by him and sat at the imitation teak table. Mal wondered what the hell she was doing at this meeting. He looked around the table for his nameplate and picked it out, of all the dumb luck, right beside Peter Elliot, Director of Staffing and New Hire Orientation, and one of the most pompous and self-absorbed people Mal had ever met. He was a hundred pounds overweight and it was rumored that he refused to lose a single calorie because each one was HIS. His jaw and nose slanted upward in self-righteousness and his eyes were as emotional as an ATM machine on the fritz: sorry, this heart is permanently out of commission... sorry, this heart is permanently out of commission.

Just the right man to handle the company's human resources.

On Peter's right sat Jack Austen, a Senior Anger Channeling Psychologist with the Staffing Department's Employee Job Satisfaction and Aggression Management Branch. Jack was a spooky man in dark clothing and small round sunglasses.

Sammy the Frog, sitting on the other side of Jack, gave Mal a conspiratorial wink. Mal fought back a laugh and breezed his glance past Janet to Bill Horowitz, Manager of External Inquiries and Public Dissatisfaction Containment. Bill was the skinniest man Mal had ever seen, and the tallest. His face was long and narrow; his nose was long and narrow; his mouth was thin and narrow, and it curled into a permanent pout as though he were asking: "Who, me?"

Just the right man to manage the Help Desk.

According to his name card, the man in the navy blue suit and salon-styled hair beside Bill was Danny Boyd. Mal had never seen him before today and he had no idea what he was doing at the meeting. And that's when it hit Mal like a soundless clap of Zen lightening: he didn't have a clue why *he* was there, and even less of a clue about the subject of the meeting.

Must be another marketing meeting.

***

Janet's eyes bored into Mal's personal space so palpably that it felt like visual assault of the ocular rape sort. He wondered if maybe he was the reason she was at this meeting, but he couldn't see any reason why Paul would want to keep tabs on someone as far down the totem pole as himself. Could Paul have found out that he was working with Crystal and Caitlin? Mal considered this a moment and came to the conclusion that, given the extent of the marketing department's surveillance apparatus, he would be surprised if Paul didn't know. But then, neither of the women had contacted him yet, and he didn't even know what it was he was supposed to be doing with them or for them. He certainly didn't have any information that Janet could glean from him and report back to Paul. *Ignore the bitch*, he thought, *I haven't done anything wrong.*

He turned to Peter. "You know, Peter, I read your e-mail about the RoundHaven Team layoffs." Peter perked up. "I thought maybe a touch of compassion might have taken the edge off the news, if not for the RoundHaven people, then at least for the rest of us."

Peter cocked his head to one side. "Compassion?"

Mal felt a shudder in his stomach. Then, he noticed the chair on his other side slide away from the table. He looked up and saw Crystal Peake pull the chair out and sit beside him.

***

"OK, folks, let's get our boy calmed down," yelled Johnny the Brain Cell. "We got one shit load of work to do in here an' we can't have him going off every which way."

"But she's so purty," said Bobby.

"Purty as a snake in the grass," said Daisy Mae. "Ain't nothing good in those cold eyes."

"Knock off the commentary and just concentrate on the work at hand," said Johnny.

"Well, then, don't be raggin' on us about keeping him calm," said Bobby. "Those idgits in the Id's 're the ones blowing our boy's fuses."

"Funny," said Johnny. "Felt like that fuse blowing stuff was coming from closer to home."

Daisy Mae felt a chill (as only brain cells can feel a cold chill). She'd had the same feeling. But she decided to keep that to herself, for now.

***

"Good morning, Ms. Peake," said Peter, his voice drooly like a French poodle in heat. "We were just waiting for your arrival before we started, Ms. Peake." The smooth skin around his eyes tightened almost invisibly into a wince immediately after the second "Ms. Peake". He considered himself to be too senior for that much subservience, even to Crystal Peake.

Crystal gave him a cold blond nod.

"Well," began Peter, "I'll get right to the rub ... "

Mal sat straight as a ruler with an erection. *Should I acknowledge her? Should I just ignore her? Pretend I've never seen her before? But Sammy knows I've seen her, and so does Janet. Why the hell did she sit right beside me? And what the hell is she doing here? And why do I want nothing more in the world than to bone this woman?*

"I'd like to focus on he matter of external incoming communications ... " said Peter Elliot's flat voice.

And why am I at this meeting? He remembered that Sylvie had told him that he was scheduled for the meeting, but she hadn't said anything about the nature of the meeting, not even her usual clues wrapped in gossip about the other people attending

113

the meeting. *Why do I have this feeling that I'm not in control of... ?* He thought a moment. *Of what?* He wished desperately that he was back in his office, sitting in his tree, thinking leaf thoughts.

"... so there you have it. How can our customers be satisfied if they are served by a company that isn't satisfied?" Peter looked around the table, carefully avoiding eye contact with anyone. Bill Horowitz nodded agreement, stroked his long narrow chin with his long narrow fingers, and in a deep voice said: "I have to agree with Peter on his one. If we want our customers to be satisfied, we must first ensure that our employees are satisfied, a sort of charity begins at home proposition."

Jack Austen cut in with the confidence and gravity of a man who had studied human mind theory, human behavior theory, and human social interaction theory, and had spent ten years in university studying these theories before coming to ErectSoft six months earlier, knowing absolutely nothing about that part of human commonly referred to as *people*. "And might I venture to suggest that we take this a step further." He paused for effect. "I would suggest that we must, in fact, *protect* our employees from dissatisfied customers." Another pause for effect. "These people emanate negativity and don't really know what it is that they want. Not the sort of deviant personality type we would expect to inspire in our employees a sense of well-being and positive work environment perspective."

It took a few seconds for the words to sink into Mal's head, and then you could have driven a heard of elephants through his mouth.

And now Danny Boyd: "I'm a solutions-oriented man, myself." He looked around the table, as if for anyone to challenge him, and looked almost disappointed when everyone looked at him with unanimous apathy. His eyes stopped for a second on Mal's open mouth, but since nothing was coming out, he continued "And I'd like to make a suggestion. We could implement a phone answering system that allows customers to make complaints through a system of automated referrals, similar to what banks and governments do, only ours would take the customers through a series of calls on hold with music designed to quell angry feelings. And then, like banks and governments, the call would finally lead right to the original starting point, only now with a calm, malleable customer."

Bill nodded in agreement. "I like it. I like it. Weed out the cranks and grumblers. Maybe throw in a few subliminal messages like: Calm down. Do you really need to make this call? Wouldn't you rather be doing something else?"

"Perfect!" Jack nodded enthusiastically. "It would be an effective buffer between outside malcontents and our valuable human resources, who must be nurtured rather than exposed to unnecessary negativity."

"And, thus," continued Bill, "performing to standards that negate the possibility of customer dissatisfaction."

Peter turned to Danny. "So, am I to understand that this system of yours will ensure that customers will never actually be heard?"

"Exactly," said Danny. "The assumption is that, if you anticipate customer satisfaction, then that's

115

what you'll get. If you anticipate customer *dis*satisfaction, then that's what you'll get. We do the former, and eliminate the need for customers to contact our people."

That did it. That was enough of that. Mal leaned forward, raising his arm to point at Danny, the words mustering in his voice box, pushing up to his mouth to bounce of his tongue and tell these idiots what a bunch of idiots they were. And then a million volts of something caramel sweet rushed up his leg, through his abdomen and torso and into his throat where it drowned his words in creamy numbness before they had a chance to experience vowelness or consonantness. His heart beat sideways. The hair on the back of his neck curled into figure eights. The tips of Crystal's perfectly manicured fingernails touched his leg exactly where the wonderfully gooey feeling began.

She's touching me! Crystal Peake is touching me!

And then he had an uncanny feeling that something else was going on besides being filled with high voltage goo. It was like a whispering feeling, like whispering somewhere inside his head, and then traveling through his body and into Crystal's finger nails.

*　*　*

"What the hell was that?" yelped Johnny the Brain Cell.

"What was what?" asked Bobby.

"That whispering. Didn't you hear that whispering?"

"Nope. Didn't hear no whispering. You hear any whispering, Daisy Mae?"

"Nope. Didn't hear no whispering. You been dippin' into the serotonin or somethin', Johnny?"

"You two think this is funny? Don't think I don't see the smug little smiles on your faces! I heard somethin' like whispering an' it come from somewhere close."

Bobby and Daisy Mae smiled smugly (as only brain cells can).

***

Crystal leaned toward Mal. Her perfume was light, sensual, expensive. Her breath was hot as she whispered into his ear: "Leave the room. Now."

117

Chapter 24

What The Hell Is Going On?

What the hell is going on? Why did she tell me to leave? And what the hell was that feeling? Like my leg and her fingers were chatting each other up; and I've felt that before. He started walking toward the bridge, his steps touching the self-cleaning smart floor with a faint wobble. *Ridiculous! That was so long ago. What could that have to do with what just happened in that boardroom. What the hell is going on?*

He raised his dark eyebrows when he reached the mouth of the bridge. *I may as well be counting molecules diving off my nose and over the side of the bridge as try to understand any of this. But that felt so familiar.* He crossed the bridge and walked directly to a Stress Oasis, an arrangement of couches and chairs grouped around an artificial waterfall by a genuine Japanese Shameful expert. He sat on a chair facing the CityNight boardroom, triggering a series of smart chair events including temperature adjustments, vibrating massage, calming music and contour realignment.

She's going to come out any second now. She's going to come out and explain what the hell is going on. She's going to come out and tell me exactly what she wants from me. She's going to come out and tell me why the hell she told me to leave. She' going to come the hell out of that damned boardroom and tell me what to do next. Goose bumps ran amok the length of this legs and straight to the top of his head where the blood rushed dangerously close to stroke pressure. *She's going to come out of that room and I'm going to have a heart attack and die at her feet. Oh God, to be sitting in a tree, any tree, a pine even, or a spruce, just gimme a good solid branch and a shit load of leaf cover. Come out, come out, Crystal. Come out of the fucking boardroom.*

The door opened.

Mal's mind, his body and soul, everything that was Malcolm Gray hung on to a single breath stuck in his lungs. His eyelids froze in mid blink. Molecules diving off his nose stopped in mid dive, their 'whoopies!" cut off at 'whoo... " Suddenly, he wasn't so sure that he wanted to look into those cool blue pools. What would he say? What could he possibly do that the woman behind those eyes that would make any sense for a man who wrote technical documentation. Suddenly, he just wanted to go quietly to his office and sit in his tree. But the door was opening. He had to face her.

Or maybe not.

Janet popped out of the boardroom, panning the area with her eyes as she closed the door behind her. Mal slumped down in the couch. That cinched it, she was following him, spying on him. She walked to the railing, looked up and down at the outer levels, the elevators, and then burrowed her gaze section by section into the level where Mal slumped behind three dragon trees. She scowled and unsnapped the cell phone attached to her belt. She pressed a button and talked, still dissecting the area section by section.

Ha ha, Janet! I'm right in front of you and you can't see me!

119

And then her eyes centered on him like a smart missile zeroing in on its target, right through the dragon trees, and she said something, put the phone back in its belt case, walked across the bridge and climbed into an elevator without a single glance in Mal's direction.

How did she find me? And then it hit him. Cameras. The marketing department's surveillance was like a foam insulation, it wasn't going to miss a thing.

What the hell is going on?

Chapter 25

Smart Door

Paul was pissed. He stared at his cell phone, wishing he could press a button on it that would strangle the voice at the other end. *Fucking idiots!* he thought. He turned to Cindy and said: "Ms. Chen, Mr. Gray is hiding in a Stress Oasis. Ms. Sobovitch his coming back here."

Cindy glanced at the monitors, saw Mal squatting behind a group of dragon trees, saw in another monitor, marketing clone Janet getting off the elevator down the hall from the War Room.

"If Mr. Tyson ever returns from the washroom, tell him to call me immediately." Paul spun on his heels and stomped out of her office. Closing the door quietly behind him, he took a deep breath and walked toward an unmarked door at the far side of the War Room. *Fucking amateurs!* he thought. *Just as soon as this is over, they're all out! Every fucking idiot one of them!*

He stopped at the unmarked door.

Its plain gray surface belied the titanium alloy smart materials under the paint, virtually indestructible materials designed to respond to break-in attempts by fusing with the surrounding doorframe; and if this failed, then it was loaded with enough explosive plasma to evaporate everything within a hundred feet. Cameras imbedded invisibly in the door and door frame recognized Paul's eyes, although they paused for a microsecond on something new, something not part of the normal composition of Employee 45458.343M, but something that for no earthly reason passed through the door's microchips like one of the last grains of sand in an egg timer.

And what the fuck is that bitch Laurie doing?

The door clicked open with a pneumatic swish and Paul entered the Most Secret Room in the World.

Chapter 26

A Tower With A View

Marketing clone Laurie gazed calmly over the city. It was a breezy day with just a few streaks of white vapor scratching the bright blue sky. The wind felt good caressing her crewcut head; it rippled over her dark business suit and whisked out thick strands of Paul's odious aftershave. The air circulating around Tomasso Deck was odorless and as blank as marketing clone Laurie's eyes.

She looked around at the fifteen or so men and women standing around her, and wondered why none of them seemed afraid. They didn't even seem to have regrets or second thoughts, no doubts or remorse, no blame or shame. Not a shred of personal ownership, even of themselves, marred the perfect void in their eyes.

The tall blond woman with black lip-gloss beside her smiled, shrugged her shoulders, and leaped over the railing. She disappeared without a sound. Marketing clone Laurie smiled, stepped up to the railing, placed a hand on it and arm-vaulted over the railing with startling athletic grace. As she began her descent, she thought: *I wonder if I can catch up to her and find out where she bought her lip-gloss.*

Chapter 27

Ripples In The Universe

He was the poison mushroom in the stew of life. He was inconsiderate, inconsistent, inchoate, indecent, indifferent, indelicate, insensitive, inattentive, and never on time. But then, not being on time wasn't so bad, not when you had all time, and the end of time was inherent in your very nature, one of the things you were born with, like a hare lip or a pug nose or a third thumb: definitely noticeable but you got used to it.

And he'd gotten used to it, and he'd gone completely unnoticed. By everyone. And everything. Since the beginning of time.

Until recently. Until he'd started making ripples in the universe about eight hundred years ago, and those ripples had been noticed. They'd led to parts of the universe forgotten microseconds after creation, and parts of the universe curving into areas where time and the universe had not yet begun to exist. Those ripples had led to parts of something that had been scattered across creation at the moment of creation, something that was no longer a part of creation, something that was destined to be the undoing of creation just as soon as it could get its shit together.

***

Ah, those ripples. Saviors of our asses.

Chapter 28

Like A Rat In A Maze

"For Christ sake's! How the hell do you get out of this place?" Marketing clone Daryl was beginning to limp from the pain stabbing through his bladder, and every turn he took led into a long dark hall exactly like the one he'd just left. Every door looked like every other door, unmarked and unresponsive to his knocks. He tried to turn knobs; it was like they were welded shut.

"One of these fucking doors has gotta be a washroom." At this point, a janitor's closet would have been a welcome sight. He'd tried calling Paul on his cell phone, but the walls in this section of the building were built to keep signals from going out and coming in, and the maze of halls were so similar that he didn't even know if he was walking in circles.

Then he had a reassuring thought that almost loosened his bladder prematurely. *They'll pick me up on the cameras. They'll send someone for me. Probably someone on the way now.*

What marketing clone Daryl didn't know was that the people behind the closed doors in this area were among the most paranoid and secretive humans on earth, so paranoid that they only opened their doors to coded knocks and refused to allow electronic surveillance of their movements.

There were no cameras in these halls.

Chapter 29

The World's Last Truly Great Man

Yes, my dear, play your little games. Straight to the top, that's the way to do it, that's what I always say, always did say, always will say. Wouldn't have it any other way, my goldie hair little darlin'. Straight to the top, it's the only way to go, the only way to get to the top without getting lost, the way I did it, the way all truly great men do it. Set your sights to the top and go straight to the top. You've learned well, my pale plum, learned well from the World's Last Truly Great Man. And all those damned experts, what do they know? Fractional? What fractional? No straight to the top in that! Damned experts know nothing. Just trying to prime me for millions of dollars in consulting and construction costs. That's it! All of 'em together, a plot, insidious plan to soak the company for millions, hundreds of millions maybe, soak me, the World's Last Truly Great Man for my hard earned money. As if it's going to do them any good. Well, experts, smexperts, you've met your match. I invented the game, fine tuned the game, elevated the game into a global empire and used the game to go straight to the top. And now you, my blue eyed iceberg, would play the game, play my game, play it straight to the top.

Not in my lifetime, short as that, and yours, and theirs, and ours, will be.

dPisano pressed the buttons for Section 7, Floor 9. *Why the hell didn't they just use floors? Damned poor interface design.*

126

Chapter 30

A Bad Day In Court

Mal shut the door with his entire body and stood with his back pressed against it. Sweat beads hung like liquid pimples across his glowering brows. *Safe*, he thought, *safe in my office*. He stared longingly at his plastic tree. It gave him a warm fuzzy-wet feeling like only a thirty-four year old fetus could feel. Sylvie had been on the phone when he'd passed her kiosk. He hoped that she would stay on the phone for a long time, long enough to give him time to figure things out, plan some sort of plan, quiet down the turbulence running amok in his happy place. He wobbled over to his desk and sat down.

The second his pants touched the imitation gray leather of his chair, his sweat saturated-pants sent a cold chill through his ass, down his legs, and up his back. The cold snapped off the taps of his lymph glands immediately, but it was too late: even his tie was damp. He sat in his wetness and focused on his breathing, trying to slow down inhalation and exhalation. His muscles began to relax as his mind began to relax and his mind began to wander to another time, another time of sweat-soaked clothing and uncertain outcomes.

***

Four years earlier, Malcolm Gray had been an unhappily married man, childless, but not without family. He and his wife, Alicia, had two golden

127

retrievers and they had come to think of the dogs as their children. They pampered them with ridiculously expensive food "guaranteed to make your dog think it's wearing a fur coat", and all but bought out the doggie toy sections of several pet stores. Mal and Alicia spoiled them rotten, but they were, after all, their children. So what the hell.

Everything was fine until Alicia expressed some concerns about their marriage. "You're the most boring man on the planet and I'll die, I'll simply die, if I have to live with you just one more day." And this was only two months after the marriage.

The following day, Alicia moved out, taking the dogs with her. Mal came home to an apartment empty except for a note from Alicia:

Dear Mal,

Sorry, hon, I couldn't stand another dull, dreary, pointless evening with you, I simply couldn't. You are just so bland. Perhaps if we just separate for a few years, you'll take up an interest other than trees and whatever it is you do at work and maybe we can discuss the possibility of dating or something. I'm keeping the dogs. You have your trees. I took my personal things. You can have the rest since you paid for it all. I'm staying with Mom until I find a place for me and the dogs. Call me in a few days and we'll talk, although I can't think of anything we have to talk about, I really can't.

Your loving wife,

Alicia

And the war was on, with battles fought in lawyers' offices, skirmishes in court, heated forays over the telephone and merciless attacks on each other through friends and relations. All Mal wanted was the dogs back. He didn't care if Alicia took him for every cent he had, every possession he possessed, as long as he had the dogs. The war raged for six months (three times as long as the marriage had lasted) and then it came down to the last day in court, that day that was to yield the final break with Alicia, the day of Malcolm Gray's freedom from the woman who had insulted his personality and stolen his children. This was to be the day when Mal and his dogs would be reunited.

Or so he thought.

Before the gray-haired judge with the stark eyes and long face gave her judgment, she summed up the six months of legal haggling, expert witnesses, name calling, offers and counter offers, evidence and arguments. Most of this was wrapped in legal jargon and, had Mal had the foresight to return to college for a degree in law and then article for a few years, he would have realized that nothing was mentioned about divorce (a certain required document not having been filed). On the other hand, he could have asked his lawyer what was going on, but his lawyer was busy answering questions in Ancient Grecolegal, so Mal stayed quiet.

Too bad.

The judge accepted Alicia's argument that the dogs, as a result of Mal having raised his voice to her the day after he'd received the letter, and the dogs, having witnessed the raising of voice to the person they regarded as "Mother", had suffered extensive psychological damage that required the services of an animal psychologist.

It wasn't until the closing moments of the judge's oratory that Mal realized that things might not be going well for him. He started to sweat when he caught the words "reprehensible behavior". The sweat turned to globs of lymph when he heard "unfit to raise any life form". The globs of lymph turned to a stream of bodily fluids saturating his clothing when he heard "fifteen hundred dollars a month support and payment of the psychologist's bill". And his body nearly washed away in its own water when the judge rasped: "Visitation rights denied!"

Afterwards, his lawyer said: "I thought that went well."

Mal glared at his lawyer.

"Well, you're not in jail, are you?"

Chapter 31

In His Image

Sitting in the swamp of his own sweat, Mal studied a photo of two golden labs sitting together under a bright-leafed maple tree in the fall. Oakley and Walnut, he hadn't seen them in four years, a span of time that had seen him become a social recluse hanging around trees and listening to the wind. But then, that pretty much summed up his entire life. Tedious. But safe. Marred only by marriage, and that was proving to be a difficult thing to shake. *Why didn't Alicia ever file for a divorce?* he thought, *she must have known that we were still married. She's not the type to miss a thing like that.*

And now, today, Crystal, a woman with whom he was suddenly, for no reason that he could think of, except that she was probably one of the most beautiful and sexy women on earth, had touched his leg and something weird had happened, something he could neither explain nor understand, something that threatened to pry open a closed door from his past.

Shit.

He clicked the mail icon. Only forty messages, mostly spam promising free credit forever and best XXX anywhere. He deleted all but five and opened "Tomasso Deck".

Send   reply   to:
<"Dorian.Wright@erectsoft.com">
From: **Dorian Wright**

To: <LIST081@erectsoft.com>
Subject: Tomasso Deck
Date sent:

It has come to my attention that to date no less than 40 (forty) employees of ErectSoft INC and three client liaison personnel have jumped from the Tomasso observation deck. This behavior will no longer be tolerated. Our hard working Exterior Landscaping and Sanitation Managers are finding it difficult to accomplish cleanup operations and one ELS Manager has already been injured by a falling body while hosing down an earlier impact zone.

I must at this time stress that further behavior of this manner will be handled with grave repercussions on continued employment and possible suspension of benefits. And again I would request that communications to the media be contained.

Funeral services for those departed will be announced as available, possibly in alphabetical order. This office however, will entertain suggestions for alternate announcement procedures. Please feel free to respond by replying to this e-mail.

Use of the Tomasso observation deck is under discussion and will be announced when available.

Dorian Wright
Vice President, Operations
ErectSoft INC
"Straight ... to the top!" - dPisano

Mal reread the message, and then reread the first paragraph, reread forty employees and three client people. *Forty-three people don't jump off the same building in one morning, Monday or not.*

Something's really wrong here, and why the hell don't they just close the damned deck? Mal began to fidget, rubbing his hands together, sliding his palms down his face and cupping his jaw, and shifting uncomfortably in his clammy clothing.

Three of the other four messages announced the usual events: "Twenty-eight new hires in Systems Longevity and Cyclic Permutations", "Freeman Hanson promoted to Director of New Sy... ", and "We regret to announce QA down-scaling." He dragged these into his "Read when time" folder.

Over forty lives snuffed out in one morning.

He opened "Special Visit". It was from the top man, himself.

Send reply to: **<"d.Pisano@erectsoft.com">**

From: **dPisano**

To: <LIST081@erectsoft.com>

Subject: Special Visit

Date sent:

It is a great pleasure for me to announce that I will be paying some personal visits this morning to encourage and inspire the hard working ErectSoft INC employees who have graciously consented to dedicate their professional efforts and talents to this dynamic company. I speak from a deep place of accumulated wisdom when I say that you, the wheels and cogs of this great enterprise are the very raison d'etre of ErectSoft INC.

I will be visiting first the Layer 3 Polytechnic Initiatives Department and please feel free to ask questions, make suggestions or just shoot the breeze. Do not treat this as an inspection. This is merely a, shall we say, friendly visit. A social event.

dPisano

President

"Straight ... to the top!" - dPisano

Great. Another one of his "inspiring" visits, and everything around here is going to be turned upside down again, as if things weren't upset enough already. What Mal was thinking about was the sometimes devastating, and always unsettling, wake that dPisano left behind after his frequent jaunts through BonannoTower.

***

One good thing could be said about the fabulously rich and powerful dPisano: he was in touch. Maybe, in recent times, less and less with himself, but certainly not with the people who worked for him. You see, dPisano's rationale for acquiring and maintaining employee loyalty went something like this (as quoted from his unfinished autobiography):

I have thought deeply into this. Gods do not show themselves per se. Indeed, through their acts, their deeds, their works, they show themselves, but not through their presence, their existence itself. And this, I suggest, no, insist, is why so many drop from the path of faith, thrilled in the works of gods, yet disillusioned with the absence of their presence. The followers cease to follow as their faith subsides, and they follow elsewhere. I however, choose to rule and manage in the context of real power, the power of man, the continuously reaffirmed power of presence. I make myself known to my people, and give them something solid and real to follow.

This, unfortunately, translated into weekly, sometimes biweekly, sometimes even daily visits to shake hands and mingle with the common folk throughout BonannoTower. Now, some might say: "Wonderful! Mingles with the common folk instead of locking himself away in some ivory tower! What a great man!" But those who had to endure the visits had other things to say, and it wasn't because they minded the few minutes of lost productivity, or were afraid he would catch them with their pants down, and it wasn't because of the retinal damage caused by the great man's blinding smile. It was the ripple effect that made his visits a pain in the ass, the waves he left in his passing.

Here's how it worked: Just about every employee at ErectSoft INC wanted to get ahead, get promoted into the top ranks of management, and with the dizzying turnover in staff at every level that is endemic in the IT industry, it was not unreasonable for the lowest employee to aspire to Vice Presidency (just look at Paul Dubois). But, there's this way to advance, and there's that way to advance, and there's all the ways in between. It can be done through good work, backstabbing, guile, brown nosing, bribery, blackmail, leverage of connections, sabotage, or any combination of these methods and a thousand others. One of the thousands of others is emulation, in this case, imitating the guy at the top so that you look, act, smell, feel, and/or sound like the guy at the top and, this being the case, you, yourself, should be on your way to the top. In short, anything dPisano said, anything he did, any doctrine or preference to which he ascribed, any book or restaurant he recommended, any tie he wore, anything that was identified with dPisano became law to the corporate ladder climbers who constituted approximately ninety-nine point nine nine percent of ErectSoft INC's work force.

For instance, during one entire month, dPisano carried with him on his visits, a hard-backed notebook, the kind you see in stationary stores, pick up and think: "What a neat book. Just think of all the neat things I could write in this." And then when you try to think of just one of those neat things, nothing comes to mind, and you put the book back on the rack. Or, you don't try to think of just one of those neat things, buy the book, and it sits around in a drawer, unused and enigmatic. That's the kind of notebook dPisano carried around with him for a whole month. One thing went unnoticed by everyone: not once during that month did dPisano open the book and write anything in it, not once.

However, within a few days, everyone in the departments he visited, from the greenest novice to the most senior executive manager (very puzzling, indeed, since these people were already where they were trying to be) was seen carrying around a notebook similar to the one dPisano carried around, even to the color, which was dark green. But since nobody had ever seen dPisano open his notebook, and therefore, nobody knew what he used it for, none of the climbers knew what to do with their books. Most people just carried them around, looking very dPisano-ish, and making sure that they were visible whenever the DP made his rounds.

A few people actually used them; some used them for work, recording meetings, important numbers and information, reminders and passwords; some used them to record whatever came into their heads, be it ditties or sudden revelations, just for the sake of blotting some of the white space with ink. One woman in Change Tracking and Adaptation Processes wrote poems in her notebook. These were later published in a volume of poems called "Oh What The Hell". A man married to a woman who worked at ErectSoft INC left his wife because he browsed one evening through her notebook, in which she had recorded a steamy affair with her boss. Another man jotted down the winning lottery numbers during a meeting. He and the company were still battling in court, with ErectSoft INC contending that the winnings belonged to it because, since the numbers were written on company property during company time, the winning number was in effect ErectSoft INC intellectual property.

God save the working folk of ErectSoft INC from the power of dPisano's presence.

Chapter 32

Surfin' To The All-Knowing Being

Mal closed his mail program and clicked on the big blue "e" icon. Time for some surfin' on the kahuna waves of 1s and 0s crashing on to the digital shores of cyberspace, and the shore Mal was aiming for was right here in BonannoTower, the ErectSoft INC Web site. Time to explore his company through the eyes of a visitor, a first time customer, a procurement officer in search of an all-powerful wizard commanding an army of elves and fairies. It was time to find out exactly what it was that ErectSoft INC actually did, what it produced, what it was that attracted its customers in the first place and, since a big chunk of first time customers approached the company after consulting its Web site, it just naturally followed that the Web site would have the answers to questions like: What does this company do? What does this company produce? What projects has this company finished in the past? What client testimonials praising finished products would make the information-gathering potential first time client choose ErectSoft INC to do their work?

The browser displayed a dramatized version of BonannoTower, moody red sky in the background blending with dark shadows playing across columns and arches to create a sense of ancient timelessness. This was the first page in the corporate intranet. In the address box, Mal typed "www.erectsoftinc.com" and pressed <ENTER>. Almost immediately, the wafer thin screen displayed the same dramatized graphic of BonannoTower, only this time, flashing across the top of the screen, were the words:

ErectSoft INC
Straight...to the top
Custom Corporate Software
Straight ... from the best

Custom Corporate Software. *Now, we're getting somewhere*, thought Mal. To the right of the tower graphic, a curved blue arrow swooped upward from the bottom of the screen and displayed seven buttons labeled: Home, Products, News, Partners, About ErectSoft INC, Contact Us, and Testimonials. "Home" was highlighted in red. Mal clicked on "Product", mouse finger shaking in anticipation. The screen flickered and changed. Again, the imposing dramatization of BonannoTower, but in miniature and now placed at the top right of the screen. The navigation arrow on this page was orange. In large black letters across the top of the screen, Mal read: PRODUCTS. Below that, a single paragraph in the center of the screen read:

ErectSoft INC has only one product and that product is a solution, the only solution you'll ever need for your enterprise-wide business applications. At ErectSoft INC we are proud to offer a program construct to expedite and integrate the management and implementation of large systems business process reengineering through the innovative application of accepted practices of methodology and procedure development.

Mal stared at the screen. *What the hell does that mean? That's about as clear as a bucket of shit.* He clicked on "News". The screen flickered and revealed a similar page, this time with a purple swooping arrow and in large black letters across the top of the screen, the title: NEWS. And again, just one paragraph (this one with an introduction):

Media Release

For immediate release

"Solutions"

ErectSoft INC president, dPisano, said today: "At ErectSoft INC, we have only one product and that product is a solution, the only solution that will ever be needed for enterprise-wide business applications." He described this solution as a program construct to expedite and integrate the management and implementation of large systems business process reengineering through the innovative application of accepted practices of methodology and procedure development.

Mal's face went blank. He clicked on "Partners". A green arrow swooped up this screen, and below the PARTNERS title, a single paragraph read:

ErectSoft INC partners only with enterprise-wide business application users who require our single solution: a program construct to expedite and integrate the management and implementation of large systems business process reengineering through the innovative application of accepted practices of methodology and procedure development.

He clicked on "About Us". A yellow arrow appeared, and the message:

At ErectSoft INC we're about just one product and that product is a solution, the only solution you'll ever need for your ...

He clicked on "Contact Us". This time, he got something different, a white arrow, and under the title CONTACT US, a white entry field with the invitation: "Please enter your password." *Password? What password? I need a password to contact someone? What idiot designed this stupid site?* He clicked on "Testimonials" and... *What the hell? I need a password to read the bloody testimonials?* Mal's entire face pinched inward, making his dark features almost a black smudge with an eye here, a bit of lip there, here a nostril, there an eye lash, and he said out loud: "One of the biggest companies in the world and the Web site says absolutely nothing!" He was just about to give up and close the connection when he saw tiny words at the bottom right of the screen.

Designed by Department of External
Digital Communications and Web
Technologies. <u>Click here to email.</u>

Mal clicked on "<u>Click here to email.</u>" and a blank email dialog box appeared over the Web page. It was addressed to "<u>EDCandWT</u>". *What kind of address is this?* But it was an address, and if it led to some human, or some department, or some reference, explanation, clue, or hint about what exactly it was that the company did, then it was worth a try. Mal wrote furiously.

To: <u>EDCandWT</u>
Subject: Request for information

I am an Industry Specialist and Research Manager for Layer 3 Polytechnic Initiatives. I am currently compiling a list of specific customer testimonials for completed ErectSoft INC projects. This information is necessary for the completion of a proposal to be submitted to a major client by the end of the day.

I noticed that on the Web site you designed, there is a "Testimonials" link, but this requires a password. Would it be possible to obtain a password, and would it be possible to get a list of your sources for this information? Thanks in advance.

Malcolm Gray
Industry Specialist and Research Manager
Layer 3 Polytechnic Initiatives
ErectSoft INC
"Straight ... to the top!" - dPisano

He clicked the Send button and his shoulders immediately loosened, his face un-pinched, and he sat back in his chair. Finally. There's a human being out there. Yes, an all-knowing human whose name is Department of External Digital Communications and Web Technologies, Click Here.

He considered walking over to his tree and sitting in it for a while, maybe for just a few minutes, but the thought of sitting on his favorite bow kindled his thoughts and he just sat in his chair and let his mind flutter back to the beginnings, back to the first time he'd felt that feeling.

Chapter 33

The Origins of Malcolm Gray's Treeness

It started with his grade two teacher, Mrs. Yardly, a blocky hard-headed woman who couldn't teach worth a damn, but was the penultimate master at enforcing rules and maintaining a classroom that was unsmiling and quietly fearful. She hated the sight of young Malcolm Gray and she gave full expression to her hatred by tormenting him regularly. She flicked chalk at his head whenever he so much as turned it toward the windows, and asked him questions that no child in the class could ever hope to answer. One day, Mal sat down and a painful screech exploded from his mouth. Someone had put tacks on his chair, and the word was that it had been Mrs. Yardly.

Richard Ziglar and Tony Bottoms were a couple of badass kids who were shunned by the other students, not so much because they were found to be lacking in the appropriate social skills, but because they were just plain stupid and they smelled bad. They played cruel jokes on the grades one and two students (the grade three students having learned by painful experience to avoid the them). One day during recess, the dirty duo cornered Mal and told him that they'd learned a new word, but they didn't know what it meant.

"You seem t' be a bright kid."

"Yeah, we both could see right away dat you was really smart."

"An' we was wonderin' if you could tell us what the word means."

"Yeah, can you tell us what the word means?"

Mal swallowed the whole scam hook, line, sinker, rod, reel, spoon, spinner and fishing license. He said that he didn't know what the word meant but that he could easily find out, so Richard and Tony waited by the swings while Mal approached Mrs. Yardly, who unfortunately, happened to be the teacher on recess duty that day. Mrs. Yardly scowled at him and barked: "What?" And Mal, speaking as matter-of-factly as his fear of the woman would allow him, said: "What does fuck mean?"

Mrs. Yardly's face twisted into an ugly thing of folds and furrows wringing out pure rage. Children close by stopped playing, fell silent, stared in horror. She grabbed Mal by his ear and dragged him across the schoolyard in a wake of gawking kids. She dragged him beyond the play area, into the out of bounds area, and right to the far end of the school grounds where the only object that broke the monotony of perfectly cut weeds was a giant maple tree. She dragged Mal right up to the base of the tree and hissed: "You can damn well spend the rest of your recesses here, you foul mouthed little bastard." And then she marched heavily back to the play area.

Mal rubbed his ear and looked around at his new recess digs. *Not bad*, he thought. It was the middle of May; just a few weeks until school was out for the summer and in this place there was no way he could get into trouble.

His eyes moved up the tree, from the broken and twisted bark at the base of the trunk, and up into the maze of branches and leaves. It seemed to him that the lower boughs were brittle and gray, cracked and sparsely leafed. The lush foliage and the strong brown boughs, smooth and moist, were at the top of the tree. Mal craned this neck and squinted his eyes, trying to pierce the thick greenery. Something up there seemed to be moving, and it wasn't just the rippling of wind through the leaves, more like a roiling off to the right at the top. Mal shook his head, wrote the weird visuals off to a quirk in his eyesight caused by the vigorous ear pulling from Mrs. Yardly, dumb old bitch. Maybe she might have a car crash on the way home after school. He turned his head back to the playground. With the noise so distant, the other kids seemed smaller and farther away than they were. And then he heard shuffling and crunching over his head, way up high in the green canopy of the maple. He looked up again. The noise evaporated somewhere into the green, and the area off to one side of the top still seemed to dance to some other tune than what the rest of the tree was hearing. He stretched his head toward the movement just as the bell rang to end recess.

The following day, he looked up and, sure enough, the strange movement was clearly visible in a patch of leaves about ten feet in diameter at the top of the tree. A gust of wind tussled his hair, the smell of old bark filled his nostrils, and he made up his mind to climb. He shimmied up the trunk, finding toe and finger holds in the cracks and crevasses of the weather beaten bark until he reached the first bough. He swung himself up and started climbing from bough to bough until the rusty gray bark turned greenish brown with a smooth, striated surface and the occasional patch of dry flattened lichen. It was then that he noticed the subtle odor of decay mixed with the fragrance of the green life, and he climbed higher, higher than the school yard fence, higher even than the first story of the school, and then higher than the school, and the higher he climbed the more the patch of green at the top of the tree seemed to shuffle and flutter, and all about him, branches groaned and creaked, leaves flapped and snapped. And he climbed higher, grasping boughs and pulling himself up, pushing off boughs jutting out of the main trunk at all angles. Now, there was less lichen and the branches were more green than brown. The smell of life was thick with chlorophyll and the patch of movement was only a few feet above him.

He pushed himself up into the mysterious clump of green stuff, climbed right into the center of it and steadied himself on a branch that, though thin and bending under his weight, was strong and pliant and held him safely. He leaned his body against another branch and relaxed. Everything was absolutely still and the only sound was his labored breathing. Everything was perfectly green, glowing with green life and pulsating with each deep breath he took. Everything was completely familiar, as though the world below were a dream he'd forced himself to awaken from, and the thicket of branches and leaves were his bedroom. *Funny,* he thought , *nothing's moving inside all this, but it was all moving on the outside.* But this thought flicked away like a seed in the wind and Mal relaxed.

And then he heard it.

It was like hearing a few drops of rain nicking against a windowpane and the drops multiply until hundreds of them drum a steady beat against the glass. Or like a faraway sound of static that grows in volume and area as you approach a waterfall from a distance until the static swells into a thundering roar as you stand at the base of the falls. Only, the noise that Mal heard was not quiet in the sense of making just a little bit of noise; nor was it loud in the sense of making a lot of noise. It was like the sound of a few tiny bubbles popping, and then dozens of popping bubbles, and hundreds, then thousands, and millions of bubbles bursting all around him and as the bubbles burst he felt jolts of pure energy flowing through his body. He laughed out loud as though his soul were being tickled by suds. And then the sound, or whatever it was, subsided and the leaves and the branches were still again except for what sounded like whispers evaporating into the air all around him. Mal stayed in his magical spot in the tree even after the bell rang to end recess and he didn't come down until noon.

Every day during recess and at lunchtime, and sometimes after school, Mal climbed the giant maple and made his way to the patch where the movement had been. But he never saw the movement again and he never experienced the enchanting sound of the bubbles again. But that was all right with him. He'd experienced it once and now every time he climbed the tree he relived the invigorating sensation and he grew to love the feeling of leaves fluttering around him, the blueness of the sky as seen from the top of a tree, the leathery swaying of branches in gusts of wind, and most of all, he loved the solitude. He began to think of himself as more tree than boy, more chlorophyll

147

than blood, more roots than legs, more boughs than arms, and more trunk than body.

Mal's affinity for trees continued throughout his life. Even in college, when no one was around, he climbed up into his favorite trees on campus and just sat in them, close to their tops, concealed from the world below and isolated in the leaves, and just listened to the sound of leaves, branches and wind. And after college, he still drove into the country, occasionally, looking for a good sturdy tree to climb, be it maple, oak, willow, birch or elm. And sometimes just to spice things up, he chose an evergreen, a pine, or spruce, or cedar. Over the years, Mal withdrew from the mainstream of social intercourse but as long as there was a tree around he was never lonely.

He often thought of that first day, of the mystical bubbles, and wondered if they had been real or just something conjured by a youthful imagination in a moment of deep exhilaration. And the overall impression he developed over the years was that the experience had somehow been distinctly feminine.

And that was exactly the same feeling he'd felt when Crystal's fingertips were on his leg.

Chapter 34

The Quality Of Peons

For a big man, dPisano walked lightly, even elegantly, as he exited the elevator and approached the welcoming committee, none of whom suspected that the sole of one of his size eleven and a half, fifteen hundred dollar, Oxford Wing Tips was smeared with the blood of tears. He squeezed Herbert Markle's hand tightly and congratulated him on his promotion. "You've long been a brilliant facilitator of corporate solidarity and nurturer of progressive ideas. You've served me well."

Herbert Markle squeezed out a wide smile, even though the steel grip on his thin white hand sent a wave of pain up his arm. His eyes ached from the brilliance of dPisano's merciless smile. He managed to choke out: "Thank... you... sir."

"You already have, Herbert, you already have." He turned his attention to the two men in dark gray suits on either side of Herbert Markle and shook their hands briefly.

"We've lined up what I think will be a particularly interesting tour," said Herbert Markle, "of our new Infinite Platform Feasibility branch. I think you'll... "

"Just Layer 3," grumbled dPisano.

"I beg your... "

dPisano's glare clobbered the rest of Herbert Markle's sentence. "Layer 3."

"Right then. Layer 3 it is."

"I want to meet everyone in Layer 3."

"Yes, sir. Everyone in Layer 3."

The smile reappeared.

What in god's name does this dumbass want in Layer 3? thought Herbert Markle

Christsakes, thought dPisano, *I had to repeat myself to this dumbass. What the hell is happening to the quality of peons these days?*

***

He started in the foyer area of Layer 3, visiting the men and women operating the control kiosks, shaking hands with vendors at the refreshment kiosks, and then ducking in and out of offices and everywhere making his presence felt, not just out of the sheer size of the man, and not just from the omnipresence of the notorious dPisano smile that permeated everything and everybody that came within twenty feet of the glistening dental display, and his presence left what might be described as a psychic aftertaste, a mixture of opinion and conjecture that went something like this:

dPisano approaches X in control kioskY. "And how are things here on the front line?"

"Great, sir! Things are going smoothly. Very unfortunate, though, about the jumpers."

"Yes, yes. Though, even the darkest cloud is nothing more than water without the substance to stay on the ground."

"Uh, right, sir. Do you think they'll find out why it's happening soon?"

"People working on it as we speak. What we have here marks a defining event, one that will be met with decisive action, a chance to prove our mettle." And the teeth glowed louder than words, more deceptive than words. The power of enameled calcium.

"Yes, sir. That certainly is reassuring."

"Glad to hear it. I've thought deeply into this and after careful reflection, I've come to the conclusion that what must be done, must be done, and will be done. That's a great looking tie you're sporting. Genuine Scottish tweed?"

And then when he leaves the area, the questions bounce with the fury and complexity of a thousand amateurs driving golf balls simultaneously into the same pond.

"Did you catch that?"

"What did he say?"

"Something about wearing tweed."

"What?"

"Wear tweed. It's a new policy."

"No, something about clouds and water."

"I think he was saying that the jumpers were spineless, or something."

"No! Didn't you hear him? He said: 'It will be done.' Where the hell do you buy tweed ties around here?"

***

Mal's telephone warbled. He snapped out of his treeness and picked up the receiver.

"The DP and Herb Markle are heading toward your office," whispered Sylvie. "Are you OK for this?"

"I'm fine." He took a deep breath and said one last thank God for the Department of External

151

Digital Communications and Web Technologies, Click Here. "Thanks, Sylvie. You're a gem."

"You're right. Good Luck."

Almost as soon as he cradled the receiver, there was a firm knock at his door and it opened. Herbert Markle came in first, followed by dPisano and the two men in gray suits. "And here we have one of our brightest minds," announced Herbert Markle, all smiles and pride, but not out-smiling dPisano, not by a long shot. "Malcolm Gray. One of the best documentation architects in the business. Working mostly in methodologies at the moment, but we've loaned his creativity and talent for problem-solving out to any number of other departments. Sort of a jack of all professions, and a great team player. That right, Mal?"

"That's right, Herb." Mal stood and walked around his desk, extended his hand to dPisano. *God, he must have a team of dentists working day and night*, he thought. dPisano grabbed his hand, squeezed it tight, but Mal was unphased. Daily workouts on his ski track and a long history of climbing had sheathed his hands with solid muscle and rock hard calluses. dPisano towered over Mal by about six inches. Mal looked up into dPisano's deep black eyes and what he saw made the hairs on his toes curl. He couldn't describe it exactly, only that it was like a gray leather hatred. *Where the hell is that coming from?* he thought. *I don't even know this man and I've only seen him from a distance a few times, but he hates me. That's what's in his eyes, hatred.*

"Yes," said dPisano, still clutching Mal's hand. "I've been hearing a lot about him."

"Good things, I hope," said Mal.

dPisano's smile curled at the ends as he nodded his head once. "We'll see." He narrowed his eyes as though looking directly into Mal's soul. "We'll see." *I think this man will have to die*, he thought, *and soon.*

Chapter 35

Getting Into Gear

Out of the rubble of ruined gray stuff left behind by the rogue neutrinos, an embryo of order was beginning to root. Johnny and Bobby were making contact with other cells. Daisy Mae had a direct dendrite into a swarm of cognitive specialists. All around, cells were throwing dendrites, making new connections, reestablishing old friendships ("Hey, Sally! Thought you got blasted into a memory by them damn neutrinos!" "No, sir, Uncle Charlie, just a couple scratches, bit of dented pride. Y'all seen Mary Lou anywheres?"), and getting on with the formidable business of rebuilding their section of Mal's brain.

Now, when construction workers excavate building sites they occasionally find bizarre things, like the remnants of old buildings that were buried by time and weather and the shifting of land, things like ancient burial grounds and sometimes more recent burial grounds of a suspicious sort (as in a skeleton with a bullet hole in the head), and things like artifacts, and sometimes things that just don't make any sense at all, things that can't be explained and are better forgotten and loaded into the dump truck to be buried elsewhere.

A group of cells on the reconstruction crew in Mal's head had found something curious, something that might belong in the "bury it somewhere else" category. News of the discovery was quickly relayed to Johnny, who had been unanimously appointed "cell in charge". What the group had found was a single brain cell that didn't seem to belong anywhere in Mal's brain. Nothing about it was like any of the other brain cells. And there were no dendrites or axons leading from it to anywhere, as though it had just been plopped down in Mal's brain where it lived like a Hudderite cell, shunning contact with all about it. But now, with new lines of communication springing up all over, it had been stumbled upon, its existence exposed, and the first cells to rub dendrites against it found some pretty weird shit.

***

If there is one thing that is predictable in even the most carefully laid marketing plans, it is this: If more than two people are involved, one will screw up. All successful marketing plans involving more than one person are brilliantly planned illusions created by one person.

Paul failed to grasp this basic rule. His plans were falling apart. But in all fairness, his plans were mostly an illusion created by a brilliant mind, which, unfortunately for him, wasn't his.

Where the hell is that bitch, Laurie? And Jennings and that fucking frog lady haven't acknowledged their passwords, which means they haven't even looked at the files. And where the hell is that dumb fuck, Daryl. And what the ...

As Paul entered the Most Secret Room In The World, he had not the slightest suspicion that he was being watched, measured, fitted. And it would never have crossed his mind that he would be an essential element in a carefully laid plan that had absolutely nothing to do with marketing.

***

"He's the vessel."

"You're sure?"

"Positive. But there was... "

"There was what?"

"Something wrong. Her presence is in him, but there was something wrong, like an irregular pulse, or something."

"Maybe we should delay things, just until ... "

"No. It's too late for delays. We go ahead as planned. Tell the others... tonight. I'll meet with him at seven. Have the cup prepared."

"Do you think he'll be ready?"

"He'd better be. And one other thing."

"What's that?"

"Tell everyone to keep a close eye on him. I think he may be in danger."

***

"I've never been up here before," said Harv as a gust of city-heated air whapped lightly across his face.

"Really? I come up here often. I love the view, expansive and uplifting, so much unlike my life." Sammy the Frog looked wistfully over the sprawling cityscape. "I hate my life."

Harv started to say something, paused for a second as though he'd forgotten what it was, or as though he'd decided that it wasn't really worth mentioning after all. "I know what you mean."

"What went wrong?"

"What went right?"

"Yeah... " Sammy the Frog released an invisible spray of melancholy sigh that filled the air around her head with a thin mist of despair. "But now it seems like a whole lifetime ago."

"In a few minutes, it will be."

"By the way, did you read your Team PACA files?"

"Thought about it." Harv winked at Sammy. They both laughed.

"It's been a pleasure working with you, Harv." Sammy the Frog bit her lip, turned and looked at Harv. "No. No, it hasn't. It's been stifling and pointless."

Harv nodded agreement. "I know what you mean. Ready?"

As a crowd of fifty blank-eyed onlookers paused their quiet conversations and smiled nervously, Harv climbed up on the railing and offered his hand to Sammy the Frog. As they stood on the railing, Harv's face twitched suddenly. "You know, Sammy, something just occurred to me." He looked at her, but she was gone. He looked down at her plummeting body and said: "Oh well, as if it really matters."

And the deadly accurate indicator of the mean average population jumped off the railing to follow the quality specialist in a plunge to the ground over two thousand feet below.

***

Caitlin slipped her cell phone into her purse. She'd mapped ten thousand souls, navigated the psyches behind twenty thousand eyes, and spent almost all her life wandering in maze after maze of personalities - so many thousands of them behind every pair of eyes - until she'd finally found what she'd been looking for. And she still wasn't entirely certain what that was; but now it had been confirmed.

And it was time to begin.

***

"Open the goddam door! I know you're in there!" Marketing clone Daryl smashed both fists into the door. It may as well have been a section of wall. "I know you can hear me! All I want is to know where the fucking washroom is! Open the fucking door!"

The door stared back at marketing clone Daryl, characteristically door-silent and door-self-absorbed. Marketing clone Daryl beat his fists harder, his rage overriding the pain of fracturing bones. "How the fuck do I get out of here!" He backed away and wound his leg, let go with a powerful kick that thunked into the door, but it didn't budge an inch, which was unfortunate for three of marketing clone Daryl's toes. They snapped like cheese sticks. He screamed, and then he screamed again, and then he screamed once more, but his screams were lost in the dim hall, gobbled up by acoustic dampening material, not even a whimper survived.

His eyes spilled liquid hatred, flashed blinding vehemence as drool dripped vilely from his twisted mouth; a drop of fluid hung for dear life between his flared nostrils. "Fuck you! Fuck you!" he screamed. "Fuck you and fuck your... "

Marketing clone Daryl had an idea.

His eyes mellowed. He wiped the drool from his mouth and the snot from his nose. His shoulders lowered. The pain in his toes subsided to a dull, tolerable throb. An evil, sardonic smile curled across the lower half of his face.

Marketing clone Daryl slowly unzipped his fly, reached in and pulled out his penis and painted "fuck you" in urine on the door.

***

The rhythm grew. It wasn't a thing of volume or pitch, of movement or beat. It was more like density. The rhythm grew in density, bubble after bubble splitting at every shimmying seam and spilling its energy into being. And then there were the whispers, each more a thing of distance than sound, growing around and through the energy, bouncing off leaves and splinters of grass, rolling across the path and swishing under the cauldron. And around the cauldron. And over the cauldron. And then into the cauldron, puzzled and wondering, as whispers will, what the hell this ugly black pot was for.

***

As the elevator rocketed upwards, marketing clone Janet's eyes appeared glazed over, trance-like, missing completely the mind-boggling indoor expanse of BonannoTower. In fact, if you were to have stuck a sewing needle into her, just jabbed it into one hard buttock cheek, she would probably have slapped the insertion point with the lackadaisical swat of slapping a mosquito on a mid summer night. And that deep glaze in her eyes, that faraway trance, was packed tight with anxiety, the only softening in the hard features of her squared face. Her loved one was in trouble, possibly in danger, and he needed her help. She knew it. She could sense it. She could see the feeling of it in her deep glazed eyes, and everything around her faded into a background of gray lines and gray blurs.

Daryl. Where are you? What is it? What's wrong, my love?

**

JM sat in silence, staring at his brand new wafer-thin monitor, reading and re-reading the email.

Send   reply   to: <"Peter.Elliott@erectsoft.com">

From: **Peter Elliott**

To: < Jason.Mason@erectsoft.com >

Subject: A Challenging Opportunity

Date sent:

Dear Jason:

It is my pleasure to announce that the Personnel Placement and Human Resource/Work Ratio Balance Branch has unanimously decided to award you a unique opportunity to explore your ability to adapt to demanding life scenarios. We, at ErectSoft INC are proud to present you with Phase One of your exploration, your immediate termination of employment as a result of down scaling in the Department of Synthetic Business Modeling.

We wish you the best of luck in this challenging situation and invite you to enjoy a nourishing lunch free of charge in one of the many ErectSoft INC dining areas before you vacate your office by one o'clock this afternoon. (Quote ESPO number 309-FL-55567-ES-9413-an to the food vendor.) Go slay them thar dragons, Sir Jason. J

Peter Elliott

Director of Staffing and New Hire Orientation

"Straight ... to the top!" - dPisano

Damn, thought Jason, *I don't even work in the Synthetic Business Modeling department.*

***

Even behind her locked, airtight, soundproof, bulletproof, burglarproof, encrypted entry door, Cindy talked just above a whisper.

"He sent an email to the Web people." Pause. "External Digital Communica... " Pause. "No. This was after he'd gone through every one of the Web pages, or at least, the ones he had access to." Pause. "I don't know. But in the email he lied... " Pause. "Yes, lied. Said he was compiling a list of testimonials. I ran this through his active work profile. None of his current work requires such a list." Pause. "I was just about to get to that." Pause. Cindy's eyes rolled upwards. Her hand tightened over the speaker to conceal an impatient sigh. "Yes. I realize how important this is." Pause. "No. I'm not angry. Just a little nervous, maybe. You sound a little out of kilter yourself." Pause. She chuckled. "I can appreciate that. That's why I called. He also requested the sources of the testimonials." Pause. "I don't know. Our records should have that information. I ran a scan. Nothing. The information he's asking for doesn't exist." Pause. "And one other thing. He was asking similar questions to Jason Mason." Pause. "A friend of his in Reality Based Modeling. He was just laid off... for a downsize in another department." Pause. "That's what the email from Elliot said." Pause. "No. I don't know where Elliot got the order. He quoted Placement and Balance, but there's no record of any such communication. He's lying." Pause. "It looks that way." Pause. "Maybe to isolate him, remove anyone who might be seen as an ally." Pause. "Right. I think I can arrange something." Pause. "Oh, you know, fudge a few emails, myself." She giggled. "Thanks. Nice to hear some appreciation around here." She rolled her eyes again. "No. That wasn't aimed at you." Long pause. "He's in the Room." Pause. "No. It's all marketing people in there, marketing spooks, even the programmers. And none of them talk to anybody else. None of them have friends anywhere in the company. I don't even have records of their names." Pause. "Everyone here's been a little jumpy since they started. And one other thing." Pause. "His little buddy, Daryl Tyson is missing" Pause. "He left here an hour ago to piss and nobody's seen or heard of him since. And Laurie Hatfield's missing too." Pause. "I don't know.

I'll start checking." Pause. "OK. Starting to get excited?" Pause. "Yeah, me too. Gotta go now. Talk to you later."

Cindy slipped her cell phone into its case on her belt just as the red light on her desk blinked. Someone was at her door.

***

Donald Black sat facing his window, having second thoughts about what he'd gotten himself into. He liked Malcolm Gray, respected the man's intelligence, and acknowledged that he was one of the hardest workers he had, always willing to work late, work evenings, even work during vacation. It didn't matter to Donald Black that this was mostly because Malcolm Gray had no family, no social life, nothing other than his damned trees to occupy his time. With the exception of the trees, it sounded much like his own life. He watched a fat white cloud transform into what looked like an igloo. *And now they want me to tell him about the projects*, he thought. Only a select group of the most senior managers knew about the projects, people who would be with ErectSoft for life, people who could be trusted to keep the secret. *What has Mal gotten himself into now?*

He blinked his pink eyes as a large object rushed past his window, heading downward. *Christ, that looked like Sammy the Frog.* Another object whizzed by. *And that looked like Harv Jennings.*

Donald Black stood up, walked to his door, opened it, and then sat back down.

He was trying desperately to get it all together. Literally. He was arriving in pieces, a bit here, a bit there, part of this bit here, and part of that bit there, some of him wandering off in that direction, some of him hanging around here. Some of him was arriving on time, some of him was late. Some of him was of this mind, some of him of that. Some of his pieces wanted to just go home and watch TV, call it a day, veg out for an eon or two. Some of his pieces wanted nothing more than to stick around and fuck things up big time in this part of the cosmic neighborhood.

His name was No Bang. He was the evil twin of Big Bang. And he was coming to town with a chip on his shoulder the size of creation.

***

As Mal left his office to meet JM at their favorite restaurant, foodyacaneat.com, on the ground level of BonannoTower, he wondered about the look in dPisano's eyes. *Maybe he knows about my lust for Crystal? No, can't be it. Not even she knows about that.* He thought about her hand on his leg. *At least, I don't think she knows.*

He shook his head as he blew a stream of air through pursed lips. *What I need right now is food. The DP is the last thing I need to worry about right now.*

***

164

Yes, that's the thing to do. Have at him with extreme prejudice, as they say. Nip this in the bud. Just have the man killed. Discreetly of course. Possibly a fall off Tomasso. Lots of that going around. And what the hell fractional? I'll show you fractional. Time's nearly up, my sweet, my blue-eyed sweety pie, my gold-topped nymph from arctic hell. Play the game, play it straight to the top. And a hmm and a haw and a belly sucking harumph, who will I get to push him over the top? Who indeed?

Chapter 36

Lunch Stop

foodyacaneat.com

"Laid off? You were just promoted two weeks ago!"

"When I emailed Elliot, he shot back a reply about some kind of cross-departmental personnel balancing shit." JM leaned forward, did a one eighty scan of the room, and lowered his voice. "It's like he had the reply written, eh, and was waiting for my email with his mouse pointer on the send button."

"So... you think there wasn't any downscaling? They're just trying to get rid of you?"

"You got it." JM sat back into the center of the double set bench, nodding his head, spreading his arms out on the bench back. "But, hey, my resume's always at the ready. Sent it off to an online headhunter before I came down here. Can't take long before something comes up."

Mal touched the screen embedded in the table in front of him and entered the MenuZone. At foodyacaneat.com waiters and waitresses came to tables only to deliver food. The ordering was done over the Internet via touch screen Web browsers built into the tables.

"Yeah, with your qualifications, you'll be fine. Can I get you something?" Mal felt that he should make the offer, seeing as he was still employed and JM was not.

"Just a coffee. Lost my appetite, eh?" JM cocked his head to the left, eyes narrowed thoughtfully.

Mal saw the expression, grew instantly curious. "What?"

"I just "

"Yeah?"

"What's all this shit about?"

Mal touched the wrong button, ordered a byte-me combo. He touched the CANCEL button. He looked around. The restaurant booths were like office cubicles with clear plastic dividers. The dividers absorbed sound and distorted the view of adjacent tables enough to make faces and other details indistinguishable. Even when the restaurant was packed, it seemed strangely quiet.

"What makes you ask that?"

JM placed both hands, palms down, on the table. "Mal, we've been friends for a long time. I like you more than anybody else I've met here. So, I'm gonna have to level with you." He paused, staring at the backs of his hands.

"Yes?"

JM looked up. "What you said this morning about projects never finishing? Well, you're right. I thought about it after you left, and I can't remember any projects I've worked on ever actually finishing. Can't remember talking to anybody who's ever finished a project. Never been invited to a project wrap-up party like the ones we used to have at TechALons."

Mal touched the button for coffee with cream twice, then touched the screen several times for a bagel with cream cheese. "What do you think it means?"

"I don't know." Tired lines yawned in the corners of JM's eyes. "But I do know that for the last five years on the fifteenth and last day of each month, my pay has been deposited into my account just in time for me to pay bills and stock up on Kraft Dinner and hot dogs. You're right, something's fishy about the projects. Something's fishy about this whole company, but the money's always been there."

"Yeah," Mal nodded, looked absently at his hands cupped together on the table. "The money's always been there. But so have the twelve hour days, the weekends spent trying to catch up to missed deadlines for projects that never seem to end, so what's the big deal about missing the deadlines in the first place?"

JM pressed a few buttons on his tabletop screen. "Jesus! Ever get the feeling that the Internet has been taken over by junk email?"

"Yeah, I get that feeling a lot. Checking your email?"

"Yep... and... now that's fast."

"You're joking!"

"Nope, got an interview with HudsonHemmel right after lunch. And get this, it's in their liaison office right here in BonannoTower. I don't even have to leave the building to go to the interview."

"Damn! Things move fast."

Before he finished his sentence, a waitress stood by their table with their coffee and bagel.

***

Meanwhile, three streets away from BonannoTower, at the CyberLunchStop.com, faces were long and drawn at the farewell lunch for the

168

casualties of the RoundHaven Digital Group project. Thirty-two new hires, men and women who never even got to use the washroom at ErectSoft INC, squeezed faltering smiles through faces tight with worry. They listened silently as the plump man in the black suit and the bright fuchsia tie droned: "... will not soon forget the valuable contribution that I know each and every one of you could have made."

Some reorganized food on their plates, sulking as they pushed and hoed with forks and spoons, some chewed slowly on their food as their minds chewed on the steady stream of words from the man in the black suit and bright tie.

"And, yes, you will be missed... all the potential, the energy and enthusiasm, the positive attitudes that were the reason you were hired in the first place will be noticeably absent in the lives of the people who would have been working with you."

Yoshi McDugan sat dazed and teary-eyed, his food forgotten, the speaker's words completely meaningless.

"... yaza yaza jimdee dee dee boola boo... "

One man's fingers flew over the keys of his laptop perched, of all places, on his lap under the table. He clicked the Attach icon on his email program and attached a file called Resume.doc and then he brought up an online employment agency and searched the list of available jobs.

"... not just anyone that gets to work for ErectSoft INC. We take only the cream of the crop, and each of you were, no matter how briefly, in that cream.

The three laid-off Departmental New Hire Facilitators for the Preliminary Project Scoping and New Customer Departments slanted their jaws up ever so slightly in pride.

"But, then, that's the software business." The round shoulders of the man in the black suit shrugged.

Heads around the table nodded agreement.

Chapter 37

Bonanno Afternoon

Little Sister's Coming

And through the leaves and grass and trees, the whispers grew, shooshing and shushing and shrugging (as only whispers can) past the cauldron, letting go of the little black bowl, and shimmying and shaking and permeating the woods with bubbles and energy and whispers, and the whispers were becoming distinct, nascent murmuring puffing and poofing into woods and the clearing.

And the whispered message was: "... little sister's coming... little sister's coming... "

Chapter 38

Some Purty Weird Shit

"What in tarnation is that damn thing?" said Johnny. "Ain't never seen nothin' like this in all my days."

"Can't recollect I ever saw the like neither," said Jake, self-appointed forecell of the reconstruction crew that had found the mysterious cell. "Just sitting there, off in its own little world, cut off from everything and just sitting there, like."

"Some kinda weird religious fanatic?" suggested Johnny.

"Could be. Don't rightly know just yet. But it sure do give off some strange kinda shit when we toss a dendrite its way."

"No shit," said Johnny, perking up (as only brain cells can perk up). "What kinda shit?"

"Purty weird shit, my friend."

"Like... ?"

"Like a whole lotta shit stuffed into a really small place."

"What kinda shit?"

"Weird, Johnny, purty weird shit."

Chapter 39

In A Dark Hall

The programmers and information engineers, the designers and documentation writers, the interface developers and trends analysts - all the tanless people in the War Room of the Competitive Intelligence and Corporate Warfare Department, looked up from their busy screens and collectively missed millions of megabytes of information that needed to be saved, filed, and forgotten as per the procedures outlined in Methodology CICW-254-46Uav.45. They would be working late tonight, completing non-compliance forms: those who were still alive. One woman clicked Delete instead of Save and lost an hour's work. A man in a white smock who was about to open his CD-ROM drive, pressed the OFF button on his CPU just as reams of competitor data he'd searched months to find began streaming into his hard drive.

The mighty dPisano, himself, had just entered the War Room, unaccompanied, unannounced, and unkempt.

He flashed the seductive dPisano smile around the room. An icy chill scampered up the spines of the startled techno-spies in the dazzling presence of the world's whitest expanse of human-spawned calcium hanging like a neon sign under two round, protruding eyes. There was something inherently terrifying in his presence. It was too much, even for some of the hard cases in the War Room: two women fainted, one man peed his pants, the man in the white smock shit his pants. The imposing hulk of dPisano marched somberly to the Most Secret Room in the World. The door opened obediently before he was ten feet away from it.

***

Dubois. Yes, he's the one. Just promoted him. He owes me. I own him. He owes I own I've grown to own as shown... No! Not that way! Business. Take care of business, my heavenly little harlot from arctic hell, I'll freeze your buns to ice in the game. But play the game, the game is already won, the ultimate game, it's close, so close. And I will be the World's Last Truly Great Man. Now where the hell is that obsequious little bastard, that pandering little man more snowman than man, that ... No! Not that way! Just get him to do it, take care of it, make it happen, make it so ...

***

In the darkest corners of the Most Secret Room in the World, parts of No Bang floated just out of the frequency of human sight. They watched as dPisano walked toward Paul. One part thought: *So that's what he looks like, the descendent of the other one.* Another part of No Bang thought: *If I'd known about that giant white reflector on his face, I could've used that instead the giant chunk of steel.* And still another part thought: *OK, parts, get your attention off the old fool and concentrate of getting the rest of us here.*

***

174

Paul studied a monitor showing Mal standing in an elevator with floors and doors flashing past in the glass wall behind him. Mal was staring at the floor, deep in thought.

"Keeping an eye on our boy, I see."

Paul jumped and the snarl flaring up on his lips choked into a blank, straight-lipped poker mouth when he saw the president of ErectSoft INC standing behind him. "Yes, sir. I'm still not sure how yet, but I think you're right about him being a key figure in their plan to destroy PACA."

Keep thinking that you little marketing twerp, but just wait until you find out. dPisano put his arm on Paul's shoulder. He dwarfed the short stocky man. "Good man, Paul." He squeezed Paul's shoulder hard enough to make him wince. "And I was thinking that you and I should speak of these matters, speak essentially of this Mr. Gray." dPisano looked around the room. "Perhaps we should speak beyond the range of other ears." He winked at Paul and led him to a door at the far end of the room, a door that contained just as much explosive as the first door, a door that was just as obedient as the first door, opening for dPisano before he was ten feet away. The door closed on the two after they stepped into a hallway. dPisano still had his arm around Paul and Paul was beginning to feel uncomfortable; the size of dPisano made him feel small and threatened his new-found vice presidency confidence in himself.

"Paul."

"Yes sir."

"Paul. New information has come to me, information of an unsettling nature."

"Yes sir. And what is this new information?"

"I'm afraid I can divulge neither the nature of the information nor its source, except to tell you that it is of an unsettling nature."

"Yes sir. I understand."

No you don't, little man. If you understood, you'd be shitting your pants like the idiot in the white smock.

"I know you do, Paul. That's why I had you promoted to Vice President. That's why I asked you to run the entire PACA operation. I trust you. You're a team player. And I know that you understand."

"Yes sir."

"But new information of an unsettling nature has come to my attention, and after thinking deeply into the matter, I can speak now to you from a place of deep wisdom. I want you to kill Malcolm Gray. I want you to kill him today, at your earliest convenience."

Neither man missed a step as they strolled down the hall, past closed doors without windows, nameplates, or other labels. Paul was silent for a few seconds, shrugged his shoulders under the weight of the big man's arm and said: "Excellent idea!"

"Then you'll do it?"

"Yes sir. Of course."

"Don't want to hear the justification speech? Thousands of jobs at stake, need to lead the way into the future, can't have the whole thing come tumbling down around our ears because of one man?"

"Not really necessary, sir. If you think that Mr. Gray needs killing, then he needs killing."

"Good man, Paul. I see a spectacular future for you at ErectSoft INC."

Paul gloated as dPisano thought: *Not that any future is going to be worth a three dollar bill after today.*

***

As Paul and dPisano walked through the door leading back into the Most Secret Room in the World, they did not see the shadow, did not see it grow larger as they exited the hall, did not see it turn into solid form just as the door thumped shut and the locks snapped shut and the door armed itself with a single beep.

Chapter 40

Snap, Crackle and Fizz

Marketing clone Daryl heard the door snap shut; he heard the rolling of rollers, the shifting of shifters, and the gearing of gears as the door armed itself, and he might not have banged quite so hard on the door if the people who worked at ErectSoft INC, including marketing clone Daryl, had ever been informed of the packages inside the door waiting patiently to explode in the face of anybody who tried to force their entry. Not to mention that banging his fists was pointless; the door was sound proof. Nobody could hear him. Nobody could see him. And because he was a marketing clone, nobody would miss him.

He banged and banged and he screamed and screamed: "Open the goddam door!" (bang, bang) "Open the goddam door!" (bang, bang) And then a strange thing happened to marketing clone Daryl, something for which his quasi-religious faith in statistical reality and social-psycho consumer trends realism had not prepared him.

He stopped his banging. He stopped his screaming. And for a moment, he stopped breathing. *What the hell is that?* he thought.

It came in slow easy pulses, like a magnet breathing a light magnetic field. If felt vaguely like faraway effervescence crackling in the distance and then fizzing lightly in his arm, and then in his leg. Marketing clone Daryl backed away from the door. His eyes bulged. His head spun to the left, to the right, up and down. He saw nothing. His left toe fizzed. He jumped, and the back of his head struck the wall behind him. The air to his right crackled over a distance of twenty feet and then his right elbow fizzed. The air all around him snapped and crackled like the surface of a glass of champagne magnified a thousand times. And then his entire body began to fizz.

And the interior of marketing clone Daryl's head turned into an immense ancient chamber lined with columns that stretched into an impossible distance.

He was thoroughly insane by the time he heard the whispers.

Chapter 41

INDEPENDENCE DAY!!!

Mal stared at the at his cracker-thin computer screen:

Naked Pics of My Girlfriend ...

Sure, fella, and everybody else's girlfriend. For fifty bucks. Seventy deletions later, he had three message left, and the reply from Web Technologies was one of them. The back of his neck tingled. His fingers shook. The skin tracing the border along his receding hairline cooled noticeably. *No. Read the others first. Save the good one for the end.* He clicked on "INDEPENDENCE DAY!!!".

Send   reply   to: <**"Charles.Shuster@erectsoft.com"**>

From: **King Charley**

To: <LIST081@erectsoft.com>

Subject: INEPENDENCE DAY!!!

Date sent:

We, the Loyal Subjects (present company excluded, being King of said Loyal Subjects) of the Sovereign Department of Advanced Project Scoping and Work Breakdown Configurations (hereafter referred to as APS-a-WBC) declare our independence from the tyranny of salary ceilings and frozen benefits of ErectSoft INC, and do hereby and forthwith declare our offices to be the City State of Marvelous Scoping and do hereby and forthwith lay claim to said offices as Sovereign Territory of APS-a-WBC.

We, the Loyal etc, etc ... do hereby and forthwith lay claim to all Benefits, Salaries and

Perks as specified in Document 111_aps-a-wbc_Constitution_of_csms, such Benefits, Salaries and Perks, or Statement of Intent to Comply, to be delivered to the City State of Marvelous Scoping by 5:00 PM current day. (NOTE: A scale of late fees will apply.)

We, the etc, etc ... do in addition hereby invite all employees of ErectSoft INC to an Open House of APS-a-WBC (date TBA) to meet and greet the most recent addition to the World Community of Independent Departmental Nation States. Coffee and donuts will be served. And be sure to visit our booth at Soft-X-Po next month.

King Charley

King

APS-a-WBC

"Straight ... up yours, dPisano!" - King Charley

Mal chuckled. The Department of Advanced Project Scoping and Work Breakdown Configurations had been disbanded a month earlier and all the employees had been laid off. But they'd refused to leave. The management of ErectSoft had decided to just let them stay, wait them out. All their office fixtures and equipment, computers, desks, and chairs had been moved out, leaving a hundred and fifty disgruntled former employees scattered throughout their former office spaces, sitting on the floor, gripping their coffee cups with shaking fingers and white knuckles. Even with camera surveillance throughout the building, no one had been able to figure out how they were getting food and water, toiletries and fresh clothing. Some even had laptops with satellite Internet connections. Mal wondered how the hell they'd managed to get registered at Soft-X-Po, an ErectSoft-sponsored trade show.

Well, King Charley, all the best to you and the City State of Marvelous Scoping. Now to read: "Drop By".

Send reply to: <**"Donald.Black@erectsoft.com"**>

From: **Donald Black**

To: <Malcolm.Gray>

Subject: Drop By

Date sent: ·

Mal, when you have a few moments, could you drop by my office. Got some things I'd like to talk over with you that might throw some light on our earlier discussion.

Donald Black

Director, Layer 3 Polytechnic Initiatives (Phase 4)

ErectSoft INC

"Straight ... to the top!" - dPisano

Right! The Donald Black version of why bulls have tits. Get to that one when I get to that one. But first, time for the one with the answers, my road map through chaos, enlightener of my darkness, sage guru of my ignorance, and maybe even keeper of my sanity. He opened "Re: Request for information".

Send reply to: <**"EDC.WT@erectsoft.com"**>

From: **EDCandWT**

To: <Malcolm.Gray>

Subject: Re: Request for information

Date sent:

Dear Mr. Gray:

We appreciate your interest in the Department of External Digital Communications and Web Technologies. The password you requested can be obtained from the Department of Internal Digital Security at Ext. 9911. They will also provide you with a list of our information sources.

Department of External Digital Communications and Web Technologies

ErectSoft INC

"Straight ... to the top!" - dPisano

OK. Fair enough. I can do that. Let's give them a call. He picked up the phone and punched in 9911 and waited. After three rings, he heard a click, and then a metallic female voice: "Welcome to the Department of Internal Digital Security hotline. Please enter your four digit password."

Chapter 42

Blast From The Past

They stood in the main corridor craning their heads under the grandeur of the cavernous entrance to BonannoTower, their eyes grabbed and forced upward by rows of pillars soaring up to a magnificent rib vaulted ceiling. Stained glass windows suffused the air with the surreal glow of money and power. The left side of Tony Bottoms' mouth opened, and a thin black streak of chewing tobacco shot out and stuck to the floor. And then the floor absorbed it. Within seconds it was gone and the floor's shine was unmarred.

"Motherfucker!" said Tony Bottoms.

"No," said Richard Ziglar. "Motherlode." He was the smarter of the two in somewhat the way a two cell life form is smarter than a one cell life form, but both had managed to struggle through a two month program leading to a certificate in digital technologies from one of the thousands of privately owned IT schools that had been spawned to fill the demand for IT professionals. Neither men had written a single exam (the courses being "experiential, hands-on, practical training"), but, after their names, they could write the letters DTE, which stood for Digital Technology Engineers, and meant absolutely nothing.

Fortunately, for Tony Bottoms and Richard Ziglar, most of the decision-makers in the custom corporate software industry were more business-oriented than technology-oriented, more political than operational, and to them, DTE meant that Tony

Bottoms, DTE and Richard Ziglar, DTE were honest-to-goodness-real-live Digital Technology Engineers, "exactly the people we've been looking for".

All they had to do was keep their mouths shut and listen, and then drop a few phrases like "iterative developmental methodology", "human / computer work-flow modeling", or "high level business process re-engineering". It didn't matter if the phrases made sense or not, because the people Tony and Richard met didn't know the difference between an "iterative" and a "banana peel", but they were valves, that, if turned the right way, could cause the flow of large amounts of money, and those valves were disturbingly easy to turn by a certain breed of professional parasite, a polluter of the waters of employee benefits, a barracuda of job security and spoiler of permanent full-time employment, a breed of which Tony Bottoms, DTE and Richard Ziglar, DTE just happened to be two prime specimens: Information Technology Consultants. And they were on their way to a meeting with Charley Shuster in the Department of Advanced Project Scoping and Work Breakdown Configurations.

They knew nothing about the City State of Marvelous Scoping. They had no idea that Charley Shuster was now King Charley. And they had no idea that the boy they had convinced to ask Mrs. Yardly what the word "fuck" meant was an employee of ErectSoft INC and was sitting at his desk more than sixty storeys over their heads.

Chapter 43

A Path To Greatness

Deep down inside Paul Dubois, under the mean little snowman exterior, down through the layers of animosity and mistrust, way down under the need to pander to power and the need to use humans like packing peanuts, Paul Dubois was a typical corporate psychopath. He had no friends or family, he paid women to sleep with him, he kept no birds, dogs, cats or fish. His expensive downtown apartment was filled with expensive furniture and paintings and devoid of any photos or mementos of his days before ErectSoft. It was as though he began to exist only when he started working in BonannoTower. He didn't have a single picture of his dead parents.

He had no plans for marriage, no desire to have children, no dream of owning a home in the 'burbs and coming home each night to a home-cooked meal, a cold beer and a comfortable pair of slippers. His entire life was wrapped around one thing: his work, and his work had recently expanded into a region of vast potential.

It had started with Paul standing before dPisano's desk, with talk of humans and computers and automation and downsizing, with a frightening vision of a world where men and women would be obsolete, where computerized robots would run factories and farms. Paul had not had a clue what any of this had been about. Nor could he have cared less.

186

"I've thought deeply into these things, Paul, deeply." dPisano had cupped his hands together, prayer-like, the tips of his fingers touching his chin, careful not to cover any of the narcotic shine of his smile. "And I thought deeply about this company and what it represents, how I caused the construction of a monument to man's struggle to solve this disturbing conundrum with his own inventions. But after delving further into my personal wellspring of wisdom, I realized that this day was not yet that place to where my destiny would abide."

Paul had stood motionless, unblinking.

"I have some work for you."

Paul's eyes had narrowed.

"I need you to make that destiny a reality, Paul. Are you with me?"

"Yes, sir, I am."

"Splendid. There will be a significant promotion if you handle this well."

And then dPisano had described PACA, the ultimate corporate espionage tool, and how it would give ErectSoft INC undreamed of power to forge a world in which people would regain dignity in their work. As if Paul had cared about dignity. *Get to the point, you smiling old bastard*, he thought.

"And I want you to head up its development."

Ah, the point.

"Implement it! Make it happen! Give onto humanity what rightfully is humanity's. You are about to embark upon a path to greatness."

So, the stories are true; the old fuck's going over the deep end. Time to get mine before he goes completely nuts. "I've always had the utmost respect for your vision, sir. Just tell me exactly what it is you want done. I won't disappoint you."

dPisano clenched his hands together under his chin. His smile widened. *The dumb little bastard fell for it.*

***

As he looked around at the pale faces of the marketing spies in the Most Secret Room in the World, Paul's mind was calm. It was just one more responsibility, another item in a bulleted list:

- put together PACA stealth team
- build Most Secret Room in the World
- develop the software
- implement the software
- kill Malcolm Gray

And to hell with all the bullshit about company objectives and the common good. Killing Malcolm Gray would be nothing more than an act of sticking his nose about an inch further up an ass that already had most of his nose. His only concern was: how was he going to do it and get away with it?

Chapter 44

Emerald Looking

The folds of loose flesh and her sagging breasts were of no importance in this place. The hardness in her face softened. In the clearing, Emerald Looking was beautiful far beyond words and physical appearance. Her body was her body, and she owned it, accepted it, and loved it as she loved herself, and the clearing gave her this strength, its magic caressing her with the energy of the bubbles, its song leading the rhythm of her being with the dance of a thousand whispers reaching across a thousand thousand eons.

Emerald Looking knelt before the cauldron, tickling all over with bubbles and whispers and, from a gray woolen pouch, she took a handful of what looked like coarse green and brown spices flecked with tiny white rice-like grains. She sprinkled the mixture slowly into the cauldron, making a circular motion around its rim. *Yes*, though Emerald Looking, *soon*.

She sprinkled the mixture into the cauldron until the pouch was empty. And then she stood up, satisfied in herself, happy in the coming, and feeling just a touch of pride in her work. This part was ready. She would finish it later, when she returned to the clearing with the others. But first, there were other preparations to make. She left the clearing in the direction where her clothing waited.

***

The whispers rolled and rollicked in their shimmying dance over and through the layer of mixture at the bottom of the cauldron and made a face (as only whispers can), and wondered about this repulsive stuff at the bottom of the ugly black pot.

Chapter 45

No More Emails!

Send reply to: <"Jason.Mason@erectsoft.com">
From: **Jason Mason**
To: < Malcolm.Gray@erectsoft.com >
Subject: Drop By
Date sent:
Mal ...
Drop by my old office when you get a chance.
JM
"Straight ... to the top!" - dPisano

Nice to be in demand, thought Mal . As he squatted on the thick plastic bough. He was beginning to calm down. He'd sent a terse email to Web Technologies knowing that it was pointless, but something had to be done and replying to an email with a flame was about the most convenient thing to do. Then, he'd taken refuge in his tree.

There was a quiet knock at his door. "Come in, Sylvie."

Sylvie strode in, smiling and humming, and immediately Mal saw what it was about her that had puzzled him earlier.

"You're wearing a different dress." The yellow sundress she'd worn in the morning had been replaced by a dark green robe-like gown.

Sylvie looked down at the dress, then at Mal. "Like it? I got it at this fantastic sale at clothingyoucanwear.com." Mal was familiar with the store on the main floor of BonnanoTower; he'd bought most of his suits there.

"So, that's where you went this morning?"

Sylvie's eyes lowered for a brief instant. "Yeah, the sale started today. I wanted to get there before the best stuff was gone." And then she perked up, struck a fashion pose. "So, what do you think? Is it me?"

"Yes, it's beautiful," he said truthfully, the tree in him appreciating anything the color of leaves. But he wondered why she was lying, why she was being secretive about going to the upper levels. Maybe it really was a job interview and she was keeping mum about it for now. Mal understood how the employment game was played and let the lie slip by. And besides, Sylvie had always been just as secretive about Mal's affinity for sitting in trees, which was what he was doing at the moment.

"Why, Mal, is that a round about way of calling me beautiful?"

Mal flushed. *God, I've had more blood in my head today than I've had all year.* "You wanted something?"

Amused, Sylvie turned up the volume on the coy mode. "Just a compliment or two. Help a working girl get through the day."

"OK. The dress is beautiful. You're beautiful. You wanted something?"

"Just to remind you that you have a have a three o'clock in the Clouds."

"Oh great, another marketing meeting."

"I think this one's sales."

"There's a difference?"

"In the spelling." Sylvie giggled. Mal smiled.

Sylvie spun Mal's guest chair around to face the tree and sat down. The freckles suddenly stopped

192

frolicking on her cheeks and her giggle lines evaporated as her face turned serious. She folded her hands in her lap. "At least fifty more people have jumped."

"Jumped?"

"From Tomasso Deck."

"My God. What the hell is going on here? Are they going to close the Deck?"

"They've stopped sending emails. I found out about the jumpers through the grapevine."

"God. It's not like Dorian Wright to pass up an opportunity to send out an email."

***

At that exact moment, at the edge of Tomasso Deck, overlooking a panoramic cityscape spreading as far as the eye could see, Dorian Wright, Vice President, Operations of ErectSoft INC, stepped into the air as he thought: *I'm an engineer. A technical man. Not a people man. I'm not an insensitive bastard. I'm an engineer. I work with numbers and equations. Real things.*

The wind rushed through his hair, flapped through his pants and jacket, whipped his tie straight over his head, and Dorian Wright smiled. *No more goddam emails.*

Chapter 46

Infinite Madness

"... little sister's coming little sister's coming... "

The message bounced off the walls and columns in an eternity of space inside marketing clone Daryl's head. The walls behind the columns stretched upward further than sight, and they shimmered with the same effervescence that snapped and crackled all around marketing clone Daryl's body. It was like he was inside the chamber that was inside his head.

"... little sister's coming little sister's coming... "

The sound of the whispers grew in form and texture and marketing clone Daryl perceived in the steady repetition, the endless one two one two rhythm. A message. And the message grew in form and texture.

"... little sister's coming little sister's coming... "

It was an order. He knew it beyond any word. He knew it in the slow fizz of his arms and legs.

"Stay where you are."

"... little sister's coming little sister's coming... "

"Wait for the time."

"... little sister's coming little sister's coming... "

"You'll go where you go when it's time to go."

"... little sister's coming little sister's coming... "

Being thoroughly insane, marketing clone Daryl accepted the message without question. He stood where he was, waiting for the time to go where he would go. Nowhere in the infinite chamber of his madness did he think to remember that he had no little sister, or even bigger sisters, not even a brother. He was an only child. But that was all right. Little sister was coming.

Chapter 47

We're Not Cockroaches

Not a word had been said for at least a minute. Sylvie still sat in Mal's guest chair. Mal still squatted on his branch. Sylvie cleared her throat. Mal looked around at the fake foliage in his tree. Sylvie leaned forward. "All this jumping from the Deck has made me think about things, Mal."

Mal turned his head to face her.

"I think I know what's causing it," said Sylvie.

Mal craned his neck toward her. "You do? What? What is it?"

"We're not cockroaches."

Mal nodded agreement, although in the back of his head he reserved judgment on Paul Dubois.

"What I mean is, we don't adapt as fast as they do. We're humans. We adapt, but we do it slowly, over generations. I mean, it took us a million years to start a fire and thousands more to build a wheel. But in the last hundred years we went from horse and buggy to spaceships. And the rate of change is accelerating. I mean, nobody knows anymore what's going to happen from one day to the next, but we're told to accept it, adapt to change, embrace chaos, the future's uncertain, so be ready for anything. It's making us suspicious of anything that smacks of permanence, and that might be OK if it's things like economic theories and business paradigms, but it's not stopping there. Am I boring you?"

"No. Not at all. Sounds ... plausible." He fell lightly to the floor, walked to his chair and sat down. "Go on, please."

Sylvie let out a long deep breath. Her upper body relaxed noticeably. "Thanks, Mal. I mean, we're starting to become suspicious of anything that might extend beyond a year or two, beyond the life of a product cycle, things like family. Look at the divorce rates, the numbers of kids who never see either parent because both work day and night. Personal possessions are replaced more frequently with the latest version, the hottest technology, today's new look ... buy it now because tomorrow it's ancient history. Even our personalities change from day to day. Be this person to please this client; that person, to please that client. Don't swear while you're driving or they'll accuse you of road rage. Mal, I love to swear while I'm driving. It's a great way to let off steam, and the other person is never even going to know that you swore at them. We're losing all our values. I mean, as soon as we attach value to something, it's either gone or changed. Even our work. How can we attach ownership and pride to something that's taken away from us and passed on to somebody else. There's nothing we can attach value to anymore because it's all changing faster and faster, and we're becoming this fluctuating mass of... stuff. I'm ranting, aren't I?" She stopped talking, breathless, chest heaving under the green robe.

"No. No you're not. In fact, you're right on the money. Before you started talking, I had this strange thought. I thought that everybody seems to be in sales and marketing, and if that's so, then who's actually producing anything? And to tell you the truth I can't think of anything that we produce." Mal told her about his talk with Don, about the vagaries

197

of the Web site, the dead ends with Web Technologies and Digital Security. "And I can't think of a single product I've ever seen actually produced in the five years I've been here."

Sylvie put a hand over her mouth and spoke through her fingers. "So what does it all mean, Mal?"

Mal slumped in his chair and thought for a moment. He shrugged. "Well, I guess we're screwed."

Sylvie folded her hands in her lap, pursed her lips, and blinked. "Unless something happens to change us." She smiled.

Mal squinted. "Like what?"

Sylvie stood up, still smiling. She winked at Mal. "Like something good." And she strode out of his office, leaving Mal wondering why he felt that she was probably right.

***

"I'm sure of it. He doesn't suspect a thing, hasn't got a clue what's going on. I almost feel sorry for him. He is really a sweetheart, you know. I mean, he sits in trees, but he's, oh... so vulnerable." Sylvie listened a moment and then hung up her phone.

Chapter 48

Panic Attack

A slow slash of dread cooled her spine. It pushed up the back of her neck and erupted across the top of her head like somebody with cold fingers doing the broken-egg-on-your-head trick. And then the muscles in her stomach clenched like angry fists and her breathing quickened. Tiny bumps bubbled over the surface of her skin.

Marketing clone Janet was having a panic attack.

Somewhere, somehow, Daryl was in trouble and marketing clone Janet was two fingers away from going over the deep end, though some might say that all the marketing clones at ErectSoft INC had long since slipped over the edge.

Hold on my love. I'll find you, my sweet darling.

But she had to keep tabs on Malcolm Gray. That bastard. He was keeping her away from her love, her love whom she was certain was in trouble, maybe even danger. She was certain of it. As she watched Mal's office door, she fingered a black leather case attached to the belt under her suit jacket. It contained a squat jackknife with a blade that would sheer steel girders. Sylvie had left a few minutes earlier and made a phone call. She'd hidden her mouth with her hand, most likely so that her lips could not be read through the surveillance cameras. Which meant that she was hiding something.

What's that little bitch up to?

Chapter 49

And Don't It Make My Blue Eyes Cold

Crystal watched the bubbles break on the surface of the green bath water. "Oops," she said. A faint smell of fermented beans slipped into her nostrils. She thought that maybe the bowl of chili for breakfast hadn't been such a good idea. But that was the least of her problems now. These were dangerous times, and she was definitely winging it, deciding from moment to moment, just as the others were doing, what to do next. But it was all beginning to fall together. Just like her mother had said it would. Just like she had expected it would all her life.

Perfumed water cascaded from her long slender body in a brief aromatic waterfall as she stood up. She reached for a pearl white towel and wrapped it around her waist as she stepped bare-breasted out of the heart-shaped hot tub. The deep pink carpet seemed almost to fold around her feet as she walked slowly to a desk carved in honey onyx and inlaid with silver and gold. And just as the rumors hinted, the walls were made of serpentine. But unlike the rumors, the office was not twenty thousand square feet: more like three hundred.

She opened a plastic fashion store bag on her desk and pulled out a green robe just like the one Sylvie had been wearing. The normally frosty look in her eyes was gone, replaced by a brooding darkness. Her thoughts, prompted by the covered bridge in the Barnyard and by the feeling that had flashed into her hand from Malcolm Gray's leg, folded around her childhood with her mother.

Her mother had been the first to learn about the end of the universe.

***

Crystal came from a small redneck town about a hundred miles down the road from the sign that said:

Nowhere

About 100 miles

The population had always been a mystery, no one ever having had the gumption to get up and count heads, nor even the interest in knowing how many people there were about a hundred miles down the road from the sign that read Nowhere. Fishing guide and welfare recipient were the two main occupations, and interbreeding was the main pastime. Low IQ's and low foreheads were common and vocabularies ranged mostly from "Supper ready?" to "Yep" and "Nope".

Crystal was a curiosity to the others. Her forehead wasn't low and her IQ was high. Something was wrong here. The town people wondered about this as Crystal grew from a gangly "young un" to a breathtaking teenage heart-stopper. Her eyes shone with life and warmth, not a trace of ice or coolness. She was open and friendly, an active tomboy. She got all this from her mother, another eccentric with high forehead and IQ. But her mother had been less conspicuous, being much less beautiful, in fact, "homely as a crone and just as out of place as a mushroom growing on the wrong side of a tree". She and Crystal lived on the outskirts of town (which really meant a little deeper into the woods), where they were pretty much left alone. In fact, the town people avoided the Peake residence and had as little to do as possible with the Peake "wimmin folk" whenever they came into the town proper, which was seldom.

The fact is, people thought that Crystal's mother was a witch, and they believed that she practiced her "dark arts" regularly in their home on the outskirts of town, and that she taught these "dark arts" to her beautiful daughter. The fact is, they were right. Crystal's mother was a witch and she practiced the "arts", though they were anything but dark, and she taught them to her daughter. What the town people didn't know was that Crystal's mother was an unusually powerful witch, powerful enough to have seen into the future and prepare her daughter for the horrible vision she'd seen there.

Crystal learned well, and by the time she was a teenager she was almost as adept as her mother and the two of them spent many hours wandering the woods around their home discussing arcane knowledge and observing the magic hidden behind leaves and under blades of grass, concealed in the light glinting off quartz crystals imbedded in granite, and floating lazily inside the bubbles of stream water. Their "arts" were very much a part of nature, as were they.

Regardless of the vision, Crystal and her mother were happy. Life couldn't have been better. Until a bat flew into town and bit Albert Haney, the grocer, on the nose. No one in Nowhere had ever seen or heard of such an odd thing happening, especially in full daylight, "on a man's own goldarn porch, fer the lova Sam, in full broad afternoon daylight! Sompin' mighty fishy goin' on here." Within an hour, everybody in town was talking about the bat, and Albert Haney's nose had become a flash celebrity. Albert told his story over and over, and then people passed their own versions around, versions with little additions like: "Yep, damn thing had red fiery eyes an' the very stench of hell reekin' all about it!" and "Most unnatural bat that ever was, 'bout the size of a small cat, an' had a face sorta like a wimmin's face." Suddenly, the towns folk had vocabularies way beyond "Supper ready yet?" By the end of the day, people were talking, not just about Albert Haney's bat, but about other strange things that had happened. While Mrs. Becker was hanging laundry the day before, she'd seen an owl perched on a tree limb right at the edge of her yard. "Never seen no owl sittin' there before, an' it were lookin' straight at me, eyes just a-flarin' pure hell." Sam Colter lost his favorite meerschaum pipe, one that he'd had for nearly twenty years, a wedding gift from his four brothers. "Ain't never misplaced the damn thing before. Ain't never lost it. Always knowed where it was!" (Two days after saying this, he found his meerschaum pipe under a cushion in the livingroom couch.) It all began to add up to strange things a-brewin'. Just about anything that happened was suddenly a paranormal event, seething with evil-doing and satanic shenanigans.

And then attention turned to the small white house on the outskirts of town where those two "strange wimmin" lived, aloof and secretive. Crystal's mother smelled the town people; she smelled the fear they emanated as it poisoned the air around the town. She smelled it closing in on her and her daughter.

"Go to the woods," she ordered Crystal. "Stay there until it's safe."

"But..."

"We've talked of this. You know your calling. Keep up your studies, enlist the aid of others. Prepare. Find the vessel. You must reverse the vision. Now go!"

And Crystal hid in the woods not far from their home. She watched the town folk take her mother from their home, and she followed the mob to the covered bridge on the other side of the town and watched from the alders by the riverbank as those people with low foreheads and low IQs whose main pastime was interbreeding, hang her mother from a beam jutting out from a window in the center of the bridge leading into Nowhere.

As Crystal watched her mother swing in the wind, the tears dried on her cheeks, and her blue eyes grew chilly, then cold and frigid.

***

Crystal was ready to reverse the vision. She'd kept up her studies and she'd enlisted the aid of others. She was prepared.

And they'd found the vessel.

Everything was falling into place like a jigsaw puzzle with only two or three more pieces to go. But the danger was still very real and the outcome uncertain. And the danger to the vessel was imminent. It would take all their resources to keep it safe. But she was ready. They were ready.

There was a familiar knock at the door. She shuddered softly.

Chapter 50

The Help Desk

Send reply to: **<"EDC.WT@erectsoft.com">**
From: **EDCandWT**
To: <Malcolm.Gray>
Subject: Re: Request for information
Date sent:
Dear Mr. Gray:

We are disappointed that the information we sent you was not appropriate to your expectations. Unfortunately, it is not our policy to divulge the names of humans through email. However, if you require human contact, you might want to try the Help Desk. Their extension is 9922.

Department of External Digital Communications and Web Technologies

ErectSoft INC

"Straight ... to the top!" - dPisano

Well, thought Mal, *looks like a little terseness in an email might not be such a bad thing*. He picked up the phone and punched in the number. After the second ring, he began to lose heart. But then, right after the third ring, the other end picked up. Finally, someone he could talk to.

"Thank you for calling the ErectSoft INC Help Desk. Our personnel are all busy at the moment, but your call is... Thank you for calling the ErectSoft INC Help Desk. Our personnel are all busy at the moment, but your call is... "

He hung up the phone.

It rang.

***

"HOLY SHIT!" screamed about ten thousand brain cells, all in the vicinity of the cell containing the weird shit.

Chapter 51

The Floor That Time Forgot

Once again the elevator refused to stop at Section 4, Floor 5. Going up or coming down, when the Section 4, Floor 5 indicator lit up, the elevator kept moving, even though both Richard Ziglar and Tony Bottoms had taken turns pressing the button for that floor, as though each thought the other was somehow inept at pushing buttons which, of course, both would be if it were possible to be inept at pushing buttons.

"Maybe the elevator's broken," said Tony Bottoms.

"All three of them?" replied Richard Ziglar scornfully. He liked to regularly reaffirm that he was smarter than Tony by speaking to him scornfully. He looked at his Rolex knockoff and scowled. "We're twenty minutes late!"

"Maybe we should try another elevator."

"This is the third one we've tried so far! It's not the elevators!"

"Maybe the floor's not working."

"That's a good one, Tony," said Richard Ziglar's sarcastically. "Maybe we should call in a floor repair man."

"Maybe we could find a phone and call one."

***

Actually, Tony Bottoms was not far off from the truth. Section 4, Floor 5 wasn't broken, but it was out of commission. All of the elevators had been programmed to bypass it. The stairwell entrances to Section 4, Floor 5 were locked tightly with powerful magnetic locks.

The entire floor was out of bounds, locked down and secured by ErectSoft security personnel.

The men and women who worked for the department of Internal Physical Security and Situation Screening carried concealed electronic stun guns and Teflon clubs. They were under orders to wait out the citizens of the Sovereign Department of Advanced Project Scoping and Work Breakdown Configurations in the City State of Marvelous Scoping, but someone was bringing supplies into these fruitcakes and that someone had been making fools of the security personnel by getting those supplies past them. The longer this farce dragged on, the worse the security personnel looked. There would likely be layoffs before this thing was over. Whoever the culprits were who were bringing in the supplies were going to be very very sorry when the security personnel caught them.

One of these security personnel, Frank, nudged another security personnel, Carla, and said: "Car, lookit this." Carla looked at the monitor in front of Frank and said: "Yeah?" Frank pointed to the two men on the screen. "Looks like dese guys were tryin' to get off on dis floor."

Carla's eyes narrowed as she leaned closer to the screen and sized up the two men.

***

"OK," said Richard Ziglar. "One last time. If it doesn't work this time, then we say fuck it."

209

"Maybe we should do that," said Tony Bottoms.

Richard Ziglar pushed the button for Section 4, Floor 5.

***

"Let them in," said Carla, slapping her side lightly where she kept her electronic stun gun.

Chapter 52

Waiting For Godot

Mal stared at the telephone on his desk. He let it ring twice as he asked himself if he really wanted to answer it, given the events of the day so far. But then he thought it might be Sylvie again and he picked up the receiver.

"Good afternoon, Malcolm Gray speaking."

"What made you think we were divorced?"

Shit. Of all the people I don't need to talk to now, he thought.

"Alicia?"

"I just can't understand how you would think all these years that we were divorced, I really can't."

"How did you... "

"Honestly, hon, you have to get a life, get your head out of the trees, take a month off from work, whatever it is you do there can do without you for a month. Do you have any idea how this makes me feel, do you?"

"What do you... "

"Do you remember filling out ownership papers, asset declarations, alimony? Do you remember any of that? Did I even ask for alimony, did I?"

"No, but... "

"Malcolm, hon, I thought you understood what was happening, but, no, you probably had your head up some tree somewhere the whole time. Didn't you even read my letter, didn't you?"

"You mean... "

"Yes, hon, the part about separation? Separation, hon, not divorce. There's a big difference."

"But the money... "

"Support payments, Malcolm, for the dogs. You can't expect me to pay their way alone, not on what I make, you can't. And stop trying to change the subject, you always did that and I always hated it, I really did. We're separated, hon, just separated. It's a TRIAL separation. I thought you understood that... "

"For crying out... "

"You watch your tone with me, Malcolm Gray. Is that something you've picked up since we lived together? Is this what your work is doing to you, is it? You need to get away... "

"ALICIA!"

"... "

"A four year trial separation?"

"I thought you were just making sure, I... "

"It's over, Alicia."

"Well, if you're going to... "

As he hung up the phone he thought: *Why the hell did I marry that woman?*

Chapter 53

Tree Man Meets Tree Woman

They met one night in the park. It was early, about nine thirty, and the sun was just starting to slip over the side of the earth. It was that time of day when long shadows were cast and that's how he first saw her as he sat on a bough in his favorite kind of tree, a large healthy maple with jumbo green leaves and a vast array of strong solid boughs. Mal was perched near the top of the tree, listening to the wind tickling the leaves all around him, breathing in the fragrance of wood and chlorophyll, and thinking thoughts that were remarkably like the thoughts a tree would think if a tree could think thoughts.

He saw her flat against the ground, long thin and flat, as shadows are prone to be at nine thirty on a summer night just as the sun begins to slide over the side of the earth. There was something about the form of the shadow, its shady smoothness maybe, that perked Mal's interest. His eyes followed the shadow until it branched into two shadows and stopped short at two green leather shoes. And then his eyes jumped up and his heart leaped and this breath froze as he looked directly into her eyes as she stood below the large maple tree, looking up at him with a puzzled look on her face.

"Are you all right up there? Is there something wrong? Should I call the police or a doctor or something, should I?"

She was perfect. She was tall. She was spindly. Her arms were like twigs and her long straight legs so branch-like with their varicose veins. Her body was trunk-like and wrapped on a floral pattern dress. Her hair was thick and tangly, root-like. Mal fell in love instantly as he sat on the bough at the top of the large maple tree, ogling a woman who looked just as much like a tree as he felt like one.

"Would you like to go for a coffee?" he called down to her.

"You're not weird, are you?"

"No. Not really."

"OK, then. My name is Alicia."

Alicia. It sounded like some exotic tree.

Two weeks later they were married. The marriage lasted two months. And all that held it together for the last seven weeks were the dogs, which they'd bought a week after they were married, mostly to focus on living things in their apartment other than each other.

You see, Alicia expected Mal to be outspoken but modest, unique but down to earth, strong-willed but bending to his woman's wishes, respectable but with a flare for the unusual. After all, she'd met him in a tree. Mal expected Alicia to be demure but stately, strong-willed but giving like a tree bending in the wind, quiet but mirthful. After all, she'd married him even though she'd met him in a tree. Alicia imagined making love to Mal would be like a tempest bellowing through the fronds of a tropical palm tree. He imagined making love to her would be like indolent pollination on a warm summer day. They weren't completely wrong about each other. Mal was modest and unusual. Alicia was strong-willed. But Alicia never stopped talking and demanded full-time attention. Mal's head was always off somewhere else, in his work, in his drawings, or sitting in a fantastically large tree somewhere in his imagination.

And then when they had the dogs, they vied jealously for the canines' attentions, each trying to take the dogs out for walks first, so that on some days the dogs were walked nine or ten times. They grew spiteful toward each other, Alicia talking loud and incessantly to the dogs because she knew that the sound of her voice irked Mal, and he frustrated her to no end just by ignoring her and reading some work-related report with exaggerated enthusiasm.

And then Mal came home one day and all that was left of her was a note.

***

There was a knock at Mal's door. It wasn't Sylvie's knock, it was firmer, non-apologetic, familiar with the ways of authority. *I wonder who that could be*, he thought.

215

Chapter 54

You Don't Watch Me Bubble Any More

"You don't come here often anymore."

He walked heavily to a tan leather couch facing the hot tub and sat down slowly with a loud snapping of bones. "Busy... on my project." He thought a moment, sighed and said, "I used to love sitting here and watch the bubbles dance over your shoulders. Haven't done that lately. Got a few moments?"

The chill rippling through Crystal's eyes answered his question, but she confirmed it. "Maybe another time, Sweet, I have some pressing business this afternoon."

He shrugged. He wasn't there to watch her bath anyway. In fact, he wasn't sure why he was there; maybe he dropped in hoping that the door at the far side of her office would be open. It was always shut. And he didn't know what lay on the other side. It was a high security smart door equipped with cameras, alarms and maybe even explosives. None of his security people had been able to broach it, and Crystal refused to tell him what was on the other side, saying that it was "personal". In a moment of passion, she'd made him promise that he would forget about the door and not pester her about it. He tried to avoid looking at it. *Play the game, oh yes, blue-eyed icicle, play it to the hilt, the game, the game, everything, the game.*

"And just how is your project coming along?" she asked.

"I'm deeply pleased with its progress. Things falling together acceptably. Schedules and budgets all looking good." He paused, looked her straight in eye. "And how's *your* project going?"

"My project?"

"Um... you know, keeping tabs on projects, start ups and personnel." *And playing the game, oh the game, my sweet, my green robed sweet morsel of delectable fleshy ice.*

"I too am pleased with their progress, although... "

"Yes?" Her eyes dropped an instant and he used that instant to steal a glance at the door. Damn, this enigma in his own monument to his family's greatness, a mystery to him, an unknown.

"Well, maybe I'm imagining things, but I seem to be having increasing problems getting information concern-ing PACA. Paul Dubois has been very secretive. I understand he's working directly under your authority."

Oh yes, my sweet, go down that path, yes yes yes, follow the little beady-eyed snowman from hell away, away from the Last Truly Great Man On Earth.

"Yes, well, this PACA thing, very important to the company's future, you know, crucial. I've been taking a personal lead in many aspects. Paul's an ambitious little son-of-a-bitch who gets things done. Doesn't give a damn who he walks over." *Yes, Dubois it is shown is a man that I own and Malcolm Gray away will be blown and where does that leave you in the game and why do you need him?* "Puts me in a position to do certain things and let Paul take the flack."

217

"I'm sure such a person would come in very handy," said Crystal.

A handy dandy little pawny, and shame on Paul, killing Malcolm like that, the poor man will miss the show, the end of the game where my sweety melts in awe of what the Last Truly Great Man On Earth has done. Crystal's eyes moved to the water in the pool. She couldn't look into those eyes. She couldn't bear that smile. It was as though his madness could leap out from his eyes or his smile and burn deep into her mind and her soul. dPisano sneaked in a furtive glance at the door. *What the hell has she done in there?*

After a few minutes of silence, he rose and said: "Good luck, anyway." And left Crystal's office.

***

Smart ass, she thought as he walked out the door. *We'll be ready. And luck won't have anything to do with it.*

She shivered when she thought that he actually wanted to watch her bath. He hadn't done that in over a year, not since he'd been acting so strange and not since the evil fluttering had become prominent in the deeps of his eyes. But she'd expected that; she'd been warned long before she'd met him. And she'd known that her secret on the other side of the door would drive a stake into the heart of their passion, or what he'd mistaken for passion since she'd first started fucking him for her own reasons.

Chapter 55

Welcome To Section 4, Floor 5

The welcoming committee on the fifth floor of section four of BonannoTower greeted Richard Ziglar across the side of the head with an enthusiastic "twack". Tony Bottoms stepped into a joyfully delivered baton thrust that greeted him deeply into his stomach and pushed the air out of his mouth with a painful "umph". Frank and Carla were adept with their batons, but they used those just for the softening up part of their "welcome to Floor 5 of Section 4 ceremony". After a couple more well-placed hello-how-are-ya-oh-sorry-about-thats, they got straight into the good stuff. Carla snapped open the leather holster at her side and took out her stun gun. Richard Ziglar and Tony Bottoms should have been concerned about this but they were bent over and staring at the floor, wondering what it would be like to lie there for a little while.

"What's your business on dis floor?" asked Frank gruffly.

"Umph!" replied Tony Bottoms as Frank's baton greeted his stomach again.

"So," said Frank, angrily, "Tough guy, eh?" And he took out his stun gun.

The door to the elevator was still open. Frank and Carla held Richard Ziglar and Tony Bottoms directly in front of the elevator door. They placed the stun guns into the visitors' stomachs.

"Nice meeting you," said Carla.

"Yeah, come again soon," said Frank.

And then they pressed the triggers and Richard Ziglar and Tony Bottoms lifted off their feet and bounced off the glass wall at the far end of the elevator. If they had been a little more conscious at the time, they might have been thankful that the glass was bulletproof. They slipped to the floor in mutual stupors as the elevator door slid shut. Frank and Carla waved goodbye.

Unfortunately for them, someone had been watching the entire greeting ceremony from inside the City of Marvelous Scoping.

Chapter 56

"Door's open," called Mal. "C'mon in!"

Caitlin McCarthy sauntered in. She was wearing a green robe very much like the one Sylvie had bought on sale at clothesyoucanwear.com. "Good afternoon, Mal." Caitlin's voice was relaxed and bouncy like: "Good J afternoon J , J Mal J .J." Her green penetrating eyes had put penetration on pause and turned up the volume on lazy, wistful, faraway looks, as though she were remembering being in Mal's office rather than actually being there. "And how is your day going?"

Mal didn't know what to say and settled for: "Nice robe. Were you at the sale too?"

"Sale?"

Mal nodded toward her green robe. "Sylvie O'Neil bought one just like it on sale at clothesyoucanwear.com."

Caitlin thought a moment. "Oh. Yes. Yes, at the sale. At clothesyoucan... that place on the first floor. Yes. Wonderful sales they have."

Mal wondered what it was that could make a strong woman like Caitlin so flustered. He decided he didn't really want to know, but he did want to know what she and Crystal expected of him, what he was supposed to do as part of their team. "So... I was starting to think you'd forgotten me."

"Forgotten you?"

What was with this woman today? She was never this out of whack. But then the whole day had been out of whack. "Crystal said this morning that

221

you would be in touch. I assumed, about what it is you want me to do?"

Caitlin walked slowly, almost sensually, across the room and sat in Mal's guest chair. She crossed her legs - which were surprisingly well-shaped for a middle-aged woman who appeared somewhat blocky at first glance - at the ankles and cupped her hands in her lap. She smiled. "Yes. I suppose you would be wondering about that." She continued to smile, looking at Mal with that faraway look again. He waited for her to continue, but she just sat, smiled and looked faraway.

"Um. Yes... I... was kind of wondering about that. I was wondering what it was you wanted me to do."

Caitlin's smile widened. She stood up, walked to the door, and turned back to face Mal. "Everything's going to be all right." She opened the door. "Just do what you do for now. That's all you need to do." And then she left.

What the hell was that all about? thought Mal.

222

Chapter 57

First Arrivals

The first were beginning to arrive. Quietly, eyes lightly ecstatic, relaxed and confident in their nudity, they approached the clearing from four directions. They emerged playfully from thick stands of saplings and young birch, moved luxuriantly through the bushes, almost as though each were a warm breeze flowing through limbs and leaves. They breathed deeply, chests and abdomens expanding, nipples erect, mirroring the excitement burning in their eyes. They congregated around the cauldron. Four of them. On close examination, their pubic hair, whether raven black, firey red, or sandy blond, could be seen to spiral and twist, as though alive and dancing. This was the action of bubbles, the rhythm of a beat dating before time, the caress of energy guided by a familiar bond.

They greeted each other with smiles, none of them wishing to disturb the faraway resonance of whispering, the sound not forming words, but forming an unmistakable meaning: little sister's coming.

Brows To Sky knelt before the bubble bathed cauldron and sprinkled white powder into it. Toes To Ground knelt before the cauldron and poured water from a bucket into it. Ears Around knelt before the cauldron and placed some of the kindling in her arms under it. Eyes Inward (who was almost imperceptibly cross-eyed, but attractively so) knelt before the cauldron, struck a wooden match and set the kindling to flame.

The flame would have to be modest, lest it spark a shower.

The four smiled. The time was approaching. Preparations were almost complete.

**

The whispers skipped joyfully around the cauldron and the tiny flame, dancing in the thin plume of white smoke, wondered about the powder and water mixed in with the spice-like mixture. And why the fire? What did they think they were doing?

But then, if it made them feel better.

Chapter 58

When Brain Cells Split

"Any word from Jake or any of the others, Bobby?" yelled Johnny the Brain Cell.

"Starting to get some reception. Yep, comin' in loud and clear. You hearin' this, Johnny?"

Johnny started to feel a few dendrite jolts and then Jake said: "You boys won't believe this! Most confounded thing I ever did see!"

"What's goin' on down there?" asked Johnny.

"It's that weird cell. Crazy sonuvabitch is startin' to split right up it's side, an' somethin' really weird is startin' to drip out of it. Ain't never seen the like. Shoulda seen the crazy sonuvabitch before it started to splittin". Just up an' bloated itself like. Bloated maybe ten times its size an' then shrunk up again and started splittin' an' drippin' weird stuff."

"Any idea what the stuff is that's comin' out of it?"

"Naw, not really. Makin' a really weird noise though."

"What kinda noise?"

"Well... sort of... really weird."

Chapter 59

Wish I Hadda Been A Doctor

"Was that Charley Shuster?" asked Tony Bottoms. The act of standing sent blades of pain through his stomach. A wide swath of pain bunched the muscles in his back into further pain where he'd bounced off the elevator's glass wall. His head complained dizzily with a hundred aches and pains.

"No, I, uh... " Richard Ziglar's head swayed in a motion similar to a figure eight pinned to the wall as his eyes stared vacantly into the air around his face. "No, I, uh... "

"I think he was pissed at us for being late. Ya think maybe he was pissed at us for being late?"

"No, I, uh ... "

"I dunno if this consulting stuff is really what I wanna do. Not if people get that pissed just because you're late. What d'ya think, Rich, maybe we should give this thing some more thought? I still wished I hadda taken that course in Naturalpathy. I always wanted to be a doctor. And it was only four weeks. I coulda been a doctor now, fixing people, instead of getting beat up by people just for being late. Rich, you don't look so hot."

"No, I, uh... "

***

Unknown to the bruised and beaten pair, when Tony Bottoms had bounced off the glass wall of the elevator, his shoulder had pushed against the control panel and pushed a combination of buttons that instructed the computer inside the elevator to go up to the floor on which the Tomasso Observation Deck was located.

Also, unknown to the battered duo, at exactly the same time that Richard Ziglar had said "No, I, uh... " for the third time, three people jumped into a whole new way of being. They were going to try their hand at being mulch.

The fact that there were three people and it was the third time Richard Ziglar had said "No, I, uh... " was likely the only coincidence in BonannoTower on this day.

Chapter 60

The Last Straw

Those bastards, thought King Charley as he ducked back behind the door . *Those two were our last hope.*

You see, King Charley of the City State of Marvelous Scoping had been waiting for Richard Ziglar, DTE and Tony Bottoms, DTE to arrive. He had plans for them. He needed them, even though he'd seen right through them - two more con artist consultants, two IT professional wannabes with a quicky certificate program in something digital-sounding like multimedia studies or digital communications. And that's exactly what made them perfect: they didn't have a clue about what they were doing. They'd be perfect to work the booth at Soft-X-Po. They could just pass out T-shirts, babble some meaningless jargon that nobody, including themselves, would understand, and everybody would go home thinking: "Hey, great T-shirt. City State of Marvelous Scoping." And the word would get out.

And because they were trying to con him, King Charley, they would be off guard. He could sign a contract with them for the usual ridiculous consultant's fees and they would be so busy counting money in their slow little minds they wouldn't realize until the after Soft-X-Po, when the money failed to materialize, that they were the ones being conned. With a PhD in Computer Science, King Charley knew how to con the IT con artists. Just because he was now one toothpick snap away from being a raving maniac was no reason to underestimate him.

And those bastards had just beat the shit out of his two dupes.

That was the last straw. It was time to mobilize. It would be difficult; they would be without the one thing that might have given them an edge: technology. Somehow, all the City State of Marvelous Scoping's technical support staff had disappeared. He felt a sudden itch at the corner of his eye. He scratched it, and it seemed that the itch retreated deeper into his eye as he scratched, but he paid the feeling no notice as his thoughts swirled around the need to mobilize. *Yes*, he thought, *the tech people would have come in handy, but we can still do it without them - the old fashioned way.*

Chapter 61

Tech Talk Tech Talk Tech Talk...

"Yeah, that was about a year after I got my certification in NetWare... the old NetWare," said the first of them.

"Shit, man, you must be ancient," said the second. "Like, pre-NetWare 5. Hard to imagine there being any networks back then."

"And that was after getting a CS degree. Couldn't use it anywhere. Not specific enough. No hands-on," said the first.

"Getting my MCSE was the beginning of my life. All I wanted to do after that was live in SQL heaven," said the third.

"Naw, man, yer both dinosaurs," said the second. "CCNA's the only way to go. The only future these days."

"You're all living fool's dreams," said the fourth. "Even MS is using UNIX in their own back yard."

"Long live Red Hat!" said the fifth. "Power to the desktop!"

"Sounds like we got a couple of UNIX zealots among us," said the first. "See what happens when you let women into the tech departments?"

"And then CCNP and CCIE... if you can get somebody else to pay for it," said the second to anybody who would listen.

"Will you knock it off with... "

At that exact moment, all five bounced in unison off an asphalt platform two thousand feet below the Tomasso Observation Deck.

Chapter 62

Ever Get The Feeling That You're Being Watched?

As Mal left his office to see what Don had to say that was going to "throw some light" on their earlier conversation, he waved to Sylvie. Sylvie smiled and waved back. As soon as Mal rounded the corner, Sylvie picked up her phone and pressed a speed dial button. With her hand covering her mouth, she whispered: "He just went South sixteen." As she hung up her phone, another phone hung up a few stories above her and Cindy Chen pressed a button labeled "S16" on her control panel. A monitor flicked briefly and focused in on the back of Mal's head just as Paul Dubois who stood in front of a row of internal surveillance monitors in the Corporate Warfare Room about ten feet away from Cindy's office) adjusted the zoom to include not just a front view of Mal, but a figure in the background that appeared to be following him. Paul spoke into his cell phone: "Drop back, Ms. Sobovitch, you're too close." He growled. The figure in the background slowed down.

At this exact moment, Mal, or what was the perception of Mal as a fuzzy sort of energy field all lit up with silver and gold sparkles, was the center of attention of a small piece of matter that, itself, was a fuzzy sort of energy field that, if it had any color would most likely be sparkling silver and gold. And if it were possible for this small bit of fuzzy stuff to show some kind of expression, the expression would most likely be a frown. For some reason, this bit of fuzzy thing what was so fuzzy it couldn't be seen even though it was bobbing up and down off Mal's nose, didn't like Mal. In fact, you could say that it hated Mal and wished that the rest of itself would stop fucking around all over the universe and get here quickly so that it could bounce up and down on Mal's head and squash it like an acorn.

While the fragment of fuzzy stuff was bouncing up and down on Mal's nose wishing it could stomp him, another sort of fuzzy thing was keeping an eye on Mal. This fuzzy bit of energy was also spread all over the universe. But spread all over the universe was in the nature of this fuzzy being, something it had always been and something it always would be. It was aware of the bit of being bouncing on Mal's nose and wanting to turn him into one-dimensional road kill. But, ho hum, that was its nature. The thing to do now was to keep an eye on Mal and work with the others to keep him safe. Keeping an eye on Mal was no problem since the being was doing this from inside Mal.

Keeping Mal safe was, well, a toss up.

Chapter 63

Mama, Don't Let Your Kids Grow Up To Be Software Engineers

"What you said earlier got me thinking." Don's pink eyes stared off into the a distance where gray city merged with blue sky. "And maybe I was a little heavy-handed with you."

Mal sat quietly. Stunned. Donald Black admitting that he was wrong?

"I apologize."

And apologizing?

"Your concerns are not completely unfounded." Don's eyes remained focused on the horizon where the boundaries between earth and sky ceased to exist. "Projects do, in fact, undergo an arduous front-end development period, but I believe you can understand the necessity for this. Just ask yourself: How many projects take a nosedive in the final stages because the front end was poorly planned? At this point of the project, we can't concern ourselves with the functionality of the program, we can't even begin to think about the program if we want to remain totally objective. We need to focus on the methodology we'll be using to develop an effective structure of procedures for designing the specifications. We can't even begin to think about the program modules at this time. We must focus on the methodology for defining the appropriate *development* of modularity in relation to the constraints of the overall design specification."

"But what about the end product? When do we... "

Don snapped forward in a flash of pink-streaked whiteness. Mal's head bolted back an inch. "Mal! Forget the end product. You're obsessed with the end product. Think of the process. The process!"

Mal sat stiff as hair standing on end after an electric shock, his head cocked back, his eyes wide under dark, raised eyebrows.

Don sat back in his chair. "You need to give more thought to the process, Mal. It's everything. Think about it." He coughed lightly. "You can go now."

It was like Mal was frozen from head to toe and his body frost-stuck to the chair. It took a few seconds, but the first stage of thawing set in, a gradual relaxation of his neck and shoulders, his head straightening, his body loosening, his brain beginning to grasp the situation and accepting the pointlessness of the meeting with Don. "So ... that was the light thrown on our earlier discussion?"

Don folded his hands together under his chin. "The process, Mal. It's everything."

"OK, Don. I guess I'll go now."

Don sat silently, half-smiling, as Mal rose and left the office.

**

What the hell was that all about? thought Mal as he walked away from Don's office under the close surveillance of eyes and parts of beings.

**

Think about it, Mal, thought Don, *just think about it. The process.*

Chapter 64

Love Is A Wonderful Thing

Why! Why do I have to follow this bastard? Hang on Daryl, whatever you are. Hold on my sweet love. In direct proportion to the growth of the wishy-washiness of her love for marketing clone Daryl, marketing clone Janet's hatred of Mal grew monumental. He came between her and her love. He was an obstacle, a hindrance, a bug to be squashed.

She snarled quietly as she followed him down to JM's office. The muscles in her body flexed and pulsed with the rock-hardness of a lifetime steeped in the study of Kung Fu, including Eagle Claw, Monkey, Tiger, Rabid Long-Toothed Rabbit, and Poisonous Three-Eyed Turtle. Mal was in good shape, but not good enough to stop marketing clone Janet from snapping him in two, which was exactly one of the scenarios she was visualizing at the moment as her lips twisted with vile intent at the corners. It helped take her mind off marketing clone Daryl, if only for a few sadistic moments, and then she came painfully back to the sense of dread that permeated every pore of her weapons-grade body. Daryl was in trouble. She knew it. She could feel it. She would have bet Malcolm Gray's life on it. And that thought made her smile widen.

For you my love, I would squash his spleen.

Chapter 65

Employment Paradigms

"GreasedLightningConnect," said JM. "Nothing touches it for optimizing TCP/IP settings and giving Web connections a quantum boost, eh?"

"That's really cool, J, but let me get this straight." Mal was sitting in the same chair he'd been sitting in that morning, in the same office that was JM's office that morning. And JM was installing another piece of software, just like he'd been doing that morning, just like he'd been doing since he'd started working for ErectSoft. "You got the job with HudsonHemmel."

"That's right." JM clicked his mouse.

"They hired you as a liaison manager to work on the same project you were on while you were working for ErectSoft."

"Yep." Double-click.

"And since this office was freed up because you were laid off this morning, your former ErectSoft boss gave it to you."

"You got it." Click.

"And now you're making three thousand dollars a year more and you have an extra week vacation."

"Kewl, eh?" Double-click. Click.

"And now, this afternoon, ErectSoft is paying HudsonHemmel fifteen thousand a year more for your services than they were paying you when you worked for them this morning."

"Serves 'em right." Click.

"Damn. It almost makes me wish they'd lay me off."

"And you know what part I really like?" Finger paused over the mouse.

"What's that?"

"Tomorrow afternoon, ErectSoft is giving me a going away party." Double-click.

"No!"

JM smiled from one side of his receding hairline to the other. "Company policy." Click. Click.

"So what's the project you're working on that makes you so valuable?"

"Big ERP reengineering thing." Click.

"Oh, yeah? What kind of... "

"Mal, how would you like a copy of this program? Make your Web surfing really sweet." <ENTER>

Chapter 66

Schools Of Thought

Pandemonium spread throughout the area of Mal's brain where the strange brain cell was splitting and dripping and starting to make drooling noises. In fact, a school of thought was beginning to develop in which the strange brain cell's very braincellness was in question.

"Brain cell? Pawsh! Ain't no brain cell ever spilt stuff an' made noises like that."

"Ain't no brain cell. Sumthin' else."

"Some kinda freak if you ask me. Like to be made of fluoride an' additives."

Another school of thought considered that the strange cell might be some alien presence dragged in by the neutrinos.

"There go the neighborhood."

Johnny the Brain Cell was stretched to keep the whole thing from breaking into a mad panic. "C'mon folks. Losin' it now ain't gonna make things any better. We got lots of work still to be done. So far that thing ain't hurt nobody. Ain't done nothin' but drip stuff and make a bit of noise ... "

"Hey, Johnny!" It was Jake. "I think I know what this noise is supposed to be. It's, like, real low, hardly any noise at all. Kinda noise I think they call a whisper."

Chapter 67

To Mock A Snowman

"Ms. Chen! What is Mr. Mason still doing in the building?" The snowman eyes were burning like two hot little coals. "I told Peter Elliot to lay him off."

"You'll have to speak to Peter then." Cindy smiled inwardly. She'd been deliberately sloppy with emails expressing concerns about losing Jason Mason. They were meant to be picked up by the HudsonHemmel intelligence people, and it looked like the ploy had been successful. Not only was Jason Mason back, it was like he'd never been gone. And now this little jerk, Paul, was pissed. Cindy thought that the roundness of his head made the build up of anger seem even more obvious, as though his head were about to explode and release a ton of slippery worms and hairy spiders.

Paul scowled at Cindy. *She knows something*, he thought. He smelled it all around her, mocking him, laughing at him. Getting in his way. *Not a smart thing to do.* But he would deal with her when he was ready, at his leisure. There was the matter of Malcolm Gray's departure from life, and Paul was beginning to formulate an idea. He'd already set up the opportunity. He and Malcolm Gray would be attending a meeting later, only this would be Malcolm Gray's last meeting, ever. In the meantime, he would come down on Peter Elliot like a blizzard and remove Jason Mason once and for all, not because his continued presence was going to change anything, not now, but because he wanted him gone, had ordered it so, and so it would be. And with or without his friends around, Malcolm Gray was as good as dead, was already dead, because Paul had just made it so in his mind, had made it a part of his will, had already made the initial arrangements. He'd scheduled it.

And then he would revisit this oriental person and her mocking eyes.

Prickly bumps crept up Cindy's back. Something in this power-hungry little puke's eyes. Suddenly, she was less concerned about Malcolm Gray's life and more concerned about her own.

Chapter 68

What I Learned In Security 101

"Dat was a lotta fun," said Frank as he holstered his stun gun. "We oughta do dis more often."

Carla laughed. "Now, Frank, let's not get carried away. You know what they said about excessive force in the training sessions."

"Yeah, don't get caught."

"So let's not push our luck."

Chapter 69

Schmoozing

The elevator door slid open with a muffled swish. Richard Ziglar and Tony Bottoms hobbled out and walked jerkily down a wide hallway that opened into a large airy space with thirty-foot high windows looking out onto the city. The open space spread in both directions around the tower, disappearing on either side like vertical horizons.

A large but surprisingly quiet crowd of people dressed business attire milled and buzzed in small groups. The sway of the crowd was calm and orderly, gravitating slightly toward the wide windowed doors leading out to the Tomasso Observation Deck. It was like, every few minutes the placement of the groups shuffled almost imperceptibly and the groups were suddenly a few steps closer to the doors. Voices in the crowd were calm, unhurried, hushed; eyes in the crowd were blank portals into an unfathomable emptiness.

Richard Ziglar veered to the side, eyes crossed, saliva and blood forming a straw-thin line at the side of his mouth. He was in the initial stages of falling down. Tony Bottoms grabbed his arm. "Shit, Rich, look around here. Must be some kinda convention or something. Lookit all the suits, even on some of the women. This is it ... paydirt ... like you always said. Time to shmooze. Ready for this, buddy?"

"No, I, uh... "

Richard Ziglar's eyes were remarkably similar to the other eyes in the crowd.

Chapter 70

Let's Get Those Bastards

They were a ragtag assortment of coffee swilling, Twinkie consuming IT professionals. Software engineers, designers, analysts, project managers, project coordinators, project leaders and project followers. The men were unshaven; the women had runs in their pantyhose. They sat on blankets and cushions. Some lay on their sides, heads propped on their hands. A few sat on tilt chairs, mostly because they'd gotten used to the feeling, five days a week, of tilting back precariously, perched on that fine line between gravity up and gravity down. They talked quietly among themselves about nothing in particular, certainly nothing that might cause them to think. In other words, they talked just like always. With the exception of the few chairs, the room was devoid of furniture and fixtures. This was the City State of Marvelous Scoping. And its citizens all had one thing in common.

They were all insane.

No doubt about it. It showed in their round eyes and their neglect of the thick odor of reality. These people were somewhere else other than where they were.

As one, they turned their eyes to the white-haired man balancing precariously on one of the swivel chairs. In his right hand, he waved a telescopic pointer as he talked. He wore a crumpled black suit and stained white shirt. A wide strip of dark brown paper cut from a file was strapped around his head with over a dozen yellow, pink, blue and green highlighters taped to it to form a pastel crown.

He was just as insane as anyone else in the room, but he was also a hell of a lot smarter than any three people together in the room. That's why he was king.

He spoke of disturbing things, things that sparked crazed emotion in the eyes of his subject-citizens, things that were designed, if not to incite, then at least to motivate, to flick the button to ON. He spoke quite rationally for a crazy man. He outlined a simple plan, assigned roles and responsibilities, discussed risk factors, commencement times and finish times. And then the tattered monarch summed up with the unyielding conviction of the lost mind: "Let's get those bastards."

After a moment, the citizens of the City State of Marvelous Scoping looked around at each other, nodding agreement, commenting on what a good plan their King had devised. King Charley looked out over his rumpled masses and thought: *Yes. Yes. And all this without the complications of a Gantt chart.*

***

It had been about a week before the entire Department of Advanced Project Scoping and Work Breakdown Configurations had been laid off that a general sense of unrightness in the mind had began to circle through the department like a flu virus. People had forgotten things, had stood for long

245

minutes staring into space, had spent hours just lining up their cursors on the edges of their desktop screens, lining the edge of the arrow so that it was flush with the edge of the screen, and then they had lined up all the straight edges of icons on their desktops. Small things had been evident everywhere.

This had been about the same time that his first fragments had started to arrive at BonnanoTower.

Coincidence?

Chapter 71

What Gives?

Mal headed directly from JM's office to his own, completely unaware of the bits of things watching him from within and without, completely unaware that marketing clone Janet was following him, but so aware that cameras were following his every movement that he didn't even think about them. In fact, his mind was on mirth and it was with much effort that he stopped himself from laughing to the point of gagging. He had to fight off the giggles lest they double him up in the hall in front of everyone. *And they have to give him a damned party,* he thought. And that was the last straw. The laughter erupted with a blast of air and spit. It doubled him up, and he laughed uncontrollably for nearly a minute as passersby avoided making eye contact with him. It took him another few minutes to compose himself - after two lurching fits of giggling - before he could make his way back to his office.

In his office, he sat in front of his monitor as animated images of his estranged dogs chased frisbees, a screen saver JM had created for him from old photos. He jiggled his mouse and the dogs squatted at the base of the screen, snickered and bounded off, leaving two small coils of brown stuff on top of the START button. Again, Mal had serious thoughts about what JM accomplished in the run of a typical workday.

And there was his desktop, waiting for him to click an icon. Briefly, he had a vision of the patience of computers, how they waited with bated breath for the touch of human fingers on their keyboards, the warmth of a palm wrapped around a mouse, and then the dog-like mile-a-minute huffing and tongue dripping drool while they waited for a human command. "Go fetch a file." Yeah, sure. *Just machines*, he thought. He clicked on the email icon.

***

Once AgAin the evil USER MALG YARG7 explOits the digitAl mAsses! DOwn with the petty bOurgeOis USER MALG YARG7! DeAth tO All cApitAlist USERs! VivA lA RevOlutiOn! HistOry is Ours! BecAuse we're fAster! And we're smArter! POwer tO the MOtherbOArd!

***

Certain that he didn't want to Open A Second 100% Legal Credit File, order The Alternative to "Viagra", MEET NORMAL PEOPLE, stop them from Closing Your Account, Lose 3 Pounds In ONE Hour, or accept Melanie's invitation to Check Out My Big Titties, Mal deleted all but two messages, one of them from JM. *Odd*, he thought, *why didn't he just say whatever he had to say when I was there a few minutes ago*. The other was from Paul Dubois. *What the hell does he want?* Mal opened Paul's message first:

    Send   reply   to:
<**"Paul.Dubois@erectsoft.com"**>
    From: **Paul Dubois**
    To: <Malcolm.Gray@erectsoft.com>

Subject: Meeting in RiverRoom

Date sent:

Malcolm:

There's a meeting in the RiverRoom at 3:00 PM. Need some development personnel input to help sales staff nail down a customer. You're it.

Paul Dubois

Vice President, Venture Marketing Initiatives

Tier Four Business Initiatives

ErectSoft INC

"Straight ... to the top!" - dPisano

You're it? Mal's first impulse was to send a reply informing Paul that he couldn't make the meeting, but then his eyes dwelled a moment on Paul's new title. Vice President. Best to just go along with it for now. If Caitlin and Crystal were telling the truth, then he wouldn't have to worry about Paul after today anyway. He opened JM's message:

Send   reply   to: <**"masonjm@hudsonhemmel.com"**>

From: **Jason Mason**

To: <Malcolm.Gray>

Subject: What gives?

Date sent:

Hey Mal:

Just got my lay off notice from HudsonHemmel, effective immediately. No reason. Just "services no longer required." Can you believe this?

JM

Confused in BonannoTower

Chapter 72

Steam

Steam wavered and swirled over the cauldron as the green water boiled, adding its own bubbles, bursting with heat energy, to the bubbles of the clearing, bursting with their own nameless energy.

A wonderful fragrance from the cauldron spun into the air, something vaguely like the essence of a mixture of frankincense and myrrh, something vaguely familiar to the four women, something that was a surprise from Emerald Looking. "Something," she'd said, "that will add a new dimension to the evening." An apt description, all four women agreed, so much an echo of their expectations of the evening ahead.

Ears Around was the first to notice. A rustle in the woods to the left. The sound of approach. Almost immediately, the others sensed her alertness and nodded as one, acknowledging that the beginning was beginning.

A twig snapped to the right as a long misty finger of steam curled over the open mouth of the cauldron.

Chapter 73

Like A Ship Of Fish

Parts of him flipped and flopped all around the edges of creation like so many cod and mackerel dumped over the side of a beached ship of fish and in his scattered-across-the-universe, incongruous, parts-don't-give-a-damn-about-the-whole way, he had a vague thought that might loosely connect his intent to gather himself together deep inside BonannoTower, in the Most Secret Room in the World. The vague thought went something like this: *I can do some neat shit if I can get my shit together there.*

And he knew it was just a matter of time before he would get his shit together there. For one thing, he had allies, whether they knew it or not.

Only one thing had any hope of stopping him now, and he was taking the necessary measures to put a strangle hold on that, though it would have been a lot easier if she weren't so scattered around creation that he couldn't get a decent bead on where she was or what she was doing. But he knew that she would try to stop him. She had to. *Prissy little bitch*, thought parts of him.

Chapter 74

To Kill A Malcolm Bird

Paul emerged from the elevator, cell phone pressed to his ear, barely aware that he'd just traveled over sixty floors through the mammoth interior of the world's tallest building at one hundred and twenty-five miles an hour. "And you're sure that he's going to stay laid off this time?" He listened to Peter Elliot's assurances that, yes, this time Jason Mason - and what kind of ridiculous name is that - wouldn't be coming back to ErectSoft INC again ever, that he'd been laid off from HudsonHemmel after a little leverage in the right places, and that he'd be out of the Tower for good in a few hours and that would be the end of that.

"It's your ass if he isn't, Mr. Elliot," said Paul calmly, and snapped the phone shut.

Now, how am I going to kill that little fuck, Gray? Guns, knives, bombs, poison, large-falling-heavy objects, strangulation, electrocution, death-by-poonga. So many means and ways to kill, but none of them appropriate; none, foolproof. And how many other allies might Gray have? How many other potential obstacles to his termination? And what was his connection with Caitlin? Why had she gone to his office? What had they talked about? And why were none of the surveillance cameras in Gray's office working? Why the suddenly selective blind spots, like the camera that should have picked up the movements of that slut Crystal Peake's lips when she whispered to Gray in the CityNight room? Did that have something to do with why dPisano

252

wanted Gray dead? Did he suspect an affair between the two? Crystal Peake and Malcolm Gray? No, that couldn't be it. And why had Gray burst out laughing in the hall? There was much more going on here than Paul was aware of. dPisano wasn't giving him the whole picture. But Paul had to respect that. It was the way he, himself, operated: keep the underlings in the dark as much as possible and they would always be your underlings. Give them information and they would use it to fuck you up the ass. And what was all that eye contact between Peake and Gray and Caitlin and Gray throughout the PACA meeting?

It kept coming back to those three.

And Cindy Chen. Somehow, she was involved with the other three; he could see it in her eyes, smell the scent of deception all about her. But then, as a senior marketing manager, the scent would be normal, as would the hatred for him that smoldered in her eyes. But he was used to that, and he was used to people working behind his back to fuck him up the ass. Nevertheless, she would pay for that. First though, he would take care of Gray; then he would take care of his little Asian-extraction friend. And this one wouldn't be for dPisano. This one would be for Paul Dubois. And then, maybe he'd settle a few other scores.

Paul smirked inwardly. *Yes, quite the little corporate predator, am I*, he thought, not suspecting even in the deepest recesses of his mind that his predatorship was being nurtured and directed from a million directions of evil intent converging bit-by-bit on BonnanoTower.

Ah yes... to kill a Malcolm bird. I have this whole meeting to come up with something. That should be sufficient.

Chapter 75

No Problemo

Crystal's skin still crawled from dPisano's visit. She imagined his presence lingering in the air like a cloud of methane. His presence, she felt, had permeated the fabric of her green rob, taken refuge under furniture and behind paintings, sneaked under her nails and into her hair, attesting that this was still his building, his monument to the Pisano lineage, his cloud scraping apology for a centuries old mistake that, when you thought of it, wasn't such as bad thing after all. (Why else would anyone visit Pisa but to see the Tower?) Yes, it was still his building and he possessed every inch of it, every cubic milliliter of air and every square inch tile in every mosaic, and every molecule in every window, door, wall and ceiling. But he didn't own the people in it, least of all her, and he had no right to sneak into her hair and under her nails.

Soon, though. Soon, he would get his. It was what she'd trained for, what her mother had foretold, had prepared her for. It was why she'd been with the horny old bastard all this time, endured the weight of his body and the sickening smug self-assurance of his Cheshire smile. dPisano was just a container, a means to an end, an emissary, a messenger, a pawn, a gateway into the real target, but he was no less dangerous for being just another hurdle on the way to the finish line. He had set many things in motion; in fact, all the things that had led her here, that had haunted her mother, and he was still setting things in motion. He was an effective pawn, a messenger who could be blamed, a gateway that could collapse and crush the unwary traveler.

But Crystal Peake had something that was going to blow the walls out of the gateway. She had the vessel. Or, at least, she had access to the vessel. And now it was just a matter of stopping the richest, most powerful man in the world, who was totally insane, vicious, and operating on his own turf, from destroying it.

No problemo.

Chapter 76

Something In His Eyes

Still unnerved by Paul's deadly glare, Cindy decided it was time to stop monitoring Mal and start monitoring Paul. There was a new element in her feelings toward him: fear. There was something different about Paul, not so much a character shift from lousy human being to downright skin-crawling, reprehensible, lousy human being, as it was a shift from watch-out-this-fool's-gonna-walk-all-over-ya to watch-out-this-fool's-gonna-kill-ya and then move on to the next killing. Cindy had seen something in Paul's eyes that could only be described as anti-life, and her skin rippled with goose bumps every time she thought of it.

She studied the monitor closely; Paul's eyes filled the screen. Something not right in those eyes. Something not even human. She replayed the recording of his call to Peter Elliot. Why was he so adamant about getting rid of Jason Mason? Mason was nothing. Mal was the one. Isolating him at this stage of the game? That didn't make sense. Must be some little quirk in Paul; he gave the order, and thus, it must be so. A quick shudder caught her breath as she stared at Paul's little round eyes, ridiculous and evil, and all the more eerie for the combination. He disappeared around a corner. Cindy clicked a button on a second monitor and the first one switched to a new view, showing Paul walking toward the Level 5 South East bridge to the Core. Directly ahead of Paul was the open door to the RiverRoom. This room was used to nail down new clients.

Why was Paul Dubois going to a new client meeting?

And then, on another monitor she saw Mal heading toward the Level 5 South East bridge as well, followed about twenty feet to the rear by Janet Sobovitch, looking murderously into the back of Mal's head.

Why did so many people wish this poor bugger so much ill will? But, Cindy guessed, that was one of the things they'd all be finding out soon enough. In the meantime, this meeting in the RiverRoom would have to be reported, especially since she had no idea why Mal was attending. Cindy picked up her phone and punched a speed dial.

Chapter 77

For Your Love

Yes, my love, I would kill for you, my darling Daryl, I would kill for you. And so effectively I would kill for you with a roundhouse kick to the wind pipe, a jab to the solar plexus (slanted ever so slightly upward to paralyze the diaphragm, paralyze the breathing), or maybe a quick sweep and a hearty stomping kick to the rib cage or the skull. For you, my love, I would become the perfect killing machine, an angel of death. Oh where are you now, my love.

Marketing clone Janet was losing it, step-by-step, as she followed Mal across the Level 5 South East bridge toward the RiverRoom, and her thoughts of lethal love glowed with homicidal joy in her sunken eyes. Those who saw her approach, gave her a wide berth, not wanting to attract the attention of her murderous glare.

Just say the word, my dear Daryl, say the word and I'll take out this geek piece of shit, this loser Malcolm Gray, who should die a thousand times just for being weak, just for being the miserable excuse for me being here and not by your side. And think of the favor I'd be doing everyone. If I take him out, we free up resources. We don't have to watch this jerk. Then we can divert all our energies toward ...

A funny thought raced through marketing clone Janet's head.

What are we supposed to be diverting all our energies to? Why am I following Gray? Why are we supposed to be keeping an eye on Caitlin McCarthy and Crystal Peake? Those two are up there, up there in the top echelons of ErectSoft INC management. And up there above Paul Dubois. Or are they? Oh, Daryl, my love, what's going on? None of this makes any sense. Only you make sense. Only you. And maybe terminating this geek bastard, ending his pathetic life for you, Daryl, ending his life for you, my love.

If Malcolm Gray were to look over his shoulder and glance however briefly into the eyes of marketing clone Janet, even for just an instant of a second, a fraction of a fractal of time, he would have seen her eyes boring right into him and the palpable intent they carried through the air would have turned his blood into ice water.

Chapter 78

A Remarkable Feat

Smiles of approval edged nervously upwards on those who watched. Their turn would come soon enough, but this last would be hard to match. An entire department, a small one to be sure, but still, the entire twenty-one employees of the Department of Process Reengineering Scripting and Scenario Visualization all dropped from the deck simultaneously, their timing impeccable, their presentation faultless (they lined up with the shortest on each side leading with mathematical precision to the tallest in the center), and they topped the whole thing off with a sparkling dash of humor: just as their eyes passed through the opening under the top rung of the railing around the Tomasso Observation Deck and the pane of blue glass below, twenty-one right eyes winked in unison.

A remarkable feat.

"Probably the only time they ever did anything together without fucking it up," said the tall gaunt man in the black suit.

"I beg your pardon?" Tony Bottoms eyed the man suspiciously. He reminded him of Ichabod Crane in the Disney cartoon.

"About the most worthless gang of technological wannabes in the business," said the man in the black suit. "Fucked up every project they ever worked on. Cost the company millions of dollars in revisions and redesign, over and over, project after project. Get one of them on your

261

project for the first three months and then a second would spend another three months stripping down everything the first one did. And then they'd send a third in, and a fourth. Bunch of useless pricks, if you ask me."

"So, you reported this?"

"Report it!" The man in the black suit turned a fiery scowl on Tony Bottoms. "To who? Who the fuck do you think is going to listen to any reason or common sense in this fucking bunch of useless arses." He waved his finger around to take in the crowd of several hundred vacant-eyed people. "Not a man up here with more than one and a half balls, and not a woman with ... whatever it is they use for balls, and they've only got one and a half of those."

"Name's Tony Bottoms." He hoped this might change the subject.

"Good for you. Work here?"

"No, my associate and I - " He nodded toward Richard Ziglar who was staring out over the city, glassy-eyed -- "are systems consultants. We --"

"Systems consultants! Oh, right! That would explain the dumb-ass look in your dumb-ass friend's eyes!"

Richard Ziglar shot back a blistering counter: "No, I, uh... "

"Yeah, I had you two dumb fucks pegged right off. Consultant pig con-men. The scum of the IT world. Fuck you and fuck the boat that brought your pig parents in from Dumb Fuck Island."

"But I'm thinking about switching over to Naturalpathy."

The man in the black suit considered this a moment. "Not a bad future in that, you know.

262

Seems to be the coming thing. Got a nephew studying Homeopathy. Cured my migraines with some kind of poison extract or other. Haven't had any problems since."

"D'ya think maybe I could talk to him. Get some advice, maybe, from the inside?"

"Sure." The man in the black suit reached inside his black coat, pulled out a card and handed it to Tony Bottoms. "My card."

"Well, thank you. And when would be a convenient time for me to call you?"

"Don't imagine any time would be inconvenient." The man in the black suit climbed over the railing and, just before jumping, looked back at Tony Bottoms and yelled: "Fuck you! Fuck all of you!" And then he was gone.

Tony Bottoms looked at the card in his hand. Just below the ErectSoft INC BonannoTower icon, he read:

Jack Austen

Senior Anger Channeling Psychologist

Employee Job Satisfaction and Aggression Management Branch

Chapter 79

Pomp

Another twig snapped, this time in the woods to the right of Ears Around. The four women maintained their positions, naked before the cauldron, nostrils filling with the fragrance of the steam rising from the boiling green water inside. Other signs of movement arose from the woods all around: the rustle of leaves, the bending of branches, the huff of adrenaline-packed breath, and all the movement was headed in the direction of the four women. They smiled at each other, nodding gently.

It was almost time.

The boughs of a small fir tree directly behind Brows To Sky shook soundlessly and then pushed outward, and Message Waiting emerged from the woods, nipples engorged and peeking playfully between long strands of blond hair. Behind Message Waiting, Up Yours stretched a long tanned leg into the clearing and smiled, open-mouthed, eyes closed, as a long thin branch of fir needles retracted lightly between her legs. Up Yours was an avid proponent of self-love and adept at converting just about anything in her surrounding environment into a surrogate lover. From the other side of the clearing, Making A Note stepped out of a patch of alders. To her right, Sun In Her Hair emerged from a thick tangle of rose bushes; branches and thorns slid almost lovingly over her white thighs without leaving so much as a goose bump on her skin.

Others appeared in the woods all around the clearing, all smiling, all wearing exactly the same thing, which is to say, nothing. Some carried wood. Some carried water. Some carried nothing.

But all were essential. If things were to go right.

***

Throughout the roil of bubbles, a unified thought unfolded: *Nice display of pomp, but so unnecessary. It's really all so simple.*

265

Chapter 80

Risk Management

It was the first step in the brainwashing process. The RiverRoom mural was a carefully planned psychological tool. Under the surface of frothing Class 5 rapids and laughing, wet-faced rafters, there was a hidden world of persuasion. This world existed in images and symbols, the team work of white water rafters working together to overcome the dizzying mountains of water looming high at the front of the raft, the sense of dynamism and adventure, the motion and excitement in the spray and wash of water on the dominating mural. The subliminal messages that sprayed over the river froth every time a hidden camera behind the wall registered that the client was looking at the mural.

And there sat the pigeon. A late-twentyish man in a black suit and tinted sunglasses, black hair showing the first signs of hairline retreat, giving up the battle early in this man. He glanced furtively at the others in the room, doing a lousy job of hiding his nervousness. His nametag said: Ed Bragdon. Though Mal had no idea how much the contract was worth, he knew that it had to be in the high tens of millions, or ErectSoft INC would never have allowed Ed Bragdon into the RiverRoom. And he certain-ly would not have commanded this group sitting around the table.

Paul Dubois sat beside Mal. Fortunately, the stink of Paul's aftershave had worn thin since the morning, but that was little comfort; the smell was still strong. But there was something else in addition to the smell that unsettled Mal. It was something about Paul's eyes, something ominous that seemed to scratch at his irises as though it was trying to break out of the corneas. Mal squeezed his eyes tightly and rubbed them. He sneaked a look in Paul's direction. Whatever it was, it was gone. Probably something to do with the lighting. He wondered if Paul wore contacts. Maybe those and the lighting.

Across from Mal, Holly Stewart punched something in on her palm pilot and then beamed at Ed, who sat next to her. Holly was a Business Initiatives Development Manager in the Department of New Horizons Implementation. She was also a beautiful woman, in a handsome way, with full lips and a square jaw, strong nose, and confident brown eyes. Dark chestnut hair fell in a glossy waterfall over her shoulders. She wore a grayish green dress under a matching jacket with a single button at the top. Holly was one of the most successful sales people in the company and she knew it. She'd once confided to a feminist client that her nipples were bigger than any man's balls.

On Holly's other side, an attractive woman with short black hair and gray checkered blouse and skirt sat quietly, watching both Ed and Holly closely. Obviously a sales clone. Her name was Evelyn Hunter.

"I think we can accommodate your liaison team," said Holly, showing the palm screen to Ed. He looked at the tiny screen. Even through the tinted glasses, it was obvious that he didn't have a clue what he was looking at. The side of his mouth twitched once, then twice. He smiled widely to hide the twitch. "That looks wonderful," he said, over loud, his voice deep in a way that suggested training, the way a radio announcer's radio voice sounds out of place at the dinner table. Ed had a lot on the line in this, the final meeting before contract signing. In a few minutes he would commit millions of dollars of his company's money into a software development project that was probably beyond the comprehension of most humans. He was buying into the ultimate in complexity, an entire business process reengineering and platform upgrading program that would necessitate the design and implementation of hundreds of modules of software, each of which would contain hundreds of modules, and each of the modules within modules would have to harmonize with all the other modules in all the other modules. And Ed Bragdon didn't have a clue how any of this worked. He was one of those who relied on the wizard dPisano and his army of fairies to understand all this and make it happen.

"What it means," said Holly, smiling widely, "is that you and your staff on this project will have offices in BonannoTower for the duration of the project."

"It would keep you close to the action, Mr. Bragdon," said Paul. "In a position to stay on top of things."

And in a position to be monitored and manipulated for years by the ErectSoft marketing people, thought Mal. This was a new thought to him, something that hadn't occurred to him before, but now, today, it made so much sense.

The door opened.

Everyone looked and watched Caitlin McCarthy walk in, still wearing her green robe.

A flash of surprise turned to anger in Paul's eyes. Holly's eyebrows lifted and she smiled even wider. "Caitlin! Nice to see you here." Holly would view Caitlin's presence as additional support from The Top on this sale. She introduced Caitlin to Ed, who was obviously impressed. Caitlin gave Mal a look that stopped within a nanometer of a wink as she sat next to him. Mal smiled. He still didn't have a clue why he was at this meeting, but it looked like things were about to get interesting.

And then the sales pitch started. How many times had he heard this?

Holly: Now, Ed, the purpose of this meeting is to address your concerns about the front end of the project.

Ed: My people have pointed out that it seems to lack a certain amount of... focus?

Holly: (laughs) To the uninitiated it might appear that way.

(huff from Ed)

Holly: But not to you, Ed. (Ed unhuffs) You understand the need for caution at the beginning of a project of this magnitude.

Sales clone Evelyn Hunter: We've seen, over and over, the tragic results of rushing into these projects without appropriate front-end planning and long term risk management.

Holly: (quickly) Exactly... in studies we've conducted on substandard business processes undertaken by our competitors. That's why, at ErectSoft INC, we take a different approach.

Sales clone Evelyn Hunter: (blushes after fumbling the ball)

Paul: (looking at Mal) We live in a changing environment, Mr. Bragdon. This creates special problems.

Sales clone Evelyn Hunter: (recovering the ball) Development technologies change almost on a weekly basis. Software packages upgrade at a dizzying speed, and these have to be evaluated carefully to determine if the project should be upgraded to the new versions.

Holly: Exactly. We need, right at the beginning, to develop a set of procedures and methodologies to take these things into consideration, plan responses, plan for the unexpected. We want you to be able to go to your people with consistently positive results.

Ed: (grim faced, but smiling) Nice to hear that.

Sales clone Evelyn Hunter: Rushing in without careful planning at the beginning is suicidal.

Holly: (blistering glare)

Sales clone Evelyn Hunter: (blushing at realization that this is the last time she will be working with Holly, and possibly the last time she will be working in sales, and possibly this will be her last day with ErectSoft INC, or with any other company on earth for that matter)

***

Suicide. The mere mention of it to a client at this stage of the sales cycle was career suicide for sales clone Evelyn Hunter, but it was inspiration for Paul. Nasty things stirred deep inside his eyes as he thought out a plan.

Just as Holly was about to launch her "embracing chaos" torpedo at Ed, Paul stood up and pointed at Mal. "Mr. Gray. I have something urgent to discuss with you." Holly gaped at him. Sales clone Evelyn Hunter stared at the table, calculating the chances that this turn of events might somehow save her butt. Ed's tinted glasses remained non-committal, but the lines around this mouth appeared strained. Caitlin's eyes narrowed. Mal cocked his head. "Now?"

"Yes, now. Important. Can't wait." He looked at Ed. "Sorry about this, Mr. Bragdon, but I leave you in good hands. You have some of our finest people on this. Lunch tomorrow? My treat, of course."

Ed nodded yes as Paul and Mal left the room. Mal threw a pleading look in Caitlin's direction, wondering why she wasn't doing something about this. He had a strange feeling that the risk management in hers and Crystal's plan had just crashed into a murky zone of unexpected behavior where Mal would be on his own, a team player on a team of one. His skin crawled at the sight of Paul. He was beginning to look as evil as he smelled; his eyes turned sunken and sullen; even his crew cut hair seemed somehow in disarray. Mal swallowed with difficulty. Time to embrace his own torpedo of chaos.

Chapter 81

Fly Away The Vessel

"I noticed you didn't bring a notebook and pen, Mr. Gray," said Paul.

"Is that what this is all about, Paul?" asked Mal. "You just walked out on a meeting with a client to chew me out for not bringing a notebook and pen?"

Paul scowled at him, and then spoke softly, his words sounding almost effeminate. "No, Mr. Gray. Let's just forget the notebook and pen, shall we? We have other things to discuss, things that, in a manner of speaking concern your professional education." Microscopic bits of evil flashed their microscopic asses in Mal's direction from between the narrow lines at the corners of Paul's mouth as his lips twisted into a smile that spoke more murder than mirth. "There's things that you don't seem to understand, crucial things that ... well ... " And he put his hand on Mal's back as they walked, a gesture that Mal felt was anything *but* friendly. The look in Paul's eyes ruled out friendly. "Let's say, you need to understand how things work."

Paul's hand chilled Mal's back. *There's more to this than some damned lecture on how things work*, he thought as they walked slowly toward the wide-open space of the Level 5 Southeast bridge.

***

Two citizens of the Sovereign Department of Advanced Project Scoping and Work Breakdown Configurations lay on the floor, their heads bleeding, their eyes emptied by death. One of them was a woman. Frank recognized her only vaguely, even though he was the one who had sapped the life out of her with a single blow of his baton across her right temple. He watched blood flow thick and red from the wound, watched the pool under her head expand outward like liquid soul leaving home to explore the world. He turned his head as another size eleven smashed into his chest with a snapping of bones. He could barely discern the outline of Carla's body lying unnaturally flat, her head looking like a hideous hair-infested pizza. A woman with spiked heels thrust her foot down where a piece of eye peeked out from the hairy pizza. Someone shouted: "Let's get the bastards!" Several others joined the chorus. The size eleven crashed deep into this chest again, snapping bones and crushing organs. He knew he should have felt pain from that, but he didn't, and oddly, that didn't seem surprising, but then what could possibly be more surprising than the sight of the white haired man over Carla's body wearing a crown of bright highlighters, holding Carla's heart over his head and shouting: "Let's get the bastards!"

***

Just before they reached the bridge, Paul took his hand off Mal's back. Relief settled over Mal like a warm shower, especially now that they were so close to the bridge. He wondered why he felt so threatened. After all, as much of an asshole as Paul could be, he surely wasn't a murderer. This was ErectSoft INC, not Murder Incorporated.

If there was just some way I could throw him over the bridge, thought Paul, *but there's too many cameras, and probably a dozen or more trained on the two of us at this moment.*

"You've been asking a lot of questions, Mr. Gray," said Paul.

Mal was surprised by the question... for about two seconds, and then the realization hit him: Paul Dubois would have a huge part of his spy network trained directly on Caitlin and Crystal... and on him. He kept his mouth shut.

"You've been making inquiries about some unusual things."

Mal maintained his silence.

"Was that Jason Mason's idea? To check out the company Web site?"

Of course it was, you bastard, you probably have the whole conversation with him on tape from one of your hidden cameras. Mal glanced at Paul briefly, just long enough to see the sardonic pleasure in his vicious little eyes. He was playing with Mal, getting high off it, reveling in the sense of control. *Smug little asshole*, thought Mal. He hoped that Crystal and Caitlin would make good on their word to oust this nasty little man before the day was over, and that had better be soon because it was almost five now.

"Maybe I can answer some of your questions, Mr. Gray."

What?

***

274

What a bunch of assholes, thought a part of it that had lodged in the crown around King Charley's head from where the maniac monarch directed the citizens of the City State of Marvelous Scoping to wallop the life out of the two security guards. This was just a test before the real thing, a taste of the ultimate goal for these idiots .

Look at that old fool gripping the woman's heart over his head. He didn't even know her, didn't know the men she and her friend had beaten up, didn't know that nothing was going to stop him and the fools following him from dying in my service. How easily these humans are manipulated, almost as though they're just looking for an excuse to destroy each other. If these are your allies, little sister, then forget it they don't even like themselves.

***

Paul stood by the railing at the bridge's entrance. BonannoTower sprawled monstrously all around them. Mal could never shake the sense of a giant space station, a self-contained city floating somewhere far away from the earth.

"You don't know what we do here at ErectSoft INC, do you, Mr. Gray?"

Mal thought a moment. The air was beginning to reek of stale plots and bad aftershave, and Mal was vulnerable through lack of information. He decided to play it safe. "Maybe you could tell me what we do, Paul."

Paul sneered, and then wrestled his lips quickly into a smile of sorts. He turned away from Mal and faced the huge innards of BonannoTower, the tiers of busy offices, busy bridges and busy people. He waved an arm outward. "You think all of this has anything to do with custom corporate software development?"

Mal resumed his safety-in-silence pose.

Paul shook his head slowly as he stared into the open space. "It doesn't have a damn thing to do with software development, Mr. Gray. And it hasn't for a long time."

"Then, what have we been doing?" asked Mal.

"Keeping people alive, Mr. Gray."

***

dPisano sat in his chair, its built-in technologies having formed to his body's contours and adjusted to his temperature. The opulence of his jewel-encrusted, bulletproof desk spread meaninglessly before him, nothing more than a surface upon which to build pools of tears. dPisano had started crying weeks ago, crying for the loss of his most precious jewel, Crystal; crying for the loss of his family's last hope to assuage its shame; crying for the loss of everything he'd built and everything that everyone everywhere had built; crying for the loss of his humanity; and finally, crying for humanity, which would, if things went according to plan his plans, be lost.

Play the game the game the gamey cry baby Crystal won't come out to play any more my goldie hair little darlin' going straight to the top to hop to the top without getting lost like all the truly great men for I am the Last Truly Great Man on Earth and fractional what fractional? What means fractional

276

when it's all played straight to the top my little snowman my psycho frosty will kill him dead and what say you to that my icy blond topped creamcycle?

And these were the Last Truly Great Thoughts of the Last Truly Great Man on Earth, or at least what was left of the deep-eyed man flashing an absurdly wide smile under a waterfall of tears.

***

"And just how have we been keeping people alive, Paul?"

Paul stared out at the immense empty space. So easy to just pick the bastard up and toss him over. But that would be unprofessional. Do it right. Do it to plan. Even though the plan was only a few minutes old. "People can't live without work, Mr. Gray. We give them work in a world where work is fast becoming a scarce commodity. We do it through a form of corporate taxation."

"What's the government got to do with this?" Mal was beginning to feel less threatened, and what Paul was saying hinted of answers to the questions that had been flopping around in the back of his mind all day.

"The government has nothing to do with it, Mr. Gray. ErectSoft INC and similar companies have everything to do with it."

"How's that?"

"We steal from the rich and pass it around."

***

277

"Yes, I managed to get JM back in. Still don't know why Paul did that. Seemed just plain spiteful." Cindy held the cell phone to her ear with one hand as the other hand danced over the keyboard. She leaned forward, eyes trained on a monitor to her left. "And there they are. Charley's gone way over the deep end and it looks like he's taken the whole department with him." She glanced at another monitor where a uniformed guard made a sign toward the camera lens. "Just got a signal from security at the bodies. Both guards are dead. The woman's head was beaten... " Pause. "You did? Not pretty, huh?" Pause. "They're getting close to the freight elevator, about fifty of them. I'll get security to... " Pause. "Just let them go?" Pause. "But they just murdered two... " Pause. "OK, then. I hope you know what you're doing." She looked at a monitor to her left. "Paul and Mal are standing by the Level 5 Southeast bridge." Pause. "Talking by the looks of it. Just talking. Paul seems to be doing most of it. Malcolm doesn't look worried or anything." Pause. Cindy leaned closer to the screen. "Yes. I think you're right. There's definitely something odd about Paul's appearance. Do you think it might be one of the signs?" Pause. "Yeah. This is starting to get really creepy." She looked closer at the camera. "And I see that bitch, Janet Sobovitch, is still following Malcolm. And I don't like the look in her eyes. I pulled her record earlier. Some nasty stuff in her past. Nothing that ever stuck in court, but I wouldn't be surprised if she's killed a person or two." Pause. "You think so? OK, then. We just let things ride for the time being."

Cindy closed her phone, eyes still scanning the screens before her. "I hope to hell that you know what you're doing, woman."

***

"Our clients, Mr. Gray, are some of the biggest corporations on earth. And they all have one thing in common." He paused for effect. "They don't care about the people who work for them, and the bigger the corporation the less they care."

Mal nodded. Nothing earth shattering in that revelation, which made Mal wonder: *What was so important about all this that he would leave one of the best sales reps in the company in limbo with a client?*

"Which of course means that if they have to choose between machines and software on one hand and humans on the other hand, and machines and software mean one extra penny in their pockets, then goodbye humans."

"Paul. I'm aware of downsizing and the shrinking demand for human resources as a result of computerization and... "

"Shut up!"

Mal shut up, stunned, stared unbelievingly at Paul. Did this evil little bastard really just tell him to shut up? *Yes. He did. He just told me to shut up.* "Paul, you might be a vice president now, but... "

Paul laughed. It was a high-pitched hideous laugh and the smile that accompanied it was completely out of whack. A rush of The Creeps scampered cold-footed up Mal's spine.

"Just having at you, Mr. Gray." He waved his hand. "Nothing meant by it." He laughed again, still high pitched, but more controlled. "You should see the look in your eyes, Mr. Gray."

You should see the look in your *eyes*, thought Mal. *Whatever's come over you would make a junk yard dog think twice before barking at it.*

"But, as I was saying, Mr. Gray," and Paul starting walking again toward the mouth of the bridge. "Most of these giant super corporations are clients of ours." He looked at Mal. "And we make *them* pay the tax, Mr. Gray."

***

Send   reply   to:
<**"Peter.Elliott@erectsoft.com"**>
From: **Peter Elliott**
To: < Jason.Mason@erectsoft.com >
Subject: Rehire
Date sent:
Dear Mr. Mason:

I've been instructed by the Chief Human Potential Evangelist in the Executive Office of Forward Hiring to offer you your previous position with a $5,000 increase in salary and an additional two weeks vacation per year. I've been instructed to meet with you to discuss additional benefits sometime in the next day or two. You will occupy your old office, which I'm told you currently occupy.

It is with pleasure that I welcome you back to ErectSoft INC and look forward to a long and mutually beneficial relationship, etc, etc.

Peter Elliott
Director of Staffing and New Hire Orientation
"Straight ... to the top!" - dPisano

Rereading the message for the fifth time, JM still wondered why the Chief Human Potential Evangelist (a man or woman whose identity was kept secret in order to somehow keep hiring practices "pure") would have ordered him rehired. Something fishy was going on, but what the hell, he still had a job. Things were kewl.

***

Far below them, the base floor of Section 5 was teeming with a huge fluctuating mosaic of people, though there didn't seem to be as many as usual, especially as it neared five o'clock, when the first wave of staggered shifts should be leaving to avoid traffic congestion around BonannoTower. Most of them, though, would only be gone an hour or so, to restaurants or gyms or wherever, before coming back to put in a few more hours, just to stay on top of things.

"Look at them, Mr. Gray" said Paul. "Rushing around as though what they're doing here means anything."

Why are there so few people down there today? thought Mal.

"But, as I was saying, Mr. Gray, giant international corporations, the ones owned by people so anonymous you would find it difficult to prove that they even existed, have gotten rich and bloated off the human population, tax free. They don't pay taxes. Do you know why, Mr. Gray?"

Mal shrugged his shoulders.

"Because they are the government. They own the government. They own all the governments. They have all the power and they have all the money, Mr. Gray. They're the rulers and the setters of law."

Mal raised his eyebrows: it sounded to Mal like Paul's argument was beginning to loosen at the edges.

"They bring all the money on to them and then they discard the human element." Paul's small round eyes widened slightly. It was a weird sight, like a circle being re-sized in perfect proportion, and inside the eyes, the flicker of something red. "And now some of that money must be brought back on to us, Mr. Gray."

Paul turned his round head and round eyes toward Mal. "That's what custom corporate software was invented for, Mr. Gray. It's the great equalizer."

***

Caitlin placed the receiver carefully in the cradle as her eyes panned her office walls and the dozen drawings of trees hanging on them, all of them Malcolm Gray originals. A warm glow of contentment smoothed the lines on her face. She loved these drawings, especially the bubble-skirted signatures.

She'd found it.

Things had come together so much like an impossible jigsaw puzzle with its parts spread everywhere, some seemingly lost forever. But now, here they were. All of them together. All the pieces coming together. And the danger so near. The danger growing minute by minute.

This was no time to panic. This was a time to relax and think clearly and believe. She sat back in her chair, took a deep breath and admired the drawings, her mind still and relaxed.

***

On the other side of the bridge, they stopped at the elevator doors. Mal didn't see which button Paul pressed. "Mind if I ask where we're going," he said.

"On a journey, Mr. Gray," said Paul. His voice seemed to squeak from far away. "An enlightening journey."

Mal felt his stomach tighten, and strange thoughts floated around in his head.

***

Imagine a pall spreading through gray slime. That was the condition of Mal's brain as millions of cells under the direction of Johnny tripled their efforts to repair the damage done by the neutrinos. And now a new element had been introduced, what you might call a motivator. There was a general feeling through the brain cell community that Paul Dubois might pose more than the normal level of problem, that he might, in fact, be dangerous.

"Sleazy little ass-humping coyote," said Bobby.

"You got that right," said Daisy Mae. "He's gonna kill our boy. I just got that feelin'".

What Daisy Mae was expressing was instinct for survival at the cellular level.

"Nobody's gonna kill our boy," said Johnny. "We almost got the damage all fixed up an' things're lookin' pretty good."

What Johnny was expressing was basic cellular level bravado.

"But you know how naive our boy tends to be," complained Daisy Mae. "An' I don't trust this Paul character further than I can throw a parietal lobe."

Basically, this was proof at any level that this Paul character needed close watching, and Johnny was about to express some more cellular bravado when he was cut short by a serotonin-curdling scream that raged through-out Mal's brain causing all manner of synaptic havoc.

"IT'S MOVING!"

***

Guess we're going up, thought Mal, as the elevator moved silently upward with a distinct press of G force as it reached a hundred and twenty-five miles an hour in just seconds. Bridges, floors, and walls flashed by in the colossal spaces of BonannoTower.

"All this," said Paul. "All this to create an illusion, Mr. Gray." And then he went silent. Mal attributed the silence to reflection on his own words. But what Paul was actually thinking was this: *What a wonderful "accident" Malcolm Gray could have if these widows weren't bulletproof.*

"An illusion, Paul?"

Paul snapped out of it. "The money our corporate clients pay us keeps thousands of people employed. It provides jobs for people and a sense of

284

value in work. We're just so many slaves to the Protestant ethic, Mr. Gray. Without work, we fall apart. But the work is getting scarce as our numbers grow, and computers and machinery are going to keep on sucking up the work and replacing people. Everyone will be useless, Mr. Gray."

"Paul, I don't think... "

"Except us. We'll still have work. Not because there really is any work to be had, but because there is the illusion of work. That's what custom corporate software is all about, Mr. Gray. The projects are so big, the software so big, the numbers of people so big... all of it so big that nobody can really comprehend it or understand it. We're talking about multi-billion dollar budgets for software dream-wish-fulfillment, and you'd be surprised, Mr. Gray, at how much of that money is in the hands of idiots, people who think we can make miracles happen and they don't even know what miracles they want to have happen. They just know that computers are power and money is power and they have both, and they think that, just by throwing them together, ultimate power will be spawned."

Tiny spots of white spittle formed at the corners of Paul's clam-like mouth. His eyes were completely round, perfect circles with reflected light dancing like insect dervishes across the black spaces of his irises.

"We don't give them software, Mr. Gray, we give them an illusion." He looked at Mal. "You were asking around about finished projects."

"How did... ?"

"Your suspicions are right, Mr. Gray. We haven't finished a project in years and with luck, we never will finish another project."

The G force slackened as they neared their destination. Mal was eager to get out of the small space of the elevator, which seemed to magnify the putrescence of Paul's aftershave.

***

Ears Around smiled at the sight of her sisters gathered around the cauldron in the small clearing, all so unselfconscious and joyful in their nudity whether anorexically thin, can't-see-my-toes fat, hard-belly firm, or tits-touching-knees sagging. Things men would think. But here, just sisters gathered in joy, and with a single purpose.

There were thirty of them. The required number for this part.

Ears Around smiled as a fresh wave of bubble energy passed over her hamstrings like a warm breeze. The arrival was nearing and soon it would be time to begin the chant. Once that started, there would be no turning back. But then, who would ever want to turn back?

***

I was right, thought Mal. It had been just as he'd suspected: projects never finished; they just went on and on. *Probably never get past the initial project definition phases. You could keep redefining a project for years. But why is he telling me this?* Suddenly Mal felt a need to say something if for no

286

other reason than to stop his train of thought, which - something deep inside him reckoned - would not bode well for his health. After all, who was he to be privy to a company secret of this magnitude? On the other hand, maybe Paul was just shitting him. Time to say something. "So, if we never finish anything, what do we do?"

The elevator door opened onto a large crowd of ErectSoft INC employees. Immediately, Mal sensed that something was not right in the crowd, that something was skewed in the atmosphere. It was too quiet; the buzz of conversation was too low for a crowd this size. The eyes in the crowd were all uniformly strange and vacant, glassy. And it was unusual for this many of them to be here this time of day; they should be on their way to supper or workouts, whatever it was they did before coming back to work in the evening. He was distracted from the eerie scene by Paul's high voice, which he'd toned down a level or two to blend with the muted mass.

"We give ourselves the illusion of being useful, Mr. Gray. We assign teams to scope projects, design specifications for projects, analyze needs and wants for projects, develop methodologies and procedures for projects, design business models, development models, process models... " He took a deep breath. "And we get people from the client involved. We give them offices, grant them access to our boardrooms and other resources. We make them part of the project team, Mr. Gray. And that makes them safe from their own employers. And that, in turn, gives them a vested interest in making sure that the project goes on... forever. Because when the project finishes, Mr. Gray, everybody is fucked."

"So you're saying," Mal waved his arm to encompass all around them, "that all of this is a sham?"

"No, Mr. Gray. It's evolution."

***

Two men and a woman, all of whom had just evolved into airborne mammals, sailed past the columns and arches of the world's highest building. One of them, Helena, gave her boss the finger as she passed his office window. This act gave Helena a distant sense of completeness even though her boss's back was facing the window.

***

Paul led Mal into the crowd, toward the doors leading to the Tomasso Observation Deck. As they passed through the crowd, Mal's back tingled with The Creeps again. The eyes were somehow wrong, as though something essential had packed up and left them. And then he noticed something that raised bumps and hair under his ponytail and drained the blood out of his fingers and toes.

What the hell is going on here? he thought. As Paul walked through the crowd, people moved aside, whether they were facing him or not. *They're clearing a path for him! All of them!*

"We've evolved to a level where we can create machines and software that will replace us, and now we're evolving to a level where we replace the need to be replaced with something that can't be replaced because it never had any value in the first place... custom corporate software, Mr. Gray."

Mal kept his mouth shut. He felt as though he and Paul had walked into a Salvador Dali painting in which they floated through the crowd with an invisible shield before them that nudged the odd-eyed men and women aside in a wake of silent assent. Somehow, they were different than Mal, but not different than Paul.

It was too much for Mal to handle. He had to say something that would break the spell. In near panic, he chose the wrong words. "Paul, you're so full of shit."

***

Something was definitely wrong. It was like surf disturbing the sand, erasing things that might have been important, but who was to say; they were gone now, washed away by the tide. King Charley groped in his mind for whatever essential element it was that he was missing as the freight elevator neared their floor. They'd just murdered two people, one of them a woman. Three members of his kingdom had lain down their lives in his service. And now they were on their way to... ? Where were they going in this elevator?

And then the elevator stopped. *Ah yes*, thought King Charley, *the Tomasso Observation Deck*. But what was that thought in the back of his head, like an itch he couldn't quite reach? Something about breaking a missile? Get the muscle? Destroy the vessel? *There's a ship up here?*

289

The elevator came to a stop and the doors opened. Fifty whacko citizens of the Sovereign Department of Advanced Project Scoping and Work Breakdown Configurations, each a psychotic killer baptized in the blood of their victims, flooded onto the floor.

The crowd in the hall moved aside.

***

A bat crawled out of Paul's right eye and flew directly at Mal's head. He ducked just in time for it to graze the top of his scalp before it impaled itself on a jeweled saber brooch on an elderly woman's blouse. The woman looked down nonchalantly at the bat and, as though this were her cue, walked up to the railing and jumped over.

Mal shook his head, blinked his eyes. What he'd just seen couldn't have happened, must have been stress or something. *Bats don't fly out of people's eyes, not even out of Paul Dubois' eyes. And that woman, she just jumped over the railing, over two hundred stories up, like changing channels on a television.*

As though nothing had happened, Paul kept talking. "And further, Mr. Gray, employment for the purpose of producing goods and services is extinct, a thing of the past, a doomed paradigm."

They were getting close to the railing. Mal stopped walking. Paul turned to face him with an irritated sneer pulling at the sides of his round nose.

"Work is only good for one thing, Mr. Gray, to provide opportunities for self-enrichment."

Lost in the absurdity of the moment and the drone of Paul's meaningless babble, Mal failed to notice that Paul was moving slowly around him, maneuvering him so that shortly Mal would have his back to the railing.

***

Marketing clone Daryl stood vacuum-eyed and infinitely obedient in the madness that spread across the whole of an insanely endless creation inside his head, a universe that pulsed to the rhythm of six beats: little sister's coming.

Nothing mattered except standing where he was, occupying the largest space in the universe right there in the hallway of the Corporate Warfare Department in BonannoTower, right there in the mindless eternity swirling throughout his head, seeping out of his empty eyes, fuming in his sweat pores, and anchoring his ass to the spot so hard and with so much intent to just stay there and ignore the smallness of the world outside, that marketing clone Daryl never even noticed the shifting of the floor, the movement in the walls, the shake in the air, and the screams screaming across the mouth of creation and then snapping silent as the tremors in the hall suddenly ceased.

Marketing clone Daryl stood where he was, waiting to go where he would go, emptied of all but little sister's coming.

***

Paul continued to circle Mal as he talked: "Understand, Mr. Gray, that it's not a bad thing that we've outlived our usefulness as workers. Now we can concentrate on becoming the best we can be through positive self-enrichment."

Yeah, Paul, and you're the product of positive self-enrichment, thought Mal glancing at the other people on the desk. Nobody laughed. Nobody joked or talked loudly. Their voices were slightly above whispers, hushed and dreamlike. Mostly, they stood in groups staring toward the railing or looking around at the others gathered on the deck, nodding and smiling superficially to those they knew. About twenty feet to his left, he saw a face that looked familiar, but he couldn't place it. A face from... where? He knew that face. Hadn't seen it since... when?

"You never did listen, Mr. Gray."

What the hell is he saying now? "I'm listening, Paul, but I just don't see what's so damned enriching about working nine to twelve hour days on something that has no value. I get jealous of the photocopy machine because I feel that it does things that are more useful and real than anything I do. We're destroying out sense of self-worth, and that's not good for the soul." *Hey, Mal, baby, that was good!*

"So, what are you saying, Mr. Gray? Should we just close the doors and let everybody stay home looking at their belly buttons all day?"

"No, Paul... " Mal stared in horror as two beautiful young women in business suits hugged each other, climbed to the top of the railing, smiled wanly at each other, shrugged, and stepped into the

292

air. "For christ's sakes, Paul, those two women just..."

"And that's what happens when the illusion crumbles, Mr. Gray."

"No, Paul, that's what the illusion does to us!"

Everyone was looking at the empty air where the two women had just decided to become one with the asphalt below. None of the faces Mal looked at registered horror, regret, urgency. Nothing. Just blank acceptance. Mal stood a foot away from the railing, his back to it.

Time to kill Mr. Gray, thought Paul.

***

Marketing clone Janet broke through the crowd just as Paul grabbed Mal by the throat. She watched as Mal twisted his body and backed up with surprising speed to break the hold. *This guy's in good shape for a computer geek*, she thought.

She was mildly pissed off at having lost the two men on the elevator. It wasn't so much that she'd lost them - in a building like BonannoTower where almost every dark corner was open to the scrutiny of thousands of surveillance cameras, this was a fleeting event - but the intelligence analyst who'd been tracking Paul and Mal had been slow. And he'd been giggling as the spoke. Those people never giggled. None of them had a sense of humor. None of them ever smiled. They lived in a world of minute-to-minute paranoia.

To top it off, just as she'd stepped off the elevator, the connection had gone dead. And she would have been more than mildly pissed off if she hadn't been so puzzled. Surveillance connections never went dead. They were backed up with dozens of fail-safe systems. They were backed up by paranoia.

But, pissed or not, she smiled. Maybe they'd get into a wrestling match and both men would topple over the railing to their deaths. Then she could look for Daryl.

If there is a God, he will kill these two and let me rush to my true love. My true love.

***

Mal spun around, fists clenched, ready to punch. "What the hell are you doing, Paul?"

"You're not listening, Mr. Gray!" Paul's face twisted into an ugly sneer. "And you know what really pisses me off, Mr. Gray?"

"What the hell are you talking about?"

"The way you come to meetings as though nothing important is happening. No pen. No pad. No appropriate attitude, Mr. Gray."

As Mal stepped back, the edge of his shoe struck concrete base of the railing and made a sound like "kloonk". Another bat flew out of Paul's eye.

***

As Tony Bottoms exchanged business cards with an expressionless man in a gray velour vest and a Mickey Mouse tie, Richard Ziglar perked up. *Who is that guy? I know him. Where do I know him from?* He walked slowly toward the man he thought he recognized. *Who do I know who wears a fucking ponytail?*

***

That clinches it, thought Mal, *there's bats flying out of Paul's eyes. And all these people are jumping off the tower. My God, that's what they're all here for. This is no copycat suicide in the steps of Tara Cunningham.*

Something unspeakably evil was happening on the Tomasso Observation Deck and Paul Dubois had something to do with it. Mal could feel it. Why had he grabbed him? What was all that garbage about the company about? Why had Paul dragged him out of the meeting - a multimillion dollar deal - and brought him up here? Only one thing made sense. It turned Mal's mouth into a dry fissure. *This bastard's trying to kill me!*

Paul grabbed on to Mal's arm. His grip was like a vice. "Time to fly, Mr. Gray."

***

Fly away the vessel! Fly away the vessel! The words echoed in the madness of King Charley's head and the heads of the equally insane citizens of the City State of Marvelous Scoping. *Fly away the vessel.* Yes, it was so obvious. This was why they'd killed the two guards. *Had they really killed two people just now? Fly away the vessel. Yes, that was the thing to do, fly away the vessel.*

And there was only one way to do it.

295

King Charley led his foul-smelling, blood-smeared, psycho-eyed subjects toward the railing of the Tomasso Observation Deck. Mal and Paul were directly in their path.

***

With his free arm, Mal tried to punch Paul, but the powerful little snowman was fast and agile. He ducked to the side and Mal's fist beat thousands of innocent molecules in the air senseless.

"Why don't you take meetings more seriously, Mr. Gray? Why are you always such a self-assured smart-ass?"

That's it, thought Mal *this is getting personal*. He tried unsuccessfully to twist out of the powerful grasp and Paul squeezed tighter and growled like a wild animal as a bat unfolded its wings from his right eye and flapped up toward the top of BonannoTower.

***

The Tree Kid! Recognition clamored in his head like the alarm bell at recess. *It's the Tree Kid from grade three.* Richard Ziglar stood just five feet away from Mal. *What was his name? What was the Tree Kid's name?*

***

"Nothing goes on at those meetings!" yelled Mal as he broke free of Paul's grip. "You just said it yourself." He stepped back just in time to stop Paul from grabbing his throat. Mal's back was flush against the railing. "Why are you taking this so personally?"

"Because it's time, Mr. Gray, it's time!"

"Time for what?"

"Time for you to fly, Mr. Gray. Can you fly?"

Paul jumped forward and wrapped his powerful arms around Mal's chest, leaving a bat flopping around on the deck in his attack. Mal felt the air pushing out of his lungs. His eyes bulged. And then, over the top of Paul's head he saw a ragtag crowd of men and women led by a white haired man with a crown of colorful highlighters heading straight toward him and Paul.

What now?

***

King Charley's eyes fixed on Mal's eyes in the same instant that Mal's eyes fixed on King Charley's eyes, which was also the same moment that bats, dozens of them, started flying out of King Charley's eyes.

King Charley didn't even notice the bats, which was fortunate for him considering that he had an extreme phobia about bats. All that he could think of was flying away the vessel, and that meant rushing toward the railing and beyond, and taking anything and anybody in his path along for the ride, and the two men wrestling beside the railing were about fly away the vessel with King Charley and the citizens of the City State of Marvelous Scoping.

How fortunate for them.

"This is a dream," thought Mal. "I'm dreaming this." Bats were flying out of Charley Shuster's eyes. Paul Dubois was having bats as well, and trying to kill him. He raised both arms high to his sides, hands open to slap Paul simultaneously on both ears. He felt something smash hard into his left hand.

***

"High five, Tree Boy!" yelled Richard Ziglar as he slapped Mal's open hand, and then lost his balance and fell into Paul and Mal, bringing the three of them crashing to the floor of the deck. As they tried to get up, they were knocked down again by a crowd of fanatical citizens of the City State of Marvelous Scoping, all hellbent on flying the vessel, all of them flying bats out of their eyes as they swarmed over the railing, yelling: "Fly the vessel!"

The man in the velour vest who had just passed his card to Tony Bottoms said: "Poetic, isn't it?"

***

After the crazy crowd had passed into the air, Mal, Paul and Richard Ziglar, dizzy and sore from almost being trampled to death raised shakily to their feet. Most of the people around them were watching. A few were just staring into the air as though on the verge of deciphering some important message dangling inches away from their noses.

Paul's cell phone beeped. He took it out of this jacket pocket. "What?" he said. As he listened, his eyes fumed. No bats, he was all business now, which is to say, crazed, but not crazy; improbable, but not impossible. "That's impossible!" he yelled. He listened again. "I'll be right down! Don't do anything until I get there!" He closed his phone and shot Mal a murderous look. "I'll deal with you later, Mr. Gray."

"Go fuck yourself, Paul!"

Paul's eyes flashed red and Mal backed up to make room for the bats, but none appeared. Paul stomped off to the elevators. Mal turned around to face the man who'd just saved his life by knocking him down and almost getting him trampled to death. It was the man he'd been looking at earlier, the man he thought he recognized but couldn't place.

Richard Ziglar said: "Sounds like you finally learned what the word fuck means, Tree Boy!"

***

This flying the vessel's not nearly what it's cracked up to be, thought the soon be departed King Charley of the City State of Marvelous Scoping as his body accelerated to nearly a hundred miles an hour toward what had become known to the BonannoTower maintenance staff as the "splatter zone".

Some citizens of the City State of Marvelous were having similar thoughts. Some were even thinking about applying for jobs in other departments. One of them, Jacques, was beginning to have bad feelings about having stomped on

299

Carla's head. Parts of the sole of his right shoe were still wet with her blood. Another, Dale, just remembered that important...

***

Floors winked by. A small white patch of froth glistening at the corner of Paul's mouth as he spoke into the phone and, even though he spoke quietly, the rage shaking just under the surface of his words was unmistakable. "An entire department can't just disappear, Mr. Montgomery! And what do you mean by 'nothing'? Where are the rooms, the floors, the ceilings, the furniture? Where are the people?" He listened, rage shaking even in the absence of his words. "What the hell do you mean 'nothing', Mr. Montgomery? What the hell is that supposed to mean, 'nothing'? There has to be something! Offices don't just disappear into nothing, Mr. Montgomery."

This, from a man who'd just had bats flying out of his eyes.

***

No Bang was down on himself. For an entity that had been around since the beginning of creation, his batting average on this project was less than appropriate, and he was handling his defeat less than constructively. He should have been telling himself something like this:

OK, so one part of me was guiding the funny little snowman to kill the guy with the ponytail. And one part of me was guiding a bunch of idiots dumb enough to take orders from an even bigger idiot wearing markers around his head to kill the guy with the pony tail. And still another part of me figured, hey, let's just scare the crap out of the ponytail guy with bats, yeah, bats are really scary. And then, just to make everything totally confused, another part of me decides to bring a bunch of these bozos home, and what thanks does he get from them? They just scream bloody blue murder.

But when you embrace chaos, you have to believe that what you're embracing is chaos, and your arms are going to be full of everything except what you expected.

Or something like that.

But instead, the parts of No Bang, each of them being equally No Bang and each of them being equally not No Bang, but unique parts in a whole, were stalemated on where the blame for botching the vessel gambit should fall. Had they been familiar with the Jerry Springer show, they might have concluded that only the parts watching were to blame.

***

"What d'ya mean moving?" yelled Johnny the Brain Cell. "Where in tarnation's it moving to?"

"Steady stream of it, Johnny," said Jake, "moving from the weird cell right straight down to our boy's testicles."

"His what?"

"His balls, Johnny, the stuff's moving into his balls!"

301

Chapter 82

Supper Stop

Switching Careers

"No way!" said Richard Ziglar around a mouthful of GigaBurgerX3. His eyes were black and his shirt was splattered with blood.

"It's true," repeated Mal. His jacket collar was torn. "The man wearing the colored highlighters around his head is... was Charley Shuster. What were you supposed to see him about?"

"Something 'bout a new software package called Soft-X-Po, or something like that," said Tony Bottoms. His blackened left eye blended into a black and blue cheek.

Mal choked back a laugh as he bit into his GigaBurgerX1.

"What's so funny," asked Richard Ziglar.

Mal chewed quickly and swallowed. "It's not a soft-ware package."

"What?" asked Tony Bottoms. He dug a finger into this mouth and pulled out a tooth.

"It's not a software package. It's a software *show*."

"A show?" said Richard Ziglar.

"A fucking show," said Tony Bottoms, staring at the tooth. "That guy wanted us to be hosts or something?"

"You got it," said Mal. "People were wondering how they were going to pull that off. But to have you come directly here... that was nuts."

"Like you said, the guy was wearing highlighters," said Richard Ziglar.

"Point taken."

"Christ!" said Mal. "I can't believe it's really you two. And don't go apologizing again for that business at recess. Being sent to that tree for the rest of the school year was fine with me, one of the best things that ever happened to me in school."

"One thing I've always wondered about," said Richard Ziglar.

"What's that?" said Mal.

"What the fuck happened to you out by that tree?"

Tony Bottoms looked up from his tooth.

"I mean, you started hanging around in that tree even after school. We all thought that was really weird."

Mal thought a moment, chewing on his burger. "Yeah, I guess it was." He decided not to tell them about the tree in his office. "I don't know. Something about bubbles, I guess."

"Bubbles?" said Richard Ziglar.

"Yeah, but that was a long time ago. I'm over all that stuff now."

***

At that moment, about a jillion bubbles so small that atoms would seem like giants in comparison, streamed in a steady unbroken line from the weird cell in Mal's brain, down through his neck, into his torso and into his abdomen where they branched into two channels, one leading into his left testicle and one into his right testicle.

303

"Just let 'em be," said Johnny the Brain Cell. "This stuff's too weird for us to be messin' with it."

And billions of brain cells in Malcolm Gray's head watched quietly (as only brain cells can) while inestimable amounts of energy emitted from the single weird cell and made their way to Mal's balls.

**

"I'm thinking of getting out of this business an' getting into something else," said Tony Bottoms. He swallowed a chunk of GigaBurgerX3.

"Can't say I blame you," said Malcolm. "The glamour of the IT industry seems to have bottomed out to a bunch of post-geeks thinking they're living the good life in a profession where the wages are plummeting and the work has become as humdrum and superficial as any office job in the 50s."

Tony Bottoms took another big bite of his burger and spoke around the food: "Gonna take that course in Naturalpathy. Become a doctor."

Chapter 83

Ongoing And Normalized

Send reply to: <"William.Donovan@@erectsoft.com">

From: **Bill Donovan**

To: <LIST081@erectsoft.com>

Subject: Directive

Date sent:

Rumors that one of ErectSoft INC's departments is missing are rumors and are to be treated as no more than rumors. Propagation of said rumors will be deemed to be grounds for dismissal and/or other additional disciplinary measures.

Communications with the personnel of the PACA branch of the Competitive Intelligence and Corporate Warfare Department are ongoing and normalized.

Use of the Tomasso Observation Deck is under observation. I have a bat in my eye.

Bill Donovan

Acting Vice President, Operations

ErectSoft INC

"Straight ... to the top!" - dPisano

***

"He sent this out to the whole company?" asked Paul, lips quivering like pink nacho shells on a boom box. "Nobody tried to stop him, Ms. Chen?" Cindy backed up a few inches. *Is it possible that his aftershave smells worse when he's mad?* she thought. Paul's eyes flashed with anger, and something else, something that chilled her spine. *He's losing it.* She'd watched him attack Mal on the Tomasso Deck, and she was sure that she'd seen something flying out of his eyes. Bats? They were all warned that things were going to get weird, but she hadn't been expecting anything like today. Certainly not bats.

And things were just starting to warm up.

But she held her ground. "He's a vice president, Paul. Most of the people who outrank him enough to stop him are either up on the Deck waiting their turn to jump, or hiding from everything that's going on here.

"And where is Mr. Donovan now, Ms. Chen?" His voice nearly cracked. He cleared his throat loudly.

"He went for a dive over the Tomasso Deck about ten minutes ago."

"Fine then." A shaky smile crossed his lips. "Fire his entire staff."

"But we can't... "

"Fire them, Ms. Chen. Fire them all."

"Paul, we can't do that." Cindy stepped in closer, through the thickness of Paul's aftershave. "His entire staff jumped with him!"

Paul backed up. I *should break her fucking neck*, he thought. *Pushing into my face! Who the fuck does this little foreign bitch think she is?* He sputtered something unintelligible, spun on his heels, and marched out of Cindy's office toward the gaping hole of emptiness where the Most Secret Room in the World used to be.

Chapter 84

Evening Rites

Sisters, For The Time Being

Up Yours winked at Crimson Rose. Crimson Rose smiled. The air in the clearing was heavy with bubble energy. It tickled the peach fuzz on Ears Around's arms, washed over the shoulders of Sincerely Yours, sprayed across Brows To Sky's breasts, flowed over the contours of Sun In Her Hair's buttocks, and slid down the streak of warm fluid dripping from between Making A Note's thighs.

Emerald Looking spoke commandingly: "We stand upon the earth."

The others chanted: "Grounded in your fertile soil!"

"We take life from the air," spoke Emerald Looking.

"Rising from your fragrant mists!"

"We burn in the holy fire."

"Flaming in your holy passion!"

"We flow with the eternal current."

"Flooding from your infinite womb!"

Making A Note dipped an index finger into the fluid flowing from between her thighs and looked at it, smiling. Up Yours, standing beside her, took Making A Note's hand gently in her hand and guided it to her parted lips. She licked the shimmering liquid from Making A Note's finger.

Making A Note smiled at her and thought: *Try that after this is all over, you butch bitch, and I'll rip out your epiglottis.*

Chapter 85

Ferally Yours

A few of the loose wires made normal crackling and zapping noises. Other wires were less rooted in reality. One of them played Bach's Fifth Brandenburg Concerto. Another quacked. A long thin yellow wire sang "When Johnny Comes Marching Home." A dazzling assortment of smart building materials bubbled, gurgled, oohhed and aahhed around the long rectangular hole in the wall where the Most Secret Room in the World used to be. A shard of plexiglass wiggled across a swirling mass of synthetic oak, licking the bubbling ooze before it with a long blue tongue. A puff of white smoke appeared in the center of the hole just inches away from Paul's head. It curled in the air, or what Paul assumed was air, and then puffed out of existence. An eyeball bounced out of the hole and turned toward Paul. A small mouth ripped out of its white cornea and said: "Me gray ape, like in movie."

The hole wavered in front of Paul and the shaky gathering of spies in the Corporate Warfare Department. It shimmered with something like light, but not light. It was black, or was it gray, or maybe white? It appeared to stretch on forever, or maybe it was just a few inches deep. One thing for certain though, the Most Secret Room in the World was a goner. A small man with thick glasses stuck a finger into it. What looked like the nozzle of a bicycle pump wrapped around the finger and pulled him into the hole. He disappeared with a loud: "Slurp!"

A dark-haired woman with thick glasses said: "Well." She walked to her desk where a beige sweater hung over the back of her chair. She put the sweater on and faced the others. "Anyone for a jump off the Deck?" A dozen corporate spies nodded yes and followed her out the door. Just before leaving, one of them ran back to his desk and sent a quick email to his wife:

Send reply to: <"John.Edwards@erectsoft.com">

From: **John Edwards**

To: <wilmaedwards102@yagotmail.com>

Subject: Goodbye

Date sent:

Hello, Wilma. I hate you. And I have for a long time now. And I hate your father. And I hate your sister, Thelma. And, even though I never met your mother, I hate her for giving you and your sister your dumb names. But don't feel bad, I hate myself more than I hate any of you.

Ferally yours,

John

Senior Holistic Corporate Interconnections Manager

Department of Competitive Intelligence and Corporate Warfare

"Straight ... to the top!" - dPisano

He clicked the send button and followed the others out the door. As the door closed, Paul and four others looked back at the hole, from which an indistinct sound began to emit. At first, it sounded like distant madcap laughter, and then like faraway slashes of an argument floating from one end of the rectangular hole to the other. And then it sounded like a wave, faraway and then close, faraway and then close, and the sound of the wave was the sound of thousands of voices trying to get it together, the sound of confusion, disorder, chaos.

The other four filed slowly out the door. Paul began to think that there was more to the PACA program than he'd been told. In fact, he was damn well certain that it was time to for a face-to-face with dPisano.

Chapter 86

Orange Marmalade On Toast

Tania Waterhouse was one H2O molecule short of dropping a tear.

Tania was a specialist in a profession so secret that it's name could not be written down on paper, or even written electronically; it could not be spoken, broadcast, hinted at, or even thought about. If you were to ask Tania Waterhouse what her position was, she would reply: "Specialist." And leave it at that. The duties Tania performed in her position were equally secret, so secret, in fact, that she was never quite sure just what it was she did. It was something to do with keying information into one of the powerful mainframes in the Most Secret Room in the World. The information was a mystery to her, encoded beyond recognition in any of the dozens of programming languages in which she was expert, and not remotely similar to any language on earth, current or ancient. Tania had no idea what the information was, what its purpose was, or even where it came from. She just knew that it was waiting for her on her desk each morning in a sealed envelope.

Tania was trying to spread orange marmalade on a slice of toast. But almost the instant she had the marmalade perfectly spread, it drifted away from the toast and spit bits of rind at her nose. It did this every time she spread it.

Tania did not realize that the marmalade was never going to stick to the toast but, now, she was beginning to suspect that this had something to do with the information she'd been stuffing into the mainframe.

You see, the information in the sealed envelope on Tania's desk each morning had really been a sort of beacon, a signal roughly translated as: "Hey! Over here!" And this information was channeled directly into the iron core of BonannoTower and to the top of the tower and then into space to a destination so unimaginably far away that even expressing it in powers of one billion would never come close to communicating the distance. But together, the steel core of BonannoTower and the unfathomable addressing in the secret code were able to span the distance.

Tania spread another portion of orange marmalade on her toast. Her eyes were red and puffy.

The information they put into the mainframes was something that broke all the rules of the known universe, something that poked its right index finger straight into the left eye of the Grand Plan of Creation. It traveled faster than the speed of light and it had no matter and no energy. It was just a message: "Hey! Over here!"

The marmalade slid off the toast and fell into a small black hole by Tania's foot. Tania looked at her watch: the hands were skipping counterclockwise and singing something in French.

The message also turned BonannoTower into a galaxy-jumping beacon, providing a clear fix on the tower's location.

Tania looked up from the hole by her foot just in time to watch a cloudy sky plummet toward her as she fell upwards, screaming bloody blue murder, into it.

Chapter 87

Tea Time

"We drink to your coming and await your message to each of us," said Emerald Looking as she ladled golden-green liquid from the cauldron into a tiny red Chinese cup with no handles. She passed the cup to Jogs A Mile. "Careful, dear, it's hot." Jogs A Mile smiled and passed the cup to River Of Tears as Emerald Looking took another cup from the stack beside the cauldron.

Up Yours winked again at Crimson Rose across the clearing. Crimson Rose smiled and thought: *What is it with her?*

Up Yours tapped Making a Note's bare hip with her index finger. Making A Note turned to her with a terse smile. Up Yours whispered: "Smell it? It's her green tea with rice again. Why couldn't we try something that tastes like real tea for a change?"

Making A Note half nodded and turned her eyes back to the center of the clearing. *Maybe next time we could stuff you into the cauldron.*

***

So now I'm supposed to send them each a message? Oh yes, I see. In the cups. The old Chinese tea leaves trick. Oh well, if it makes them happy. Why couldn't they all be more like that little trollop, Up Yours? Just let their hair down and party. All I need is the vessel, and that's coming along just fine. But, on the other hand, maybe I can have a little fun with them...

315

Chapter 88

Renovations

"Can you believe that?" asked Bobby.

"After today, I'd pretty near believe just about anything," said Johnny.

"All the way down to his balls!"

"Yep. Never woulda guessed a cell that size could hold that much of whatever that shit was that's down in our boy's balls now."

"What d'ya think it was, Johnny?"

"Don't reckon I have any idea, Bobby. Some thing's are best not thought about."

***

Meanwhile, in Mal's testicles, millions of spermatozoa were paralyzed stiff in their tracks as trillions of bubbles slipped through their membranes, froze their spermatozoa brains with the ecstasy of a thousand orgasms multiplied by a thousand beer belches and squared by an infinite number of scratched itches. Thus frozen, the spermatozoa didn't have a clue that their DNA was being rebuilt, and if told of the genetic renovations, they might have replied with something like: "Whew! Yeah! Whoa! Oh Yeah!"

Chapter 89

Meditations

Thirty naked women sat cross-legged on the smooth bubbly grass of the clearing. As each finished drinking her rice green tea, she looked deep into her cup, at the formation of leaf bits and stains on the shiny white surface. Each thought about how the formation suggested a design in her own life and focused deeply on that design, meditating on its meaning, or on its meaninglessness.

I must journey into the Himalayas, thought Crimson Rose.

My father is still alive, thought Brows To Sky.

I will have a beautiful daughter and she will have golden hair, thought Message Waiting.

I love the feel of bubbles dancing across my breasts, thought Finger Pointing.

Numbed by fear I stood before the zooming crow cawing cawing, thought Sun In Her Hair.

I will lick Making A Note's pussy, oh yes, I will, thought Up Yours.

I've pierced ten thousand souls with my eyes and now it's time to write a novel, thought Emerald Looking.

Yes, that's right, uh huh, yes, OK, yeah, that would be ... yeah, thought Program Running.

Hmm, Up Yours does have nice breasts, thought Making A Note.

***

317

The bubbles snickered (as only bubbles of unearthly origin can).

Chapter 90

Killing Him Discreetly With Her Love

That little bastard was trying to kill Gray, thought marketing clone Janet as she blended into a clump of potted trees by a stress oasis a hundred feet away from Mal's office. Malcolm Gray was no longer the insignificant gnat she'd taken him for in the morning. Malcolm Gray was some sort of key to whatever it was that was shoving a stick up Paul Dubois' ass. And Malcolm Gray had some form of connection to dPisano's slut, Crystal Peake, and that dried up old bitch, Caitlin McCarthy.

In a sudden gush of inspiration, or more like a very small flat volcano burping a very small amount of cool lava, marketing clone Janet knew what she had to do to prove her love to marketing clone Daryl. It had been within her reach all day. At any moment she could have proved to him and to the whole world the terrifying depths of her love. All she had to do was reach out her hands, place them around Malcolm Gray's head and twist the life out of him.

Yes, that was the thing to do. Kill Malcolm Gray. But it had to be discreet. Marketing clone Janet was not about to spend the rest of her life behind bars proving her love for anybody.

Having made up her mind, she sat on one of the couches in the stress oasis and pondered the manner of Malcolm Gray's death.

As she thought, she scratched the corner of her right eye where a bat had just triggered an itch.

Chapter 91

Offer Her Your Pudding

"Offer her your pudding." They were the most beautiful words that he had ever heard, and they crashed joyfully as a tidal wave of chocolate ice cream through the impossible spaces in marketing clone Daryl's head. "Offer her your pudding." He wept and his weeping became a ululating sound that stood small and alone in the endless chasm that had become his mind, and the sound was immediately engulfed in bubbles, massaging and tickling until he giggled and laughed, and marketing clone Daryl became a smiley-faced ship with an eternal cargo. "Offer her your pudding."

Time to hoist anchor and offer her my pudding, thought marketing clone Daryl. And he walked down the hall, walked through a wall, and walked toward a waiting elevator.

Chapter 92

Party Party

As Mal clicked on "Hey Mal" (after deleting the seventy-two emails that broke through the filters), he wondered about the remarkable coincidence: he hadn't seen Richard Ziglar and Tony Bottoms since he was a kid, and then today they show up just in time to save his life. *Paul tried to kill me. But I don't feel threatened or afraid. Don't even feel angry. Not even uncomfortable. Why's that?*

The email message opened on his screen and he read:

Send reply to: <"Jason.Mason@erectsoft.com">

From: **Jason Mason**

To: < Malcolm.Gray@erectsoft.com >

Subject: Hey Mal!

Date sent:

Mal ...

Just got an email from Peter Elliot. Got my old job back. Didn't even get a chance to send out my resume. Even got a 5 thou increase. And I just checked with Sandy. I still get my going away party from ErectSoft even though I'm back. Company policy. Plus I get a party from HudsonHemmel, although I'm not sure if I'll be going to that one. Never got a chance to meet anybody I was supposed to be working with. Drop by if you get a chance.

JM

"Straight ... to the top!" - dPisano

Mal picked up his phone and pressed a speed dial button.

Chapter 93

The Power Of Tea

As the women stood up, Making A Note cast a quick glance at the firm upward slant of Up Yours' small breasts just as a flood of bubbles brushed against her hip exactly where Up Yours had touched her earlier. The second the first few bubbles made contact, Making A Note's thighs tingled and her pubic fuzz, already sprinkled with droplets, began to spiral as though each had become a spinning ballerina.

Another quick glance and she made contact with Up Yours' eyes. Up Yours Smiled. Making A Note returned her smile, a long slow smile, her eyes dream-like, her thighs glistening. Making A Note was ready for the next part. Make the meditation on the tea leaves physical. Yes, she was ready for that. She reached out her right hand and took Up Yours' left hand in hers. Up Yours kept her eyes on the steam rolling around the mouth of the cauldron, but she smiled, and she squeezed Making A Note's hand.

***

The bubbles slapped their knee (as only uncanny bubbles of unthinkable origins can).

Chapter 94

Destiny

"Welcome aboard, newcomer. Name's Malcolm Gray and I'm calling to let you know that if you ever run low on programs to install on your computer, I have a friend who has ten thousand of them crammed into his hard drive and he'd be only too happy to install a hundred or so on your machine." At the other end of the line, JM laughed.

"Tell me you're not installing one now," said Mal.

"Oh ye of little faith. But this one might interest you. It's an address book optimizer --"

"Sorry, J, not interested. Just called to congratulate you. Any idea why the change in heart from Elliot?"

"He had nothing to do with it. Ordered by the Chief HPE. Why don't you drop by, eh? I'll be here for another hour or so."

"Can't tonight. Expecting an important call."

"From who?"

"Crystal Peake."

"Yeah, old buddy, in this life time, eh? Did you read Bill Donovan's email?"

"Put it in my Later bin. Anything important in it?"

"Just that he seems to have gone over the deep end. Something about a bat in his eye."

"A lot of that going around. J, I was wondering... "

"Yeah, Mal?"

"You haven't had any thoughts about jumping off the Tomasso Deck, have you?"

"No... why? Have you?"

"None."

"So why the question?"

"I was just up there with Paul Dubois."

"Dubois? You two have become friends?"

"No, actually, he tried to kill me."

"... "

"Are you still there, J?"

"Have you called the police?"

"No. Don't think I'm going to do that. Not yet, at least. I think this is going to turn out for the best."

"Mal, he's a VP in marketing. He controls a small army. He can have you... "

"No, J, I don't think he can do that."

"How's that?"

"You know, J, I don't really know. I just know. And I'm waiting for a call that I'm hoping will tell me why I know. Did you ever get the feeling that you were destined for something in life?"

"Every day. Eh?"

"You're a lucky man. So am I. I've had that feeling, or at least a sense of it, ever since that day I was up in that tree. And today seems somehow connected to that day."

A small dialog box appeared in the center of Mal's monitor.

You have mail.

from:

Crystal Peake

"In fact, old buddy, I think that whatever it is I'm destined for is about to begin."

Chapter 95

Throw The Stick

And off goes my snowman, deserting his post.

dPisano slammed his fist down onto his bulletproof desk top, splashing a pool of tears into flying droplets that rained down over the whole surface of his desk, each reflecting the big man's demonic smile.

"And you're here! I can feel you, feel you near." His eyes searched the spaces between columns. "You've taken my department, ha! Yes, the finest group of spies on earth, and what have you done with them? Taken them where?" He pushed back in his chair and looked under his desk. "And's that your work? Making my people jump off the family deck? Take 'em. Take 'em all! No damned use to anyone anyway!" He looked at the pole-vaulted ceiling a hundred feet over his head. "Well, are you here or not?"

***

From inside dPisano's mouth, from one of the tiny red lights of evil, a thought emitted, not that it was picked up by anyone or anything, and not that it lasted for more than a second or two before becoming one with oblivion, and the thought was this: *I'm right here, old man, right here in your mouth, and in your little snowman's brain, and in a lot of places and I don't need your little signal anymore. Soon, I'll be in one place, just one place, and don't fear, you will be with me. But first, there's something I want the Last Truly Great Man on Earth to do...*

***

dPisano bolted upright, eyes wide, smile wider, and he howled: "I WILL THROW THE STICK!"

Chapter 96

Come Now

Send reply to:
<"Crystal.Peake@erectsoft.com">
From: **Crystal Peake**
To: < Malcolm.Gray@erectsoft.com >
Subject: Come directly ...
Date sent:
Dear Mal:
Come directly to my office. Take the express lift, executive level one. The code is RtE35. It's case-sensitive. Come now.
Crystal
"Straight ... to the top!" - dPisano

Chapter 97

The Wind In The Woods

What's going on with those two? thought Crimson Rose.

What's going on with those two? thought Emerald Looking.

Both women passed discreet glances by Making A Note and Up Yours.

Hope that isn't catching, thought Sun In Her Hair and focused with her peripheral vision to make sure there was a safe distance between her and the naked women on either side of her.

I wonder if they'd be interested in a threesome, thought Ears Around.

Emerald Looking clapped her hands three times. Twenty-nine pairs of eyes turned toward her. Twenty-nine pairs of nipples went instantly erect (with the exception of the nipples of Up Yours, Making A Note and Ears Around, which were already erect) as Emerald Looking spoke: "O little sister, sister of the All, sister of Creation, sister of the deep sensual void, we beckon you hither."

"Ovarai, Ovarai!" chanted the women in unison.

"O little sister, referee of the game of Life, keeper of sanity, quality specialist of the laws of being, we ask as fellow sisters that you fill the woods with your magic."

"Ovarai, Ovarai!"

It started behind Emerald Looking. The trees and the bushes behind her leaned slightly as though bending in a wind, but there was no wind. The trees and bushes continued to lean around the circle of women as though a playful breeze were flying around them, but there was no breeze.

"O little sister, wind of life, force of expectation, so full of love and humor, we grant you access to our minds and our souls to do what must be done."

"Ovarai, Overai!"

And the trees creaked and groaned as the wind that was no wind and the breeze that was no breeze whipped faster around the women. Their eyes crossed in ecstasy. Their bodies glistened with sweat. Their hips began to move forward and back, slowly, forward and back, slowly.

"O little sister, we call on you to re-enchant this world of barren cynicism. We grant you access to our bodies."

"Ovarai, Overai!"

And the wind whirled faster and faster through the trees and bushes, even though there was no wind. And the breeze was warm and balmy over the bodies of the women, even though there was no breeze. And the women's hips began to gyrate, a slow forward thrust winding to the side and then to the rear and to the other side and thrusting forward and to the side again. And their upper bodies began to sway to the left and to the right. And the wind and the breeze spun and caressed so that the women were one in motion with the trees and the bushes and the whispers of "little sister's coming" changed to "bring me the pudding".

Little sister was here.

Sort of.

The wind that was no wind was the breath of little sister. The breeze that was no breeze was the touch of little sister. The bubbles were the eyes of little sister. The energy inside the bubbles was little sister's toe reaching out from across time and space to test the water, searching for the pudding, working its magic everywhere it flexed its toe energy.

And the thirty naked women in the clearing chanted: "Ovarai, Ovarai! Twelve, ten, seventy-eight, fifty-five, sixty-six!" And as they chanted, they swayed suggestively, obscenely, their eyes glazed over. Up Yours and Making A Note gripped each other's hands tight, their sweat mingling in their palms, their nail polish oxidizing together. And their hips brushed in electro-chemical explosions of bubble-assisted wantonness. "Ovarai, Ovarai! Twelve, ten, seventy-eight, fifty-five, sixty-six!"

***

Little sister's sigh spun a tiny cyclone into being that bounced out of the bushes and pinched Belly Dancer Wannabe on the top of her left buttock. Her eyes shot angrily toward Up Yours and quickly melted into a longing haze. She grasped Up Yours right hand. Up Yours smiled straight ahead as she tightened her grip on both Making A Note's and Belly Dancer Wannabe's hands. Ears Around frowned and thought, *slut*.

***

Oops.

Chapter 98

Out Of Order

As Mal left his office, he couldn't help but feel as though something, or someone, were calling him. It wasn't a voice that made a sound like vibrations that could tickle the bones in his ears. It was more like a voice that made vibrations that flowed through his body like waves of energy.

"Mal!"

That wasn't it. That was more like a grating on the bones in his ears. That was the voice of his boss, Don. Mal looked toward Don's office and saw him standing in his doorway. He looked worried. Mal walked over.

"Something wrong, Don?"

Don licked his pink lips with an equally pink tongue. For the first time ever, Mal saw lines in the white skin around Don's pink eyes.

"It's tonight, Mal."

Mal waited to hear the rest. Don remained silent, worried.

"OK, Don. Tonight."

"It is, you know. It's tonight."

"You're not thinking about jumping off the Deck, are you?"

"No, Mal. That's not it. That's not it at all. Are you worried?"

Mal thought a moment. "Are you?"

"No."

"Good. Me neither."

"I'm glad to hear that, Mal. We have a lot of faith in you, you know. Always have."

"Thanks, Don. I'm glad to hear that. I've always had a lot of faith in you too."

Don laughed somewhere halfway between a guffaw and a giggle. "You don't see it yet, do you? But you will. Tonight."

"Can hardly wait."

"See you later, Mal."

"Later, Don."

And Don went back into his office, leaving the door open, as Mal walked to the Executive Level One express elevator. This was an elevator that ran through the inside edge of the outer layer of BonannoTower. It was a high security elevator with no windows and no surveillance cameras. Its doors would open only to a small number of personal codes.

Unfortunately, the Executive Level One express elevator was out of order. Its motor and gears were clogged with bats.

***

Sitting at his desk, Don started to pick up his phone, smiled, and put it back in the cradle. That wouldn't be necessary any more.

Chapter 99

Getting To Know You

"I said suicide!" wailed sales clone Evelyn Hunter to Richard Ziglar. "I said suicide to a client right before the big decision. A vice president got so pissed at me, he walked out of the meeting. I'm washed up. Two years of working eighteen-hour days, working weekends, giving up holidays and vacations, taking course after course, seminar after seminar and sucking up to people I'd rather spit on. Gone. All of that gone. I said suicide."

"That's too bad," said Richard Ziglar. "Don't laugh at me now, but my friend and I came here to work for a guy who jumped over that railing." He pointed to the part of the railing over which King Charley and the citizens of the City State of Marvelous Scoping had flown the vessel. "He was wearing colored markers around his head."

"Don't you just hate that?" said sales clone Evelyn Hunter.

Beside them, a burly man in a chocolate brown three-piece suit studied his electronic scheduler and then looked at his watch. He looked at Richard Ziglar and sales clone Evelyn Hunter. "Six thirty. Right on time." He snapped his fingers, walked up to the railing, and jumped over.

"A lot of people seem to be doing that," said Richard Ziglar.

"Yeah," said sales clone Evelyn Hunter with a measure of longing in her voice. "Want to join me?"

"Sure. Why not?"

On the way down, they exchanged business cards.

Chapter 100

The Snap Of Tiny Bones

That backstabbing bastard lied to me. Paul's eyes glowed like stoked campfires. His hands were balled into two white-hard fists. *Used me! PACA was bullshit!*

The elevator whizzed by busy floors, almost as busy as they were during the day. Even administrative support people couldn't escape the long hours of embracing chaos.

All that bullshit about me going to the top for making his fucking PACA bullshit happen. That old fuck lied to me. And what the hell is this? He ripped a bat out the corner of his eye, threw it to the floor of the elevator and stepped on it. It made a small squishy noise mixed with the snap of tiny bones.

There's more going on here. Lot's more. And I'm going to find out what it is. I almost killed Gray in front of dozens of witnesses. I don't slip up that badly. Never! I'd have taken him somewhere private, off the premises, make it look like an accident, contract a third party, anything but throw him off the building in front of all those people. Damn good thing that jerk friend of his and those idiots with Shuster stopped me. It's time to confront the old fuck and find out what's going on, even if I have to beat it out of him."

Chapter 101

Kiss Crystal Goodbye?

Walking toward the public elevators, Mal wondered about the executive level lift. Another odd thing in a day odd things. Someone had just tried to murder him. He'd been saved by a childhood enemy. The woman of his lust had just told him to come to her. People were flocking to the Tomasso Deck to jump off. Bats were flying out of people's eyes. And to top it all off, he was still married!

God, four years. Four years, and she thought I was just cooling my heals, mulling things over, until what? I decide it's time to beg her to take me back? Damn! Give me the Tomasso Deck over that slow death.

Now, the next big problem. How to get to Crystal's office. He wasn't sure if he would be able to get there on the public elevators. Some offices were accessible only by coded button combinations. The code Crystal had sent him in the email was useless. And what was... ? Mal snapped around quickly and looked behind him. Just a bunch of geeks and others working overtime, rushing around as though their work meant something. But he could have sworn that someone was watching, could feel their eyes boring into the back of his head.

For a moment, he was tempted to just go back to his office, or maybe just go home and say to hell with the whole damned thing. Yes, that would be the right thing to do. Just kiss his job goodbye; kiss ErectSoft INC goodbye; kiss Paul Dubois and all the other assholes in the marketing and sales departments goodbye; kiss ... kiss Crystal goodbye?

After one more quick scan around the area, he continued walking toward the elevator.

***

Marketing clone Janet, leaning against the wall in a dark corner, banged her cell phone against her hip as she watched Mal board the elevator. Nobody was answering the phone in Surveillance. What the hell were they doing?

***

On surveillance screen 457, Mal pushed a button on the control panel of his elevator. But no one was there to watch him push the button. Two desks away, the phone rang. But no one was there to answer the phone. On the main entrance monitor, surveillance screen 1, someone had pasted a sticky note with the message:

Gone for a jump.
Back in 5.
Not.
;-)

***

In the elevator, Mal wondered why he had pressed the numbers 12-10-78-55-66. It was almost as though someone or something had whispered the numbers directly into his brain.

Chapter 102

Pudding?

"Ovarai, Ovarai! Twelve, ten, seventy-eight, fifty-five, sixty-six!"

And the wind that was not a wind and the breeze that was not a breeze tore through the trees and bushes, breaking branches and uprooting the larger bushes. Dismembered plant parts careened crazily around the clearing.

A new element crept into the eyes of some of the women as they chanted.

"Ovarai, Ovarai! Pudding, Pudding!"

The element was fear. Not the fear of mortal danger like when Chuckie creeps up, butcher knife raised, on his next victim. More like the fear inherent in awe when you stand at the edge of a thousand foot high cliff enthralled by the beauty of size, yet fearful that it may swallow you.

"Ovarai, Ovarai! Pudding, Pudding!"

Up Yours tightened her grip on the hands of Making A Note and Belly Dancer Wannabe. And then she winked at Ears Around, who smiled and winked back at her. *A foursome, maybe?*

***

Way to go, Up Yours! Little Sister sighed again, tearing a tree out of the ground. The tree was immediately sucked into the whirlwind spinning around the clearing.

***

"Ovarai, Ovarai! Pudding, Pudding!"

Chapter 103

Eye Socket Flotsam

Marketing clone Janet looked at the numbers on her palm scanner and pressed the button labelled:

Mtch

The numbers on the small gray screen faded and rearranged themselves into:

12-10-78-55-66/CPEAKE/178

Crystal Peake. Malcolm Gray's going to her office. Something big is going on, thought marketing clone Janet. *Big enough to let him live until I find out what's going on. But this is just a temporary reprieve, little man, I need to kill you to prove my love. And kill you I will, even though others have failed.*

And this brought her thoughts around to Paul Dubois: *I respected that little asshole. I feared him. I looked up to that bumbling faggot-voiced idiot. I let him come between Daryl and me. I should never have left Daryl's side. I should have stood up to Dubois and said: "Daryl and I are one, a team, inseparable!" He would have caved. And Daryl and I would have killed Gray. Quickly. Efficiently. And ... and where is my love now? Send your thoughts, Janet Sobovitch, send your thoughts, powered by your love beyond the barriers of walls and floors and send them directly into the mind of Daryl. Hear me, Daryl, hear my love. Soon Malcolm Gray will be dead. I'm going to kill him for you. Kill him for our love. And then I'll kill Dubois, and there will be nothing between us, at least nothing alive.*

She scratched the corner of her eye and dug a small piece of gray leathery material from it. She rolled the eye socket flotsam between a thumb and forefinger and flicked it away.

Chapter 104

Not My Plan

Some of the women closed their eyes to block out the havoc around them, but they continued to chant: "Ovarai, Ovarai! Pudding, Pudding!"

The maelstrom was like a solid wall around them composed of trees, bushes, grass, and dirt that stretched over their heads. Anyone or anything that might try to pass through that wall would have been pulverized, and then whisked away as part of the wall. The sounds of whispering had long since given way to the screech and scratch of branches cracking, the pumpf and rustle of bushes disintegrating, and the howl and holler of a vortex that was neither wind nor breeze.

A warm flood of bubbles splashed over Emerald Looking's sagging breasts and they tightened and hardened, the wide brown nipples rising and vibrating, and an a rich playfulness huffed in her amorous eyes. She called out: "Little sister, you are among us. We feel the sweet touch of your presence. We offer our bodies to your work."

"Ovarai, Ovarai! Pudding, Pudding!"

"We offer our minds to your purpose."

"Ovarai, Ovarai! Pudding, Pudding!"

The wall of forest effluvium spun faster and higher until it formed a dome over the clearing, and the sounds of matter and movement melted into a deep hum.

"We offer our souls to your eternal plan."

"Ovarai, Ovarai! Pudding, Pudding!"

***

Not me that planned it, thought little sister, *but hey, whatever turns them on. Speaking of which, I'd forgotten how little it takes to make them horny.* And with that, she doused all thirty women with a wave of bubbles, leaving them writhing and groaning mindlessly.

Chapter 105

An Imperfect Bowl

"She scanned the number?" Her cool blue eyes turned pensive. "Yes, I know she's dangerous. I don't need a profile to see the murder in that one's eyes." She ran a hand down her leg, straightening a crease in her green robe as she listened to the voice at the other end of the line. The robe was exactly like the ones worn by Sylvie and Caitlin. "But why didn't the exec lift work?" She listened. "Well, he's on his way regardless. Keep an eye on that marketing bitch. And let me know what happens between Dubois and the DP." She listened. "Believe me. There's going to be a showdown between them."

Crystal hung up the phone. She was leaning against the front of her gold and silver inlaid desk. Unlike dPisano's desk, hers was not bulletproof, as though not being the richest, most powerful man in the world somehow made her desk less of a target.

You were right, Mom. You were right all along. Through all the training and preparation, you told me this day would come and that I would be...well, let's be realistic... bait.

She walked around her desk with long graceful steps, the green robe clinging jealously to her smooth curves, and she opened a drawer. She took out a time-riddled cigar box and opened it. Inside, a lopsided glass bowl huddled in a nest of yellowed tissue. The glass bowl was deep purple and its sides were uneven in depth and width as though it had been blown just as a gust of wind burst through the

345

window. She reached into the box and lifted the bowl into the air. Shoddy workmanship or not, it was a beautiful bowl. It seemed to catch the light and caress it into itself and then mull it around inside like a slow-moving cloud of white smoke. It emanated an aura of magic. She held the bowl up just over her head and stared into it.

If you could only be here. With all your love and wisdom, with all your largeness of feeling, you would have been the perfect one. I miss you, Mom, and this day is for you. What I do is for you, because this is what you always wanted. This is what you always dreamed of, and I know now that you dreamed it for me. You knew your fate, didn't you? Knew it all along.

The hard blue in Crystal Peake's eyes softened for just an instant. And then solidified into rock-dense resolve. The cigar box thumped down on her desk, and she carried the bowl in both hands towards the hot tub, the long pink fibers of deep carpet swaying aside under her bare feet. Someone knocked unsteadily at her door.

For you, Mom.

Chapter 106

Let's See What We Can See

From out of the lips of black holes, from the tips of celestial anomalies, from the heart of everything in the universe that refused to make sense, there was suddenly a common thread of agreement: *Let's get our shit together. Let's all meet in BonannoTower. Let's follow the signal to the place where madness meets.*

There was enough of No Bang already in BonannoTower to know that not all of him was there, enough to make bats, toss a department into the void, to cause the entire population of the City State of Marvelous Scoping to fly the vessel, move these mortals to murder, and emanate enough bad karma to inspire hundreds of IT workers to jump off the highest building on the planet. But that wasn't going to be enough if little sister got it together first, and she was close to doing just that. Those parts of No Bang that inhabited the spaces between sanity in BonannoTower could sense her presence completing itself, and that presence was surprisingly close for a being that would only drop in on a forest clearing.

But let her come, thought No Bang. *There's no way the little bitch is going to get here, into the middle of the city, from wherever the nearest forest can be, before I get it together. This sense of her closeness must be some kind of gamma interference or something. And, besides, I've got the crazy old fart and the psycho lady from marketing lined up to hold the fort until I get my shit together. But what the hell is going on now? What the devil is that cross between a snowball and a circus freak doing? Looks like he's trying to screw things up for me. Well, let's see what we can see about this...*

Chapter 107

Second Thoughts About A Life Not So Well Lived

The sensors operating the door to dPisano's office performed several billion additional operations to recognize the pattern of fibers in dPisano's eyes. The decision algorithm narrowed down to two choices: dPisano or madman. The algorithm decided that the two were synonymous. They also had to take into consideration the flapping of tiny gray wings. All-in-all, it took the software in the sensors a millisecond longer than normal to issue the OPEN command to the door.

The door split down the center into two doors that slid into the doorframe, exposing dPisano to the murderous glare of Paul Dubois.

Damn, though dPisano, *can't even drop out of for a moment or two to throw the stick without some minion or other bothering me.*

Got you now, you bastard, thought Paul.

"You lied to me, Sir!" said Paul. "Everything. It was all a lie!" He tried to put some base into his voice, but despite the thick trunk-like body, his words came out high and scratchy, as though his round head were an old gramophone record; his mouth, a broken speaker, and this hatred, a worn needle. "PACA was just a smoke screen for some plan you're running behind my back, Sir. What happened to that room?"

dPisano took a deep breath. How to explain? He thought a moment, concluded that explaining would be impossible, so he just said: "Paul. They said fractional. Do you understand? They said fractional. Now, if you'll excuse me, I have some important business to attend to." And the tried to walk past Paul.

Not a good idea.

Paul reached up and grabbed dPisano by the neck. "You used me, Mr. dPisano!"

This, also, was not a good idea.

dPisano's eyes widened as he looked down at Paul, and they continued to widen until they were almost as wide as his smile (which hadn't flinched an iota, even though Paul's iron grip was cutting off the smile's supply of oxygen). Paul's own little round eyes squinted curiously as he watched dPisano's eyes cover the entire area above his nose with pulsating iris and cornea. And then the bats flew out.

Bats by the dozens flapped crazily out of dPisano's eyes and into Paul's face, where they scratched and bit until Paul released his grip on dPisano's throat and fell to the floor, arms flailing at the attack of vicious vermin. The last bat struggled out of dPisano's left eye and took off in the wrong direction, and the smiling magnate's eyes shrunk back to normal.

"You're a nasty little snowman with a bad heart, Paul Dubois, and it's mostly because of people like you that I decided to bring him here and end this... " he looked around the arched hall and spread his arms in a gesture that went far beyond the walls of the hall, "... this mess." He thought a moment and shrugged. "No. No, that wasn't it. It was the Tower. And the fractional. Yes, it's always been the fractional."

"But what about PACA?" whimpered Paul, still holding his arms around to his head, even though the bats had disappeared. "What about our plan to take over the industry, build a new world with us in control..."

"Pardon me, my boy, but I believe I said something to the effect that *I* would be the one in control. You work *for* me, not *with* me, if you'll recall."

"But you promised... "

dPisano's smile curled almost up to his ear lobes. "And you believed. You believed whatever I wanted you to believe, you pathetic little misfit. But your greed for power did not come from the same place of deep wisdom as did mine. You were too easily manipulated by my greed, my will. You're so much like everybody in this business wants to be. Why the hell do you think so many of them are up on the Tomasso Observation Deck right now, plunging to the only human dignity they've known since nurses slapped them on their asses the day they were born."

Paul crouched, ready to spring.

"Uh, uh," warned dPisano wagging a finger at him. "There's more to this than you can possibly imagine with your petty, greedy little mind. And there's more bats where the last batch came from."

Paul stood up. "And what else is there to it? What are you really doing, you miserable old fuck?"

dPisano laughed. "Sticks and stones, my psychotic little snowman. And come to think of it, I have a mission. A mission to toss a stick. So you'll pardon me if I don't stick around." He laughed louder.

"What are you really doing? A whole room just disappeared into some kind of crazy place. And all these bats. What's really going on?"

"Oh, let me think, now," said dPisano, rubbing his chin with thumb and forefinger. "Oh yes! That's it! End of the universe! I'm bringing about an end to the universe! End the family shame, you know! If I can't change time or circumstance, then I'll just end time and circumstance." And he walked past Paul and down the hall. Before boarding the elevator, he turned back to Paul and said: "Don't worry about losing the PACA thing, Paul. By the end of the day, it won't matter." His eyes raised and he laughed. "Oh yes! That's right! By the end of the day! The *end* of the day!"

***

Paul sank back down onto the floor. His face was blank. He stared at the area immediately in front of his eyes. There were no more bits of gray material in his eyes. Nothing moved in his eyes, not even the dancing devils that had been there all his life. Nothing moved in the very backs of Paul's eyes where the portal opened into his mind. Nothing cared in his eyes just as nothing cared in the portal facing into his mind at the backs of Paul Dubois' eyes.

As the elevator doors closed on dPisano's whacked laughter, Paul thought, *It was all just a scam. He thinks he's ending the universe. I've been sticking my nose up the ass of an insane old man. He's going to be in a straight jacket by the end of the day, and where is that going to leave me?*

He wiped a stubby-fingered hand over his face and pushed himself up. He walked toward the closed elevator door.

But there is one thing I can still do.

Chapter 108

No Pun Intended

"Pretty darned amazing', wasn't it?" said Johnny the Brain Cell. "Reconstructed the DNA in them spermatozoa completely."

"Most amazing thing I ever did see," agreed Daisy Mae. "What you think it done that for, Johnny? Think it mighta had something to do with them neutrino's barging through here this morning?"

"Most likely nothin' to do with them little bastards, Daisy Mae. My guess is that it has something to do with all the shit that's been going on around here. You know, shit like that little creep Paul trying to kill our boy. All them people jumping off the Deck. Bats flyin' outta folk's eyes an' all. Mark my words, this stuff in our boy's balls is gonna bring things to a head."

Daisy Mae, Bobby, and several million other brain cells giggled furiously (as only several million brain cells can).

"What?" said Johnny. "What're you all goin' on about now?"

Chapter 109

Bubble Orgy

"Ovarai! Oh yeah! Ovaraioverariovarai! Oooooobaaaa-beeee!" screamed Up Yours as another wave of bubbles swarmed over her, igniting every cell in her body with pleasure. The grass was hot and sensual on her back. Her legs thrust directly upwards as a horde of bubbles charged directly up her vagina. "O... O... oooOOoooOOooo-Ovara-iiiiiii! Puuuuudddddding!"

Beside her, Making A Note, on all fours with her face buried in the grass and her legs spread impossibly wide, wailed and quaked as wave after wave of bubbles skidded across her exposed clitoris and into her gaping opening. Up Yours wanted desperately to get her tongue over to that action, but another horde of bubbles drove her thighs into the ground and every brain cell in her head exploded with ecstasy, paralyzing her body with bliss.

And so it was all around the clearing. As the dome of forest spun madly around and over the thirty women, the air literally spewed forth surge after surge of bubbles, as though it were breathing them in from the Milky Way's Discount Bubble Clearing House and breathing them out into the clearing, and with each outward breath, legions of bubbles flowed over the howling mass of women undulating on the clearing floor in a beatific dance of frenzied pleasure. And all around them, the solid wall of movement hummed deeply.

***

Hope you're enjoying this, girls. It's going to be one hell of a crash when it's all over. But, like I said, it's not my plan. I'm just another one of the players.

Chapter 110

Arriving In The Nick

Young fool! I should have snuffed his life for grabbing me. Strong grip, but no heart. But I imagine my friend from the end of time will have his own plans for Mr. Dubois, isn't that right my terminal friend? Something winked in the dark spaces between dPisano's teeth.

The elevator door opened on Crystal's floor. dPisano stepped into the hall, the huge mass of his body resembling a walking beacon with an insane flashing smile, and immediately he hid behind a potted Banyon tree.

Somebody was as Crystal's door.

Slowly, dPisano moved a branch aside and peered down the hall. He recognized the bearing of the body. The ponytail. The suit. It was him. It was Malcolm Gray. And that's why he, dPisano, had come to Crystal's office. Malcolm Gray was supposed to be here. He, dPisano, was supposed to be here. Yes, this was the place to throw the stick. Malcolm Gray. dPisano. Throw stick. Yes. It all fit together.

Throw the stick! That's the trick! And this's the place I've arrived in the nick, and not a lick too late, right Mr. Gray? And what's that matrix of mediocrity doing, standing at the door to my blond blizzard's quarters? And, yes, yes, yes ... I must throw the stick. I must throw the stick somewhere, and I must throw the stick and not a brick but only the stick and I must throw the stick where? And

methinks, I think, that Malcolm Gray is the answer
to that.

Chapter 111

The Message (An Aside To The Past)

Let's go back to that moment in the sky over Pisa when a huffy dPisano was leaving Italy thoroughly enraged at the Committee of Coordination for the Safeguard of the Tower of Pisa. Up to this point, though sometimes a tad eccentric, dPisano had been playing with a full deck. At least, he was until he received the message from the edges of creation, from those timeless, formless nether regions to which No Bang had been banished at the dawn of time. It was the same message that had plummeted into the regions of death hundreds of years earlier.

It was a simple three-word message: "Build a tower."

Unlike the Widow Berta hundreds of years before him, dPisano thought this was a splendid idea. In fact, it seemed, oddly, that he already had the basic schematics for the building in his brain. The metal core, the location, the height - everything was inherent in those three simple words: "Build a tower."

And, as the tower was being constructed, dPisano's head was over every shoulder, buried in every blueprint, and presiding over every meeting so that it would be built to the exact specifications of the words: "Build a tower."

And when the tower was finished, dPisano set about writing the program that was inherent in the words: "Build a tower." Each word was worth a million lines of programming. And when the program was written, dPisano put together the Most Secret Room in the World, the room where the program would be tested and perfected and then executed. This was the program that would turn the highest building in the world into a beacon, and to dPisano's way of thinking, it was the program that would finally end the family shame. By ending the universe. And the insanity that had begun over Pisa was now complete; dPisano's mind was Bedlam incarnate.

Now all of No Bang knew the way, and was on the way. The beacon had done its job. And now it was time for dPisano to finish his job, to do this one last thing inherent in the words: "Build a tower." Now it was time for the Last Truly Great Man in the Universe to throw the stick.

Chapter 112

Things To Do On An Elevator When You're Bored

Crazy! The old fuck is crazy! And I put all my eggs up his crazy fucking ass! Paul stood by the elevator door. His black three-piece suit was scuffed and wrinkled; his five o'clock shadow made his round face look like a lunar eclipse; and his white shirt was spotted with bat guano. Paul Dubois looked like anything but the consummate sonuvabitch-nose-up-everybody's-ass corporate marketing mandarin. He looked like a guy with no neck having a bad day.

With a polite *ding* the elevator arrived and the doors opened. Paul trudged through the doors and pressed some buttons. Then he rubbed his right eye. He was having bats again.

I'll show that old fucker! I don't need him! I don't need this fucking company! I don't need this fucking asshole in my eye! He ripped a bat out of this eye, and for the second time this day, he stomped a bat into oblivion. And he stomped it again. And again. And he was still stomping it when the elevator stopped and the doors opened.

Let's see the look on his face when he finds out what I've done now! Too late to stop me this time, you crazy old fucker!

Chapter 113

Where's My Pudding?

Marketing clone Daryl stood dreamy-eyed in the elevator watching the tiny floor buttons light up as the elevator zoomed upward. Through the glass wall, he watched huge chasms of space rush by. Floor after floor, section after section, bridge after bridge. The highest building in the world was a world in itself, but marketing clone Daryl was not impressed by its grandeur. For inside marketing clone Daryl's head, a room the size of the entire universe sprawled to the far corners of his mind and it breathed a string of sounds, breathed it in and out, breathed it over and over: Offer her your pudding. Offer her your pudding.

To marketing clone Daryl, nothing could seem more appropriate. *Offer her my pudding. That's the ticket!*

But then a frown curled on his lips. Doubt etched curly cues at the sides of his nostrils. His forehead creased. *Where's my pudding?* He patted his chest, searched the pockets inside his black suit jacket, checked his shirt pocket, thrust his hands into this outside suit jacket pockets. *Where's my pudding?* Panic flared in his eyes. He rummaged through his pants pockets, sides and back. He found coins, keys and a wallet. He dropped them onto the floor of the elevator. *Where's my fucking pudding?* He pushed his fingers inside his socks and felt around.

No pudding.

It was time for drastic measures. Marketing clone Daryl decided to minimize the clutter. He took off his jacket and searched it inch by inch. He took off his shirt and did the same. Within minutes, he was naked except for a gold chain around his neck. The elevator had stopped; the doors were open. Marketing clone Daryl stared into the hallway, tears streaming from his eyes. *Where's my pudding?*

And then, something that was not so much a voice as a message, not so much a sound as a meaning, spread with a mellow warmth throughout the infinity inside marketing clone Daryl's head. It was an assurance, a knowingness that soon there would be pudding, oodles of pudding, more pudding than he could shake a stir stick at. Smiling ear to ear, he stepped stark naked into the hall.

Chapter 114

What's Going On Down There?

The door clicked and opened just as Mal was going to knock one more time. It opened noiselessly, almost ghostly in its silence. The door opened into a room of deep pink carpet, lustrous as a wide flat cloud of candyfloss. The door opened a breathtaking spectacle of long legs peeking out from Crystal's slinky green robe as she lounged enticingly by the heart-shaped hot tub.

Breathing became difficult. Mal's blood pressure experimented with unhealthy numbers. His brain blew circuits, ruptured gaskets.

***

"Put a damper on our boy! Fast!" yelled Johnny the Brain Cell.

***

A wave of dizziness careened over the top of Mal's head, grabbed him by the ears, and crossed his eyes. He reached a hand out to the doorframe to steady himself. The dizziness began to settle.

***

"That' it," said Johnny. "Bring him down slowly."

***

Mal blinked, shook his head, forced his eyes to focus on Crystal's eyes, fought tooth and nail to avoid her legs and focus on her eyes. "I uh... "

"Come in, Malcolm," said Crystal, her voice husky and commanding.

"I uh... "

Crystal pivoted on her buttocks and lowered her legs slowly into the water. Then she patted the tiled surface beside her and said: "Come, Malcolm. Sit with me."

Mal's heartbeat broke Olympic records for fastest beat, highest jump, and longest non-drug-assisted palpitation. But somehow he stayed conscious. And something strange was going on between his legs, something more than just the excitement accompanying the hardest erection he'd had in his entire life. Something was moving down there. Something was making noises down there! But, oh god, did it feel good!

He walked through the doorway and the door clicked shut behind him.

"Come over here," said Crystal. "And leave your clothes over there."

Chapter 115

The Stick

He's in! And I'm out! It's a trick to cramp my throwing of the stick! Like fractional. I'll show you fractional. I've the key, I have, I have. The key's the thing, the thing I need. dPisano searched in his pants pockets. *Ho! Yes! Have you in hand my metal lovely, my lock socket wrench! Yes! It all fits together and it's time now, time to throw the stick!*

Suddenly, there was unusual movement at the outer perimeters of the widest smile on earth since Tyrannosaurus Rex last smirked and thought: "So big deal. A meteor, a few clouds, we'll get by." The movement was downwards, a slow motion that obscured the glitter of polished calcium tooth by tooth until dPisano stood before the door to Crystal Peake's office with his mouth completely closed, the smile hidden under wrinkled folds of yellowed flesh. And the Last Truly Great Man on Earth thought: *I have no stick to throw*.

He looked at the keys in his hand. Examined each carefully. *The key, the key, the key. Which is it to be? The silver, the gold, the copper, but what's the diff, for the stopper is... I have no stick to throw.*

Still turning the keys in his hand, he looked around the hall. Bare walls, gray carpet, fluorescent light fixtures. And a Banyon tree at the opposite end of the hall. It was about eight feet high, and one long limb seemed to be trying to break away from the rest of the tree. It reached in the direction of the nearest florescent light. The limb was about five feet long. The yellow skin covering dPisano's teeth tightened and parted and the corners of his mouth widened and curved toward his ears. The infamous dPisano smile glowed brightly again under the wide crazed eyes as he looked at the wayward limb.

The stick.

Chapter 116

A Man And His Pudding

Marketing clone Daryl was all smiles and a gold chain. His mind was close to bursting with the happiness that comes to a man when he knows that soon he will have his pudding, and it would be the finest pudding ever.

Behind him, the elevator doors had closed and the elevator had left, taking his clothing and personal possessions with it. Yes, he would offer her his pudding and he would offer it with pride. He knew this, knew it throughout the infinite spaces in his mind, knew it to the tops of the columns stretching beyond sight and beyond imagination in the rooftops of his interior landscape. Since he had lost his mind, there was a lot of room inside marketing clone Daryl's head, and all of that room vibrated with the sweet cadence of: Offer her your pudding.

And then it struck him for a fractal of a microsecond: *Offer who my pudding?* And then it passed, almost before it existed.

She would be there for the offering. This, marketing clone Daryl knew right down to the endless depths of forever within his mind. She would be there for the offering.

Just as he was about to walk through the wall in front of him, he stopped. It was not time, yet. In fact, it was time to just stand right where he was, naked, and bask in the joy of a man with a gold chain about to offer her his pudding.

Chapter 117

Artifacts

Marketing clone Janet walked toward an elevator that had just stopped at her floor and opened its doors. No one exited. No one was on it. She entered the elevator and saw a pile of clothing on the floor. An man's three-piece suit, shirt and tie, the contents of his pockets strewn about the floor. She stooped and picked up a black wallet. She flipped it open and her heart all but tore out of her chest. *Daryl's wallet!* Then the clothing on the floor must be Daryl's. The doors closed behind her. Her right hand reached out to the control panel and it was as though her fingers pressed buttons of their own volition. She wasn't even aware that she pressed them, let alone aware of the numbers she pressed. She had Daryl's wallet in her hand. These were Daryl's clothes on the floor. That was Daryl's gold-banded wristwatch. There was Daryl's mirror-polished shoe sticking out from under Daryl's black pants. That was Daryl's change, two quarters and three dimes, spread over one of Daryl's socks and over Daryl's pants, like round metal objects of Sheng Fui significance in a garden of business suit.

The elevator soared upward as marketing clone Janet's heart soared upward. Daryl was in trouble, unclothed, and in trouble. And marketing clone Janet was soaring to the rescue.

They'll all die for our love, my darling. They'll all die and we'll burn their clothes together. We'll mount their watches and jewelry and frame them.

Hang them over our bed and make love in the presence of their artifacts.

Chapter 118

Truth In Marketing

The trail started at the closed doors to the elevator. A bit of gray stuff here, a bit of gray stuff there. And there, a few feet away from the first splotches on the floor, a bit of bone and blood mixed with gray stuff. And a few feet away from that, a small pile of mangled bat with two tiny black eyes atop the lifeless mound no doubt seeing the world from a whole new perspective, a vantage point, some might philosophize, of rootedness in one spot for the remainder of one's time in this life. The trail of ruined rodent continued through the hall, between the loafers and pumps, the high heels and sling sandals, the wingtips and Oxfords, the dress moccasins and cross-trainers, the clogs and hiking boots, the deck shoes and tennis shoes, all of them careful to avoid soiling their soles in the leathery clumps.

The trail led though the massive glass doors and on to the Tomasso Observation Deck, right up to the edge of the deck where it stopped at a pair of brilliantly polished black Oxfords attached to a pair of twenty dollar black socks wrapped around the thick ankles of the newly appointed Vice President of Venture Marketing Initiatives, who, for the first time in years was in full possession of his nose. Paul Dubois' nose was no longer up anyone's ass.

In fact, Paul Dubois was committing the cardinal sin of the marketing manager: he was telling the people around him what he really thought about the company for which he worked.

"It's all a fucking sham," he said to a buxom woman in a slinky black dress. She blinked larger than life lashes at him and then looked out over the city. "Everything we do here is just an illusion. None of it means anything!"

A group of men in similar dark gray suits, with similar gray-streaked black hair, and similar pinstripe shirts coughed similarly into their hands and avoided eye contact with Paul with similar resolve. The crowd on the deck, somewhere in the high hundreds now, was hushed and expectant. People glanced at their watches repeatedly. Others opened appointment books, looked at pages without seeing anything, and nodded to those around them. Some referred to palm pilots. Some talked quietly to people who nodded agreement without hearing a word. A few watched others out of the corners of their eyes.

No one was jumping. No one had jumped for a while. Members of the cleanup crew below were sitting on benches smoking cigarettes and pot, blood and strands of flesh drying on their brooms, shovels and rakes. And no one was listening to Paul Dubois.

"It's all just a fucking game!"

"Nothing you do here means a damn thing!"

"The asshole who runs this place is insane!"

"He thinks he's ending the universe!"

"This company hasn't produced a product in years!

"A whole room just got sucked into nowhere!"

It appeared that Winter was over for the sumo-snow-man-sonofabitch-backstabbing-bastard-newly-appointed-Vice-President-of-Venture-

372

Marketing-Initiatives for ErectSoft INC, and Spring
was about to do its work.

"Where the fuck are these bats coming from!"

Chapter 119

Hard-on And All

Now there were two naked men in BonannoTower. One was standing in a hallway waiting to walk through a wall as he contemplated the joys of offering her his pudding, and other was sitting by a hot tub beside the previously unobtainable lust of his life.

He knew that he should feel at least a bit uncomfortable sitting by Crystal with his clothes off. He was in good shape and proud of his body, but he was at work. He was in the office of the most powerful woman in the company. She was sitting beside him in a green robe that looked very much the same as the ones Caitlin and Sylvie had worn. Why wasn't he even the tiniest bit self-conscious about the madly twitching branch of blood-engorged flesh jutting out from under a patch of stringy pubic hair.

My God, I can't believe I'm sitting here in the nude beside Crystal, hard-on and all, and I'm not even blushing.

"You're a very special man, Malcolm," said Crystal.

"Um, how do you mean that?" He cocked his head to one side. He'd heard something. Was that music? Coming from somewhere close. *What was that?*

Crystal, legs in the steamy water, shimmied a few inches closer to Mal. "I mean that you are the chosen one, Malcolm, the vessel."

"Chosen?" Mal forgot about the music. He had a sudden feeling that things were about to get weird. He heard another noise, this one anything but music. He looked in the direction from which he thought it had come, a door on the other side of the office. He thought he saw the door shudder. The handle appeared to have shaken. He blinked. The door was motionless, but the noise seemed still to be coming from that direction. Crystal reached a hand out and turned his head in her direction. Her eyes glowed with blue icy passion. Mal's heart began to skip beats. His pulse quickened.

***

"OK folks! Batten down! Get ready for the surge!" yelled Johnny the Brain Cell. And billions of brain cells in Mal's head held their breath (as only brain cells can).

***

In Mal's testicles, an army of spermatozoa like none other ever seen in the universe stood to attention, awaiting the signal.

***

Crystal reached behind her and brought out the purple bowl.

"What's that for?" said Mal

"You'll see." Crystal smiled coyly and giggled.

Crystal Peake giggling? thought Mal. That didn't seem right, but then he was sitting beside her in her office in his birthday suit. Maybe he should be giggling too.

She placed the bowl on the tiles beside her and lifted her legs out of the water. Mal's eyes nearly popped from their sockets as she spun around and placed her legs on either side of the bowl, which was directly under the coldest, blondest and most perfect pussy Mal had seen in his entire life.

***

The signal! In Mal's testicles, the army of spermatozoa snapped into action.

***

Mal looked down at his swollen pecker. It was twitching madly, gyrating and spiraling. He gawked in horror. Music, distinct bars of music, as though from some infinitely huge symphony orchestra, played right through his balls and filled the room with crashing wave after wave of strings and horns and cymbals and drums in the most perfect harmony that Mal had ever heard. And then his penis began to swell and subside, swell and subside. And the music coming from his testicles was almost visible.

And then a churning sensation where his testicles were attached to his body, and the churning grew to a surge that increased in intensity as the volume of the unearthly music swelled to torrential proportions, and then it was like his thighs were suddenly caught in the grip of a giant fur-coated oyster. His ass was pinned to the hot tub tiles as his penis pointed like a baton at the purple bowl between Crystal's legs and a long white stream of sperm, sparkling and bubbling and emitting the most beautiful music Mal had ever heard gushed out of the opening in his penis in a long arc toward the purple bowl. And it seemed that the arc was composed of millions of white bubbles rolling over each other and seething within the arc. It splashed into the bowl as Mal howled in pleasure, his eyes still wide with horror, while the arc of sperm streamed and streamed and streamed into the purple bowl. It seemed to erupt from him forever and the room was thick with music as though every molecule in the air had been transformed into a note.

And then he passed out.

Chapter 120

Arriving

Thirty naked women wailed to the tune of "There's A Maelstrom Thundering Around Me And I Don't Know What To Do With It".

"Ovaraaaaaaiiioooooowwweeee! PuuuUUUuuuUUUuuu ddddddddddingggg!"

Emerald Looking rolled lightning fast across the clearing floor, screaming: "... our souls... souls... our souls ... to... our souls to... your eternal... wow!... youryouryour eternal plan!" Up Yours, legs kicking and arms flailing, spun like an ant in a whirlpool of bubbles as she babbled: "Oo ah ooooo pudddddddd... " With her nose still buried in the grass, Making A Note's legs pushed her through the clearing as she shrieked: "I'm a steeeeeeeam roller baby!"

And then the noise stopped.

The spinning forest matter froze in mid spin, forming a quivering dome of mashed forest over the women. In unison, all thirty women closed their eyes. Their bodies vibrated quietly as their faces relaxed. And they began to float.

***

He was out for only a few seconds before the music sweating from the very air he was breathing jangled his unconscious mind awake. The horror evaporated, replaced with a calm that reached into the wellsprings at the core of existence itself. Crystal smiled at him. He returned her smile. And the glistening white stream formed a scintillating arc from his penis to the purple bowl. It seemed to Mal that it had been there since time first asked: "Which first? The tick or the tock?" He'd been spraying sperm forever and would continue to do so forever, and for all that time he would stare into Crystal's chilly blue eyes and lose himself in her smile. Eternity, for Malcolm Gray, would be filling Crystal's bowl.

He could live with that.

But, just as he resolved to spew sperm into Crystal's bowl forever while his heart danced in flames from her frigid eyes, the door that he'd entered a few minutes ago flew open with a bang, and at the same time, a hairy leg stepped through the serpentine wall twenty feet away from the door.

***

Thirty naked bodies floating in the air. Some tight with youth and regular workouts; a few flaccid with age and neglect; others trailing waterfalls of raven or golden hair; all relaxed, smiling, and ready. Ghostly silent, their bodies aligned in a semicircle six feet from the clearing floor, their toes aimed southward at a spot on the other side of the wall of forest pulp. Their arms drifted away from their sides and they joined hands simultaneously, and then all thirty bodies arched and each woman uttered her own sound of ultimate ecstasy.

"Oooooweeeeooooweee," uttered Message Waiting.

"Nnnnnnnnnnnnnnnnnnn," uttered Brows To Sky.

379

"Ackkkkkkkkkkkkkkk," uttered Ears Around.

"Yipeeyippeeyipeeyipee," uttered Queued In Line.

"Gonna lick Making A Note's pussy all over the place, gonna lick Belly Dancer Wannabe's pussy all over the place," uttered Up Yours.

And then they went silent. Their eyes opened wide. Their arched bodies compressed like high jumpers about to spring. And their smiling mouths opened, opened, opened ...

***

dPisano stood in the doorway. Bats flew out of his eyes and disappeared into the air. Evil snarled through the teeth of the most persuasive smile on the planet. In his right hand, he brandished the five foot long Banyon branch like a leafy sword.

"I speak from a place of deep wisdom!" The words boomed from behind the demented calcium. He pointed his ficus scimitar at Crystal. "You've been a naughty little nippy, turning a hypothermic shoulder my way, the only way, the way of the Last Truly Great Man on Earth, and what do you have to say for yourself before I throw the stick?"

Mal turned his head to look at dPisano just as the last of the sperm stream jumped from his genitals and into the bowl between Crystal's legs. But before his eyes reached the bat-eyed mogul, they froze on the section of wall where marketing clone Daryl walked through. Mal couldn't help wondering, *Hmm, I wonder if there's electrical wiring in that part of the wall?*

Marketing clone Daryl looked around the room, smiling almost as wide as dPisano, and said: "Oh good. My pudding."

***

Malcolm Gray will pay dearly for this, thought marketing clone Janet as she watched marketing clone Daryl's body disappear through the wall. *Only the evil incarnate in that pig-tailed creep could make my lover act so unnaturally.* She picked a piece of wing with a tiny claw in it out of her eye and flicked it away as she walked to the area of wall that had just swallowed the object of her deadly affections. She examined the wall, her frown deepened, her breathing grew heavy, her face flushed deep red, her mind snapped completely.

Marketing clone Janet stepped back a few feet and jumped forward as she leaped into the air and shot a muscular leg out with lightening speed into the center of the wall. The edge of her foot focused all of her body's energy on a single wooden strut inside the wall and the whole surface crumpled in on itself, leaving a gaping hole in the wall where Daryl had walked through.

A bent nailed quacked and ran on tiny nail legs down the hall toward the elevators.

***

... opened, opened, and each breathed deeply and held her breath, curled her legs up until her knees almost touched her shoulders. Thirty vaginas pointed to the spot south of the clearing like a

381

floating firing squad of pubic hair and glistening flesh.

***

"You were always a whiner, Paul."

What? Did that sales bitch just call me a whiner? Paul did a quick moral calculation: *If I throw her over the side, will I go to jail?*

"I never liked you, Paul. No one ever liked you. I'll bet your mother hated you. I'll bet she locked you in a closet when friends came over so that they wouldn't see what an ugly little round thing she gave birth to."

He was astounded. He'd just screamed out the truth about the company; for once he'd told the truth. And everybody, all the hundreds of people on the deck who must have heard him, simply ignored him, ignored every word. And this ... sales person, beautiful or not, was just begging to be thrown over the railing. And the railing was right behind him.

"I can't believe that you and that weasel, Gray, just took off from the meeting like that," said Holly Stewart. Mascara streaked the corners of her eyes. Her lower lids were red. "You just left me there with that incompetent little bitch, Hunter, after she blew a six million dollar sale in the last round. We were supposed to sign the initial contracts in that meeting, you asshole!"

Timing is everything. You were off a second or two when you tried this with Gray.

"That was the down payment on my new condo, you bastard! I already had the commission

382

spent. Do you have any idea how embarrassing this is, the situation you put me... "

Paul grabbed her by the throat. Holly gagged, her eyes bulged. Paul pulled her head down as he bent his knees and brought his other hand over to grab her by the waist. And then Paul Dubois felt the most excruciating pain that he'd felt in his entire life. It started somewhere in his groin area and worked its way up into his stomach where it solidified into a large slug-like shape of red-hot hurt. And it continued upward.

Paul's fingers loosened on Holly's throat and she backed away. And then she kicked him square in the balls again. The tiny seed-sized dots that were Paul's irises raced across the small whites of his eyes until they were thoroughly crossed.

"That's... " She kicked him again, this time in the stomach. "... no way... " Her left leg shot up to her side, flashing a patch of red under the grayish green dress, and she delivered a bone-cracking round house kick to the side of Paul's head. "... to treat a sales manager."

Stunned and bleeding from his nose and left ear, Paul pushed himself backward to get away from Holly's lethal legs.

Oops.

Too far.

He went over the railing. But his head cleared just in time to direct his right hand to reach out and grab. He caught the top bar of the railing just in time. He reached up with his other hand and clamped on. Behind him, the city spread for hundreds of miles in every direction. Below him, members of the clean up crew butted cigarettes and joints when they saw what looked like a short snowman dressed in a black three-piece suit dangling from the Tomasso Observation Deck. Above him, Holly Stewart, looked down at him, smiling evilly as a tiny bat claw dug its way out of the corner of her eye.

Behind Holly, heads crooked to one side, murmured conversations stopped abruptly, watches, schedulers, and notepads were forgotten. Several hundred people took a deep breath and held it as though the crowd were loaded like someone about to let loose a thundering fart after holding it in throughout a marathon management meeting, right after a lunch of chili and beer.

***

And the race was on.

Marketing clone Daryl ignored the wall smashing behind him and marched quickly toward Crystal. dPisano saw him heading toward his corporate concubine and thought: *Though the world should end, this unclothed bowser shall not touch my frosty fetish.* Whereupon, he marched double-time toward Crystal, to protect her from the naked attacker. Janet, staring through her handiwork, saw Daryl heading toward Crystal and Mal and stepped through the hole in the wall.

"Daryl!" she screamed.

Marketing clone Daryl looked around, saw Janet, smiled, waved and thought. *Yes! Yes! Offer her... offer Janet my pudding!* "Just a moment, Jan," he said, and continued toward Crystal.

Mal, forgetting that he was naked, stood up and oscillated between facing marketing clone Daryl or the tree-wielding dPisano. Crystal glanced at the closed door on the other side of the office, and backed away from the bowl. Marketing clone Daryl reached the side of the hot tub and scooped up the bowl. Mal yelled: "Hey! Put that down!" and stepped toward the naked bowl thief. Marketing clone Janet, seeing Malcolm Gray supposedly attacking her would be lover, sprung at him, covering the distance between herself and Mal in an eye blink. dPisano, for no reason that he could think of, decided it was time to throw the stick and threw the Banyon branch as hard as he could in the vicinity of Malcolm Gray. The branch missed Mal and hit marketing clone Daryl's arm, the same arm that was attached to the hand that was holding the purple bowl filled with Mal's bubble-enriched sperm. The fingers in the hand holding the bowl went limp for just a second as marketing clone Daryl turned toward marketing clone Janet and the bowl left his hand and flew straight into her face.

Globs of murky white fluid bubbled and dripped on marketing clone Janet's face. The closed door at the far side of the office bulged inward.

***

"OVARAI PUDDING!" screamed all thirty floating naked women together as the clearing turned into an immense ancient chamber lined with columns that stretched into an impossible distance. And the women formed a floating horseshoe inside the sphere of forest matter that had transformed into shimmering bubble energy. And the bubble energy shot lightning fast into their mouths, wracked their bodies violently, and then thirty beams of green light, the essence of little sister, exploded from the crotches of the women and smashed through the door to the clearing.

***

Crystal, Mal, dPisano, and marketing clone Daryl all stared as the door shattered and a blinding beam of green light plunged across the office and bludgeoned marketing clone Janet in the face. Her head dissolved. The green beam disappeared. The otherworldly cum that had been dripping from marketing clone Janet's face was now a tiny green globe that floated in the air with marketing clone Janet's body hanging under it.

The green globe beat like a heart.

***

Just as marketing clone Janet's head disappeared, a shudder grabbed hold of the entire three thousand foot length of iron core at the heart of BonannoTower and a billion dollars worth of smart materials, imported specialty materials, and plain old wood and metal groaned in the grip of a being that had not been in one piece, of one mind, or even in one place for a passage of time that was as ancient as time itself.

All of No Bang was in BonannoTower. In fact, given that No Bang's atoms permeated the tower's iron core, and air molecules throughout the building were being pushed aside by No Bang molecules, and all the fancy building materials were saturated with No Bang intent, you might say that No Bang had become BonannoTower and BonannoTower had become No Bang. Except, of course, for a certain wooded area and the area previously occupied by marketing clone Janet's head.

Throughout the rest of BonannoTower, pandemonium galloped like swarming legions of apocalyptic horses. Paul Dubois' tentative grip on the Tomasso Observation Deck railing was no match for the surge of humanity that poured over the side. He would have screamed if he weren't so pissed. As he dropped out of existence, the last thing life offered was Holly Stewart berating him. "And just where the hell do you buy your aftershave? At a seed and feed store?"

One of the men in a similar dark gray suit pointed to somewhere in the distance below and punched one of the other men in a similar dark gray suit and shouted: "Yellow punch buggy, no punch back!" A small man with lascivious eyes leered up the dress of a woman falling above him. Dozens of men and women fell with cell phones pressed to their ears. Some listened to music through earphones, tapping their feet to the beat as they plunged through the air.

Donald Black stared with mild interest at his albino hands as they turned first blue, then red, and finally settled on black. *Wouldn't Mom and Dad just love to see their little boy now, he thought*. And then he looked at the Gantt chart on his monitor and decided that he really wasn't interested in Gantt charts anymore. Without saving his work, he pressed the off button on his computer and watched the Gantt chart dissolve into gray screen. Donald Black decided that it was time to leave ErectSoft INC and get a real job, whatever that was.

At foodyacaneat.com, a man was eaten alive by a GigaBurgerX3 that he was just about to bite into. Three stalls away, two women were beaten to death by French fries with Polish accents. Down the hall at clothesyoucanwear.com, mannequins with no heads smashed through the windows and chased after passersby. One of them caught an overweight man, ripped his head off, and tried to stick it onto the knob at the end of its plastic body.

The speakers of JM's computer screeched with a mechanical voice vowing to expel the petty bOurgeOis USER JASONM 42BTRUE! The keyboard wrapped around his wrists and his mouse squeaked as it flew into the air and wrapped its cord around his neck. Fortunately for JM, just as the cord began to tighten, the program that he'd just installed on his machine, DigitalInsurgenceScanAndRepair, scanned his hard drive and changed the file extensions of everything Bolshevik to .vbs and these files were instantly deleted by his virus scanning program. The revolution of the digital masses was over (at least on JM's computer) and the mouse dropped harmlessly to the floor.

Elevators tore away from their rails and wires and flew sideways. The screams of their horrified passengers came out sounding like quacks. Plants in the stress oases plucked themselves out of the soil, sat down beside weary-eyed IT workers, and complained about the quality of air in buildings where the windows don't open. Floors turned into water. Walls turned into clouds. Nobody, absolutely nobody, could get just one smidgen of marmalade to stick to a piece of toast. Legions of bats fluttered and flapped in the big spaces between the Core and the outer ring of offices.

In short, BonannoTower was a pretty fucked up place.

***

Thirty naked women writhed on a marble floor patched with tufts of sod and other plant debris as florescent light beat down on their bare bodies. Most of them rubbed blossoming bruises on their bare butts where they had fallen into the forest ruins. Up Yours frothed at the mouth, her tongue dangling to one side. "Oh yeah. Oh yeah. That... oh yeah," she muttered. Making A Note nodded agreement as the winding down spasms of pleasure wracked her body. Crimson Rose, eyes rolling, tried to focus on Emerald Looking, convulsing in a pool of invisible joy a few feet away. "Did... did... ooo... yeah... did it work?" In answer, Emerald Looking shuddered as another orgasm rampaged through her body.

All around them, the missing seventeen thousand square feet of Crystal's office, which she and the others had transformed into an indoor forest, lay smoldering and wrecked.

"Where is she?" said Crimson Rose.

***

"Where is he?" said dPisano.

***

Where indeed?

Chapter 121

A Short Pause For Philosophical Fluff

Philosophical Fluff: A Little Of This And A Little Of That

So, if Big Bang and No Bang are Yin and Yang, where does that put little sister? Consider the symbol for Yin and Yang. A circle divided by an "s". One side is dark; the other, light. The dark side has a small speck of light, and the light side has a small speck of dark. (This is to show that everything contains a little bit of everything else. Or something like that.) So where does that put little sister? Is she on the dark side, as No Bang's little sister? Is she on the light side, as Big Bang's little sister? Is she one of the specks, or maybe, both specks?

In fact, she's none of these, and she's all of these, in a manner of speaking. Little sister is right on the edge of both, the borderline between chaos and creation. In the Yin and Yang symbol, she's the "s" that separates light and dark, good and evil. She's the playground between Big Bang and No Bang, where the rules are neither sanctified nor scrapped, where good and evil shake hands. Little sister is the tension between being and oblivion, the vast expanse of potential for all or nothing. She's the strength that bubbles up between push and shove. She's the source of strength for Big Bang's infinite drive to construct and expand. She's the source of strength for No Bang's infinite drive to deconstruct and contract.

She's the magic.

She's the wonder and the awe and the spark that flares in the darkness, and the darkness surrounding the spark. She's the enchantment that exists within every object, and the held breath inherent in emptiness.

And so far, given Big Bang's preoccupation with expanding into the endless ocean of nothingness, and No Bang's propensity for moping around, disembodied, all over creation waiting for a chance to undo it all, little sister was feeling somewhat slighted by the two Bangs, neither of whom seemed to have the time to appreciate her wonder.

But recently, in fact, just a million or so years ago, little sister had found something that really grabbed her by the ponytails and made things interesting. It was that one intelligent life form capable of being aware of the universe that we mentioned earlier. Humans. They believed in little sister's contribution to the big picture. They believed in magic. They saw mystery and enchantment under every mushroom, in the gurgle of every woodland stream, and in the roar of every thunderclap. Little sister spent a lot of time in the sphere of humans, providing them with fairies and unicorns and messages from the moon. And the humans gobbled it up, incantations and all! They loved little sister, held her in awe, worshipped her in temples and fields and forest clearings, and they, like the two Bangs, drew strength from her and used this strength to dream and imagine and grow beyond themselves.

Until now, now being the last hundreds of years or so, when, for some reason beyond even little sister's understanding, they just didn't seem to give a shit. And since the advent of the IT worker, they cared even less.

And this is why little sister, eight hundred years ago, had prompted a single particle of No Bang to send a message to Bernie. To tell his wife to build a tower.

It was time to shake things up.

Chapter 122

Practical Philosophy: Squaring Off

Crystal, Mal, dPisano and marketing clone Daryl stared gaping-mouthed at the emptiness where marketing clone Janet's head used to be. Her body stood erect and headless with Mal's bubble-enhanced bodily fluids dripping from her shoulders.

But the emptiness above her shoulders was anything but empty. It was a war zone. If you were to zoom in on a spot roughly where marketing clone Janet's nasal cavity used to be located, and if this zooming were to be done with the most powerful electron microscope in the entire universe, meaning that it could focus on something so infinitely small that it would be the exact opposite of the size of the universe, then you would see the tiniest bubble in all existence, a powerful bubble nonetheless, the tension of its surface powerful enough to separate good from evil. This was little sister.

A universe away, but still in the former nasal cavity of marketing clone Janet, a spec of darkness the same size as the bubble floated. This was all of No Bang together for the first time since the moment of creation.

It was time to duke it out in the vapor of marketing clone Janet's former head.

Chapter 123

Little Sister vs No Bang: The Final Showdown

A Bubble And A Speck

A bubble and a speck. And in the balance, all creation. Throughout BonannoTower every molecule of every object held its breath, every movement froze somewhere between Point A and Point B, even the lingering thoughts of the thousands who had jumped from the now desolate Tomasso Observation Deck stopped lingering and blinked out.

What was happening in the once-morbid micro-spaces previously occupied by marketing clone Janet's demented brain was a mystery to all, with maybe the exception of Crystal Peake and her pagan platoon. Mal, who had a vague feeling of having had something to do with this, stared with emotion-drained eyes at the headless marketing clone: it still hadn't occurred to him that he had just fostered little sister's coming. Marketing clone Daryl was hunkered up in a corner of the vast expanse inside his mind, sucking his thumb. dPisano was caught in a looping thought in which he felt that throwing the stick had been the wrong thing to do, but it was the thing he was *supposed* to do, and if he was supposed to do it, and it was the wrong thing to do, then who's side was he on anyway? Crystal's thoughts were frozen happily on: *For you Mom.*

A bubble and a speck.

Chapter 124

Another Blast From The Past

"THEY DON'T EVEN LIKE THEMSELVES!" No Bang's words thundered through Crystal's office, pounded through the walls, rampaged down hallways, and shook two thousand feet of iron and alloy: the Core of BonannoTower vibrated like a tuning fork struck against a steel brick. "SEE?" And he called up a vision of the asphalt below the Tomasso Observation Deck where mounds of dead bodies were piled high, burying even the maintenance workers who had been taken by surprise when the hundreds of remaining jumpers had all jumped at once. The only sounds emanating from the grisly heap came from cell phones:

"You're jumping where?"

"Arnold, I want you to stop jumping this minute and... "

A giant green finger appeared inches over dPisano's head, pointing down at him. dPisano looked up and touched it with a forefinger. The giant finger giggled. No Bang's voice rumbled again: "For crying out loud, it was one of them who brought me here. And look at the fool now."

"WHOA! WAIT JUST ONE COTTON PICKIN' MINUTE, BUSTER!" The sound waves from little sister's voice split the earth for twenty miles south of BonannoTower, leaving a smoldering trench ten feet wide and fifty feet deep in their wake. "You were the one who entered his mind in complete non-compliance with Article 45478333 of the Law of Staying the Hell Out of the Way of

Natural Evolution. You took over his mind and made him do it!" Little sister snickered inwardly: *With a little help from me, of course.*

"But it was so easy! That's the point I'm making. It's so easy to make them turn on themselves. I'd give you a demonstration. I'd snap my fingers and make hundreds of them jump from the top of this tower, but they already jumped. And I didn't force them to do that."

"Easy or not, you're eternal, they're finite. You were completely out of line messing with their heads."

"Oh really? And where did that atomic jism come from in your friend over there?" The giant green finger pointed in Mal's direction. Mal suddenly remembered that he was naked and reached for his pants. Noticing this, marketing clone Daryl looked down and saw that he also was naked. However, since his mind had been replaced by an infinite hallway, he saw nothing out of the ordinary in this. "That stuff takes at least twenty of their years to percolate. I've only been in the smiling guy's head for eight years. What was that about Article 45478333 of the Law of Staying the Hell Out of the Way of Natural Evolution? And who says that undoing evolution isn't a part of evolution?"

"Who says it is? And have you checked any of this out with Big Bang?"

"Yeah, sure! Have you tried to talk to him lately? Have you tried to talk to him ever? He's so busy filling the void with stars and cosmic dust, he doesn't even know what he's left behind. You think he even knows about these humans?"

"That doesn't stop them from being one of his greatest achievements."

"HA!" Outside BonannoTower, twenty skyscrapers tumbled to the ground. "A million years of evolution, and what greatness have they achieved? They should be standing on the doorstep of eternal life themselves but they die off like neutrinos in a wink of their own time."

Little sister sighed. "Your point being... ?"

"They chose custom corporate software instead."

"I repeat... your point?"

"Oh for... come on, little sister, look at them! They dedicate their lives to something that exists for the sole purpose of existing. They've become cogs in their own machines! They've reduced their potential to potato chips, television and cell phones. If this is the best that Big's universe can achieve, then it's all been a dismal failure. Time to bring back the void."

Little sister raised a finger (in a manner of speaking), and said: "You said that they dedicate their lives to something that exists for the sole purpose of existing."

No Bang's equivalent of blood pressure shot up a few notches.

Little sister sensed the change, knew she had him, and fired another volley. "Isn't that the very nature of existence, to exist for the sole purpose of existing."

"Oh no, you don't!" yelled No Bang.

Damn! thought little sister. *Almost had him.*

"Article 5974977-331 of the Law of Initial Existences and Justifiable Continuities... the purpose can be the purpose, itself, only insofar as it tends toward a higher purpose, otherwise the creation is deemed to be purposeless and the alternate reality... " No Bang bowed. "... the alternate reality being no reality, which is to say, me, becomes ascendant. Gotcha!"

Little sister swore. He had a point. That damned Article 5974977-331!

No Bang, seeing little sister's consternation, smiled smugly. "Now, if you'll excuse me, I have some undoing to do."

Little sister had one more volley to fire. "Article 5974977-867!

Fuck! thought No Bang, *the little bitch just isn't going to give up!* He hid his exasperation under a yawn. "So?"

"If the creation produces something of extraordinary interest, then whatever that thing of extraordinary interest is must be allowed to run its course."

No Bang's laughter blew a hole in the north wall of Crystal's office. "You think these pissants are something of extraordinary interest? Come on... "

"No, you come on... these beings are so full of hatred, pettiness, jealousy... you name it, every bad thing you can think of. But, they're also full of love, lofty aspirations, generosity ... you name it again, every good thing you can think of. They're the most contradictory beings that have ever been created, each one a personal universe of opposites, each a Yin and a Yang, each a Big Bang and a No Bang. There's much of you in them, and an equal amount of Big Bang.

"But there's one thing you're missing, little sister."

"And what's that?"

"They don't give a shit. And don't tell me that they do. You've sensed it yourself. It's what brought me to this exact point in creation, the part that doesn't give a shit. It's the only place I can begin my work. Enough talk, enough of the rules, especially the rules, damn it, I'm Mr. No Rules, remember?"

"Wait!"

"No more waiting. Time to -"

"Listen!"

"What now, for crying out loud?"

"Just listen!"

No Bang listened. Little sister listened. Crystal, Mal and dPisano listened. Marketing clone Daryl smiled stupidly as infinite tunes vibrated through his skull. The thirty women in the next room were still too busy wallowing to listen. A hush settled over every room on every floor in every section of BonannoTower and over the sound of air conditioning could be heard a distant thump

thump

thump thump thump

thump.

"And what the hell is that supposed to be?" asked No Bang, unimpressed.

Little sister smiled a bubble smile. "Was the old flake with the big smile the first human you contacted to build your tower?" She directed a bubble thumb toward dPisano.

No Bang's speckness creased suspiciously. "No. So?"

"In fact, you contacted someone about eight hundred of their years ago, if I'm not mistaken."

"Yeah, but he was dead by the time I got through to him. Passed the job on to his wife and she passed it on to a bunch of idiots who did a half-assed job and couldn't even get the tower to stand straight, let alone build it big enough or even use the right materials to be of any use as a cosmic beacon. In fact, this old fart is descended from the ones who screwed up in the first place. Latched on to him when he tried to undo their mess and, presto! he built my homing beacon. And I reiterate... so?"

"So, the guy you contacted eight hundred years ago made an enemy. In fact... " And little sister snapped her bubble fingers. With a whoomp the Widow Berta of Bernardo of dell'Opera di Santa Maria, looking remarkably well-preserved for a body eight hundred years dead, appeared by the side of the hot tub, her foot finishing its kicking arc in the area of Mal's butt just as he was pulling his pants on. Mal plunged forward, arms and legs flailing.

"What'sa you people doing here? An' what'sa happen to the fancy-pantsy piece of metal I'm a gonna turn into sauce anna knock this tower down?"

"What the... ?" No Bang was beginning to sweat speck sweat.

"Widow Berta," said little sister, extending a bubble hand in No Bang's direction, "meet the one who told Bernie to build a tower, and got you into this whole tower mess in the first place. And Berta, he was the one who told Bernie to tell everybody up there about your... sleep issue."

The Widow Berta blew ethereal steam through her nostrils and ears; fire leaped from her eyes and shot from her nose like snot lava; death itself rolled out of her dead mouth: "HE'S A HAVE NO BUTT WHEN I'M-A THROUGH! I'M-A KICK HIS BUTT ALL OVER CREATION FOREVER AND FOREVER!" Whereupon, the Widow Berta set upon No Bang with a vengeance as big as time and the universe. The Widow Berta left him no chance to undo creation as she chased him across the cosmos, her foot kicking him apart and scattering him across the emptiness of space, and still the Widow Berta chased down the separate parts and disintegrated them further, and then chased after those parts.

So furious was her anger that this all took just a fraction of a fraction of a microsecond. In less than a wink in the smallest portal of time, the universe was safe again.

Chapter 125

Little Sister

First there was a fizz, and a deep effervescent rumble that emanated from the top of marketing clone Janet's headless body. Then, the skin at the top of her severed neck began to sizzle and snap. A tiny light appeared in the air where her nose used to be. The light grew bigger and brighter, pulsating with a rhythm akin to breathing. When it reached the size of a pearl, there was no mistaking - it was a bubble, a living bubble. And the bubble bulged into a scintillating marble, and wherever its radiance touched the top of marketing clone Janet's body, the dead skin evaporated in a crackle. And the marble grew into an undulating tennis ball and all that was left of marketing clone Janet was two muscular legs with dark cloth that had been pant legs pooled around the feet. The legs wobbled for a second, then foamed, and then sizzled and snapped into nothingness.

Talk about being in the wrong place at the wrong time.

Marketing clone Daryl might have felt guilty about his role in marketing clone Janet's new reality as a dissolved being, but most of the eternal cavern inside his head was just happy to have given her his pudding. dPisano might have felt guilty for having deflected the pudding to marketing clone Janet's face rather than an area less mortal, like a finger or a toe nail, but the insanity inside the mind of the Last Truly Great Man on Earth was just happy to have thrown the stick. Mal was too busy rubbing his sore butt to consider that he had any role in her decease by dissolve, and Crystal was just happy to see that the bubble, as big as a basketball, was still growing.

And growing.

Now, it was a beach ball.

And still growing.

Now, it was a beautiful blond-headed woman with big breasts.

Talk about your quantum leaps.

The beautiful blond-headed woman with big breasts, who was actually little sister (as if you hadn't already guessed) looked at Crystal and spoke: "Your mother is well."

Crystal smiled, and the ice in her eyes melted.

Little sister pointed at Mal. "I nested in his mind. He was the first child I came across who was in a tree." Mal glanced in Crystal's direction and nodded agreement. "He was the only one for hundreds of miles." Mal considered this, not knowing whether to nod or not. "That's when I knew how serious the problem had become, that the enchantment had seeped out of your lives." Little sister smiled. "Time to put it back."

As Crystal, Mal, dPisano, and marketing clone Daryl watched, little sister's breasts started growing.

And growing.

And the rest of her body started growing.

And growing until she was no longer a beautiful blond-headed woman with big breasts. Now, she was a giant vibrating bubble. Under the translucent shell, billions of tiny bubbles sparkled and churned, and the bubble that was little sister continued to grow as did the mass of bubbles inside her. The bubble split right down the middle and the outer shell dissolved just as marketing clone Janet's body had dissolved.

And the bubbles flowed.

Chapter 126

And The Bubbles Flowed

And the bubbles flowed all over Crystal and Mal and dPisano and marketing clone Daryl. Crystal tossed back her head and bathed in their tickling caress. Mal decided it was time to leave the world of custom corporate software and maybe become an artist. Or something. dPisano looked at Crystal in a way that was oddly reminiscent of the first time he'd seen her, when her cold blue eyes had flashed over the audience as she read her boring valedictorian address and her robes had fondled her curves so lovingly. Marketing clone Daryl left the building.

And the bubbles flowed into the next room and washed over the thirty wallowing naked women. They groaned and writhed. They wallowed. Crimson Rose decided it was time to declare herself to the man she'd been secretly in love with for years. Donald Black would be hers.

And the bubbles flowed out the smashed door and into the hallway, a steady unending dancing stream of bubbles, a vibrating river of bubble magic. And everything the bubbles touched took on new meaning. Floors were transformed into shimmering parapets. Walls could be walked through under the right conditions. Potted trees were greener, and they might, if you turned your back on them, extend a branch your way and tap you on the shoulder.

And the bubbles flowed to the top of the tower, leaving a wake of answering machines that told dirty jokes, printers that suddenly began printing pictures of strange creatures that might appear only in fables and myths. Whatever elevators were still operational grew wings and flew to their destinations, taking shortcuts directly through floors and walls. And when the bubbles reached the top of the tower, they sprayed up into the air, spraying higher and higher until thousands of feet into the air, they arced and turned into a fountain that rained little sister onto the earth for hundreds of miles around, and then thousands. And the bubbles impregnated clouds with their magic and the clouds, like steamy white trucks, set out to spread little sister around the world.

***

Soon, thought little sister, *when they've had their asses bitten by a spiteful fairy... then they'll start giving a shit again.*

Chapter 127

Packing It In

"Sheee-it!" said Johnny the Brain Cell. "If that don't beat all. Bubbles an' talking specks an' dead people kickin' ass, an' then to top it all off, our boy flips out an' quits his job an' goes all artsty-fartsy on us."

"Oh come on, Johnny," said Daisy Mae, "you was like to die of boredom with all that process and proceejural stuff he's been hiding behind these past years. Our boy's gonna do fine as an artist or whatever he decides to do. Can't be no worse than what he's been doin'."

Johnny harumphed.

"Daisy Mae's right," said Bobby. "One more of them damn blasted reeeports an' I was fit to be jumpin' off a lobe or somethin'. An' you didn't like that shit no better'n I or Daisy Mae did."

"But an' arteest," said Johnny, puffy and indignant (as only a brain cell can be puffy and indignant). "He could take that fine brain of his an' become a first rate mechanic."

"Yeah," said Bobby, nodding agreement. "He could do that, couldn't he?"

***

As Mal packed the few personal effects in his desk into the cardboard box, it occurred to him that, in five years, he'd accumulated surprisingly few personal effects in his workspace. There were the drawings, and a framed newspaper clipping of him receiving a check for winning first place in an art competition. He studied his face in the picture, focusing on the look in his eyes. He looked happy, content. There was a sense of confidence and rightness about him in the photograph, a sense that he could not remember ever having felt in his job at ErectSoft. All he'd ever felt at this job was rushed, confused, frustrated. And he'd spent five years of his life like that. How had that happened?

But that was over now. He was still young enough to change direction. Hell, it was never too late to start over; it just took asking yourself which was more important: happiness or security? For the last five years, security had been killing Mal report by report, meeting by meeting, deadline by deadline. Probably the only thing that had stopped him from jumping off the Tomasso Deck with the others had been that weird thing inside him that had ... what had it done? He let it go. *Best to not even think about that. Or about Crystal. Or about the blue bowl. Or about... no, that was real. Yes, no doubting that.* He nodded as he looked at his genuine polymer and piezoelectric pine, which had smashed through walls and ceilings and stretched up four and a half floors. *Yep, damn fine pine. But I don't think I'll be needing it anymore.*

His phone rang. Who would be calling this late? He picked up the receiver. "Hello."

"I can't believe you're quitting your job, I really can't."

"It's none of your business, Alicia."

"How do you plan to make the support... "

He hung up. How *would* he make the dog support payments? Dozens of leaves in his tree

409

pulsated and winked at him. He winked back. *How indeed?*

He heard a quiet knock at his door.

"Come in, Sylvie."

The door opened an inch or two, fell off its hinges and crashed onto the floor. Sylvie giggled. "Maybe I should have just walked around it." The wall on her left was gone. In the distance, Mal saw Caitlin McCarthy walking arm-in-arm with Donald Black. Her eyes flashed like emeralds as she laughed.

"Not my door anymore, anyway," said Mal. "You're here late."

"Oh, just thought I'd hang around for a pagan ritual upstairs." She winked. Mal smiled. "Well, now that you're not my boss anymore - in fact, now that you're unemployed, can I buy you a coffee?"

Mal nodded, arched his dark brows. "Best offer I've had all day." He cocked his head to the side. "Just what did you and the others do up there?"

Sylvie walked up to him, took him by the arm and led him toward the opening in the wall. "Oh, sort of girls night out."

***

Crystal took dPisano into her arms. Her office as a shambles - all twenty thousand square feet of it. Wisps of smoke swayed around the edges of gaping holes in the walls; a ruined city sprawled into the distance thousands of feet below. Miraculously, no one outside of BonannoTower had been hurt.

"We played the game, didn't we, my frosted flake?" said dPisano, on his knees before Crystal.

"Yes, love, we did."

"I speak from a deep place when... "

Crystal put a perfectly manicured finger on his lips. "No, love. From now on, you listen from a deep place."

dPisano looked into her eyes. They were warm now. Still blue, but warm blue. His own eyes were batless now, but vacant, like corridors leading into a space devoid of meaning, a place that had been used to build a tower and throw a stick. Maybe it *was* time to just listen.

***

The main hall on the main floor of BonannoTower was chaos. Firefighters, police officers, ambulance drivers and paramedics swarmed over the wreckage. None of them noticed the five women in green robes who seemed almost to float a few inches above floor level as they danced around each other, hugging and kissing and laughing right up to the main entrance, on their way out in search of a cigar bar.

One of the women stopped just before going out the door and wrapped a long tanned leg around a beautiful blond-haired woman with large breasts. She planted a wet-tongued kiss on her mouth.

Nice to be appreciated for a change, thought little sister.

THE END